MATCHED TO THE *Alien* PRINCE

MATCHED TO THE *Alien* PRINCE

DANIELLE FORREST

The Eternal Scribe Publishing
Indianapolis, IN

CHAPTER ONE

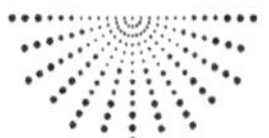

Something about that first step was absolutely terrifying.

Justine stood on the threshold of her home, staring out at the suburban community beyond. It felt so quiet, so peaceful. It was weird, like coming home after a long vacation and your space just felt off, like you were entering somewhere new rather than somewhere you'd been countless times before.

Continuing to move forward, she scanned the street, flinching as a car drove by. Her heart pounded, and the instinctual urge to run back inside hit her. She resisted, but still tensed, her leg twinging as the movement put undo strain on an injury that had only recently been freed from a walking boot.

When she reached the sidewalk, it felt like a monumental accomplishment. She hadn't been this far from her home on her own in months, not since her injury. She looked over at the empty driveway. The cement was cracked in one spot where the harsh winter had proven too much for it. It, too, felt odd, like it was wrong that there wasn't a car in the drive.

What if he comes home?

What if he sees me walking down the street?

What will he say?

What will he do?

Every panicked thought sent her heart racing, creating threats where there were none.

It's only a few miles. That's nothing, she thought, trying to convince herself as she turned, walking toward the stop sign at the end of the road. But every time she put weight on her right leg, it reminded her that she wasn't the same person she used to be.

In more ways than one.

No, she couldn't rely on her old ideas of what she was capable of. She couldn't rely on her once strong self anymore. That wasn't her. That woman was gone, stolen by Brian in one too many fits of anger, one too many snide remarks.

"How did I get here?" she said as she reached the stop sign. Her right leg was already aching, protesting the exertion.

And she'd only just started.

Justine turned, focusing on the map she'd created in her head. She'd had no choice but to memorize the route since Brian had confiscated her cell phone months ago. It was dumb luck that she'd even managed to connect to a neighbor's Wi-Fi at all. It wouldn't have been possible months ago, when she was still almost completely immobile, sprawled out on the couch with nothing but some streaming services to entertain her.

And the worst part was that he'd been better since the injury. Him controlling every moment of her life had been better than before. Before, she'd been careful about her every action, her every word, all to preserve the peace. Anything could trigger him, and somehow she'd fallen into a pattern of going to extremes to appease him. He'd never hurt her physically, but he'd insulted her and denigrated her, and she'd taken it for the sake of fixing their broken relationship.

That is... until the "incident."

That's what he always called it. The "incident." He couldn't seem to call it an accident, but he also couldn't seem to admit his part in it, either. There was often this look in his eyes when the topic came up, like even without saying it, he was blaming her.

Or was that just my mind playing tricks on me?

She was honestly a little afraid to know the truth. She didn't *want* to know the truth. What was worse, someone psychologically abusing you or making up a fantasy that someone was abusing you to explain your issues?

After a few more blocks, she began to actually *feel* the way the one bone bowed, deformed as punishment for not breaking when the other one did. She could feel the distortion of the bone, which caused her gait to become more and more awkward with each step. It hurt, but she ignored it, because it also felt good to walk in two shoes again. Real shoes. For the first time in months, she could walk without rolling her right foot, her right leg constantly feeling longer than her left.

It was freeing, but with each step, the nagging fear grew, a fear built upon years of insidious mind games. Even now, with that "incident" threatening to resurface from the back of her mind, she still wanted to believe he was the smiling, charming man she'd met years ago. She wanted to believe her instincts and judgment couldn't have been that far off. She wanted to believe that she wasn't this weak thing that couldn't even stand up for herself.

I'm standing up for myself now.

"Isn't that what counts?" she said out loud, then cringed when she spotted someone within earshot, someone who might have heard her talking to herself.

Does he think I'm crazy?

She watched him carefully for several long moments as she

approached the next intersection, looking for indicators in his facial expressions and body language.

He seemed oblivious.

She sighed a breath of relief when she spotted the earbuds in his ears.

It's fine.

You're fine.

Just get to Amira's place.

That was her plan: get to Amira's place. Anything after that was beyond her ken, a reality so far into the future it didn't bear thinking about.

And yet, what if Amira didn't take her in? What if she didn't help her? She hadn't told her college friend that she was coming over, let alone that she was arriving with nothing but the clothes on her back. Would she turn her away? They hadn't really talked in months, after all. Her injury and Brian's subsequent overprotectiveness had separated her from everyone she knew, and she'd only managed to reconnect with Amira a couple days ago.

She supposed that was the impetus for all this, reconnecting with an old friend. Amira had been excited to hear from her again, immediately asking her what she'd been up to and where she'd been. Justine had been reticent, not knowing what to say. What *could* she say? There was just so much, and all of it felt... impossible. Her fingers had frozen on the keyboard. Even typing the words had seemed an impossible feat, like doing so made it real. She wasn't sure she could handle that yet.

As her walk continued, she tried not to think about what she was leaving behind and what Brian would think when he got home.

Or worse, what he would *do*.

Instead, she tried to clear her mind, focusing on the physical things. The constant uneven pace of her footfalls. The swing of her arms. The bellows of her breath. The heat of the sun against her skin. She focused on each crossroads, trying to determine how far she'd traveled and how much longer she had to go.

It felt like an eternity.

Before long, she started to tire, none of her muscles being accustomed to this level of activity. She'd spent the last six months mostly sitting on a couch, her broken leg slowly withering away. When the doctor had finally removed the cast, her right leg had been half the size of her left.

Maybe I shouldn't have done this.

Maybe she'd been unrealistic and overestimated her abilities. Walking several miles to her friend's apartment was probably more of an undertaking than she was ready for.

But what else could she have done? She had no phone, no money, nothing. Brian had seen to it that she couldn't have left him if she tried.

Watch me, she thought to herself in a rare moment of gumption.

She supposed a similar moment had inspired this trip as well. She'd been sitting in the doctor's office, listening as he told her she could officially stop using the walking boot. Brian had been his "normal" charming self, smiling and nodding along with the doctor's instructions, acting as if he was a parent in an appointment with an injured child rather than a monster ensuring her silence.

For whatever reason, Justine had sat there feeling annoyed with Brian, annoyed with his facade, annoyed with their farce of a relationship, annoyed with her own passivity. She imagined her old self telling him to go fuck off. She imagined standing up and shoving him out of the room, then turning to the doctor and declaring, "He did this. He broke my leg."

It made her think of an offhand comment one of the doctors had made. "I've never seen this kind of break outside of child abuse." She remembered her cheeks heating at the statement, but the doctor had been staring at the x-rays, so he'd neither seen her blush nor the way Brian had stiffened, as if the statement was a direct accusation.

Justine, stop it, she told herself as she realized she was doing it again. She was letting her mind wander, letting it dwell on things she was better off forgetting.

I don't need him.

He's dead to me.

He's my past.

She said the words in her head over and over again like a mantra, eventually using it like a metronome to set her pace, each word a beat as her foot hit the concrete.

She got lost in that rhythm, and the bad memories faded for a spell. As they lost their power over her, her awareness of the day's heat intensified. She began to notice the way sweat beaded on her face and how the sun beat down on her skin. She wanted so desperately to be indoors and wished she were already there.

Because I certainly don't wish I was back home.

Justine tensed and stopped, willing the looming memories to recede once more. It took all her focus not to think about them. Her eyes widened, and she held her breath as she kept her mind blank, forcing him out of her thoughts by sheer force of will.

Finally, she started her mantra again.

I don't need him.

He's dead to me.

He's my past.

After several iterations, she continued down the sidewalk, then turned onto a road that had no sidewalk at all. She transitioned to walking in the narrow gutter on the left side of the road.

This neighborhood was a little poorer and older than the one she'd left. The yards were a little less manicured, the buildings a little more worn around the edges, and the vehicles had a few more years on them. It was the type of place that served as a buffer zone, protecting the well-off neighborhoods from the seedier ones. She imagined each house filled with hardworking families trying to make do on incomes that kept them out of poverty, but not by much.

Recognizing where she was, she picked up her pace, although by this time, her leg was screaming at her. Each step was painful, and she wanted nothing more than to sit down and not get up again.

But I'm so close. Just a little farther, and I can sit with Amira, where there's air conditioning.

The air conditioning was what did it for her. Her pace picked up even further in spite of the sharp pain shooting up her right leg every time her foot hit the pavement. Her limp became more pronounced, and she wished she'd thought to grab her crutches. She'd stopped using them when she started using the walking boot, so it hadn't occurred to her to bring them, but it would have helped, would have taken a little of the burden off her weakened limb.

After a few more minutes, the street opened up into an apartment complex. Plain brick buildings rose from concrete parking lots while mature trees softened the experience. Because it was the middle of the day, few cars cluttered the scene. Most people were at work.

From this distance, the buildings looked homey and nice, the community a quiet oasis. She could even hear birds chirping somewhere. It made her smile, like the universe was telling her this was the right choice.

As she walked through the apartment complex, looking for building 1703, her limp became almost absurd. She felt like Igor from Frankenstein, her gait rolling and thumping again and again as it became more of a struggle to put weight on her bad leg. Even so, she was hopeful. As she grew closer, the buildings looked worn and rundown, but even *that* couldn't hold back her optimism.

I'm here, she thought. *I made it!*

She felt proud, proud that she'd escaped, proud that she'd reached her destination. And Brian couldn't stop her because he didn't have a clue. She eagerly searched the buildings, looking for her friend's address.

"There!" she said aloud as she spotted 1703, her hand automatically lifting to point at the numbers on the face of the building. The 0 was missing, but she could still see where it had hung there for years, the brick behind it now a different color.

She picked up her pace, but it was hard. Her leg didn't want to cooperate, but her enthusiasm wouldn't let it slow her down. She practically hopped now as she crossed over the grass to get to the front door.

Justine pulled the door open. It was unlocked and exposed a carpeted area between the apartments, with stairs creeping up to the second floor. She glanced at the numbers on the door of the closest apartment and decided Amira was probably upstairs.

Of course.

She rolled her eyes, but gamely walked over to the stairs and reached out for both railings, basically using them as crutches as she hopped step by step to the second floor.

When she reached the top, she recognized Amira's door immediately. It was the one with a beautiful tapestry hanging on it, decorated with the Muslim crescent and star symbol. She crossed the space and stood slightly to the right of the door. Her hand reached out to the tapestry, tracing the crescent. Amira had always been very up front about her religion, sort of like, "If you don't like it, tough. This is me." It was part of the reason they'd gotten along so well. They had different interests and different beliefs, but they'd approached those things with the same zeal and disregard for the opinions of others.

Just thinking of the old days, which felt so distant now, had tears rolling down her face. Suddenly, she wondered if she belonged here anymore. She wasn't the same strong, opinionated person she'd been the last time they'd seen each other. Would Amira even like her anymore? Or would she see her as weak and easily manipulated? Would she look upon her with disgust for bending to Brian's tactics?

Of course, she will. That's who I am now, isn't it?

She pressed her palm against the door as the tears reached her chin and started flowing down her neck. She sniffed as the cold from the metal door seeped into her skin.

Just knock, damn it!

She took in a shaky breath and wiped her cheeks, but it would be obvious that she'd been crying. There would be no hiding that. She curled her hand into a fist, still resting against the door, and whispered under her breath, "You can do this. You've gotten this far. Just knock."

Justine pulled her hand back and rapped her knuckles against the green-painted metal. The sound reverberated through the hallway, causing her to jump.

Knock it off! He doesn't know you're here. No one's gonna harm you.

As she finished berating herself, noises drifted from inside the apartment as someone approached.

Suddenly, it occurred to her that she hadn't brought a gift. Almost from the moment the thought popped into her head, she felt silly for even thinking it. This wasn't a normal situation, and Justine wasn't a normal guest. No one in their right mind would expect her to bring a gift on today of all days.

What's wrong with me?

When the door opened, her voice quavered when she said, "As salaam alaikum."

On autopilot, Amira muttered, "Wa Alaikum Assalam. Justine?"

Justine felt awkward as she sat on the couch in her friend's living room. She wanted to curl up into a ball, but her leg was achy from the walk and she was hesitant to put her feet on the upholstery. Amira had always been so particular about keeping her home clean.

"Here," Amira said as she approached from the kitchen with some tea.

Justine accepted the cup, a small smile gracing her face as the heat radiated into her hands from the smooth ceramic material. She closed her eyes, enjoying the creature comfort, but it only brought into starker relief how tight the skin on her face felt, a souvenir of the tears she'd shed only minutes before. She opened them again, now looking around the tidy room. There was no television here as there was in most living rooms. Instead, a couch and several comfy chairs and end tables encircled a coffee table. It was the layout of a room intended for socializing. Unfortunately, Justine wasn't feeling very social right now.

After handing her the tea, Amira turned and headed back to the kitchen as Justine's gaze wandered to the walls. There weren't any pictures, just little creative cross-stitch projects in Arabic. Some were short and sweet, things Amira had likely made in her free time. Others were longer, full paragraphs in that elegant script, the designs reminding her of illuminated manuscripts.

I wish I knew what it meant.

But she only knew a little bit of Arabic, and she'd never learned to read the language. What she *did* know, she'd learned back in college. During one of their "lessons," she remembered asking why all Amira's artwork was just writing. Amira had said, "I love my religion. It's beautiful. Don't Christians use inspirational phrases as decoration as well?"

Amira interrupted Justine's thoughts by returning to the room with a tray, which she set on the table. She sat down in a chair across from Justine and started adding lemon to her own tea. The tray was loaded down with cheese, crackers, nuts, and fruit, and Justine felt even worse for not bringing a gift.

I'm a terrible guest.

She looked down at her teacup. "I'm sorry."

Amira paused. "For what?"

Justine tucked a non-existent stray hair behind her ear. "For barging in on you like this."

Amira scoffed, waving off the apology. "You are always welcome in my home. Never forget that." She scooted forward in her seat, resting her forearms against her legs. "So, because I'm not very good at subtlety, I'm just going to get right to the heart of it. What do you need, Justine?"

She looked up. Amira almost seemed serene, like a holy woman or something. Her hijab was a subdued black today, and she was wearing "house clothes," as she called them. Yoga pants and a loose, long-sleeved tunic made her look beyond the cares of this world in Justine's eyes. Probably, on any other day, the outfit would have just looked relaxed, comfy, maybe even frumpy, but right then, Amira was her anchor, her life raft, and that made her sublime.

Justine opened her mouth, but no words came out. What could she say? How could she admit what she'd let happen? It seemed impossible, so she started with the basics. "I left him," she said simply.

Amira didn't immediately speak, instead rotating her cup with her fingertips as she seemed to stare deep into Justine's soul. "We're happy about this, yes?"

Justine nodded hesitantly. It had been a long time since she'd said or done anything against Brian, and she could almost *feel* the weight of his hand on her shoulder, that physical reminder he always used to steer her actions and words.

"Then good," Amira said, leaning back in her seat with a smile as she took a sip of her tea. Yet, beyond the smile, she could see a shrewdness in her friend's gaze. Like she saw exactly what Justine had been through, but was too polite to say anything.

Justine also sat back and took a sip. The tea was strong, but the heat suffused her insides, making her almost sigh in contentment. She relaxed into the couch little by little, only realizing as each muscle eased just how tense she'd still been. Being in this room, in this haven, was allowing her to let go for the first time in a long time.

Far too long.

The minutes dragged by in mutual silence, each of them awkwardly focused on their drinks while intermittently casting furtive glances at each other. Eventually, Amira put her tea down and stood. "It's far too quiet. I'm going to put something on." She walked over to the mantel and started fiddling with a small speaker there, then stepping back with satisfaction when some soft instrumental jazz started playing. "There. That's better." She turned and smiled. "I've always liked music like this. Just reminds me of the beauty of the world Allah created, the beauty of people sometimes."

"Not all people are beautiful," Justine said, thinking of Brian, who was as dark inside as he was charming outside.

Amira turned to her, her expression solemn. "I know. Sometimes, the best we can do is leave behind those influences that will lead us astray."

Justine nodded distractedly as her mind's eye started focusing on darker things. Amira's statement hit too close to home, and a part of her wanted to unburden herself, to tell her friend everything. She needed to get this off her chest. She needed to tell someone, but would it do any good? Or would it just needlessly burden Amira with something she didn't deserve to carry?

It felt like an impossible decision, a terrible choice no person should ever have to make, so instead of deciding, she looked up at her friend and said, "Can I stay here?"

Amira's mouth stretched into a slow smile, her eyes soft with emotion. "Of course you can."

There was a massive relief with those words. Justine felt lighter, and she couldn't help smiling as well. "Thanks," she said as her hope suddenly became a very real thing, something she could see and touch and believe in.

I'm gonna be okay.
I'm gonna be safe.
Finally.

The rest of the morning and afternoon passed without incident. They ate snacks and listened to music. During one of the ad breaks, a segment came on about some alien matchmaking service, which had spurred the conversation on for quite a while, giving Justine an appreciated reprieve from her problems.

"Can you imagine?" Amira's voice had held a combination of curiosity and distaste. "An alien."

"Well, maybe they're like us. Maybe they just want companionship, love."

"I mean, that may very well be, but I could never leave Earth."

"I could see the appeal." Those words had slipped from Justine's lips like a carefully held secret.

"You'd leave?" Amira had sounded hurt at the idea.

Realizing what she'd done, Justine had backpedaled. She'd stuttered as she'd looked up at Amira, begging with her eyes for her friend to understand. "Oh no, Amira. It's not like that. I'd never want to leave you. You're the one thing I have going for me right now."

Compassion and pity had instantly taken the hurt's place. "Oh, Justine."

Neither of them had known what to say after that. Eventually, Amira had excused herself, saying she had work to do, and she'd shown Justine to the room she would stay in. It was a simple room, clearly intended for visiting family members, with a space set aside in the corner for prayer. There was even a qibla compass on a side table so a visitor not familiar with the space would know which direction to face.

Alone and with nothing to do, Justine had sat down on the bed, keenly aware of the way the mattress contoured beneath her weight. She'd sat that way for some time, just staring at her surroundings, not wanting to think, but also not knowing what to do, either. Her life was too much of a blank slate now, and it left her feeling paralyzed.

At some point, she'd propped some pillows against the headboard and turned on the TV, hoping to get lost in some mindless entertainment.

That had been hours ago, and now she wondered if Amira had finished work for the day. Back before Brian, Amira had worked at home as an astrophysicist. She still remembered the setup, the stratification of the room, with a desk and working space on one side of the bed and her religious paraphernalia on the other.

Eventually, Justine got up and went to the window, wondering what time it was. It was broad daylight, which this time of year meant it could be as late as almost ten o'clock. She could see one of the parking lots from here, could see as the spaces began filling with people arriving home from work. A part of her, the part driven by fear, started to ramp up as car after car arrived.

What if one of them is Brian?

What if he's found me?

"That's ridiculous," she said, trying to be quiet. "He doesn't know where I am. He has no way of knowing. I got away clean."

Or did I?

What if she forgot to wipe her browser history? What if he got access to her social media accounts? What if he was tracking her computer somehow?

The more time passed, the more credit she seemed to give him, like he had supernatural powers or something.

Then the doorbell rang.

It's him.

She panicked, her gaze spinning around the room, looking for an out, looking for somewhere she could hide. Her brain revved in neutral, unable to click into gear.

"I'll get it!" Amira called out.

Amira's steps clomped down the hallway, making Justine want to cry out, "No!" She wanted to tell her to pretend they weren't home, but her words stayed lodged in her throat, and suddenly, she could barely breathe. She dropped to her knees, holding her neck and gasping for breath.

No. He can't find me. I can't go back. I just can't.

Murmurs filtered to her from the other room, unintelligible as the blood rushed in her ears. Moments later, the door clicked closed, and Amira yelled across the apartment. "How would you like some Indian takeout?"

Justine paused, her panic and paranoia momentarily dispelled. The pressure eased slightly, and she waited for someone else to speak, maybe the person who'd knocked on the door.

"Justine?" Amira said, sounding concerned.

"Sure," she replied, her voice squeaking. "Sounds good," she continued, this time a bit more normal in tone.

She pushed her way up from the floor, the harsh yarn of the carpet digging into her hands. Her legs were sluggish and sore as she limped across the room and pushed out into the hall. She still half expected Brian to be standing there at the entryway, waiting for her. Amira was in the kitchen, a package in front of her and her phone in her hand. Justine let out a sigh of relief and continued forward.

"What shall we order?" Amira asked, but then abruptly quieted as she looked up at Justine.

"Butter chicken?" Justine said, trying to act normal.

Amira's smile was obviously forced, but she barreled forward, pretending everything was fine. "Cool." She looked back down at the phone in her hand, her fingers selecting options on the screen, then set the phone down on the counter. "There. Should be about half an hour."

Trying to distract herself from the looming panic attack, she turned her focus to the box on the counter. "What's in the package?"

"Nothing important." Amira rapped her fingers against the

cardboard, the material thumping dully with each tap. "Just a new hijab. I couldn't resist. It was *gorgeous*."

"Do you want to try it on while we wait?"

Amira looked coy at first, but then burst into a smile, nodded her head eagerly, and rushed off to her bedroom with the small box.

Justine turned and settled into a chair in the living room, leaning a little to the side to get a view of the hallway. She tried to relax, but she was still tense from the doorbell ringing.

It's gonna happen again, silly, when the food arrives. Calm down.

She swallowed heavily and tried to relax her muscles, but she feared it wouldn't last. She was skittish as hell right now and suspected every little noise was going to startle her for quite some time.

This is what he did to me.

She took a deep breath in and out, repeating it again and again until Amira's door opened and she stepped out, experimentally touching the material on her head and neck. "What do you think?" she said as she reached the living room. She spun around, arms spread wide, before facing Justine once more. "Isn't is gorgeous?"

It was a jewel-toned material with silver accents. The accents ran along the edge closest to her face. The material wasn't any specific color, but transitioned from teal to purple to blue.

"It's fantastic. Do you have something special you plan to wear it with?"

Amira nodded. "I have a holiday dress that should match it perfectly."

"Awesome."

She sat down on the couch and continued to touch the

hijab, playing with the corners near her shoulder, adjusting the areas where she'd pinned it in place.

"How's your job going?"

Amira nodded. "Good. Real good. Although, sometimes I fantasize about finding work at a mosque or something."

"Really? I know you love your religion, but is that really what you want? I thought you loved astrophysics."

She bit her lip. "I *do* love my work. Really, I think it's more of a fantasy. I have this grandiose idea in my head of revolutionizing Islam and making it more modern, but it seems so egotistical. It also seems impossibly large, like it's more than one person can do. And you're right, I don't think it's what I want to do. I love my religion, but everyone needs balance, right? It's too easy to get caught up in a microcosm and lose perspective. I would hate that. I wouldn't even recognize myself anymore, I think. Plus, we both know I'm not known for holding my tongue." She chuckled.

Justine laughed along with her, and it surprised her so much she stopped mid laugh. When was the last time she'd laughed? "No, you're not. But that's why we get along." Saying it was automatic, something she'd said or thought countless times before. But this time, it stopped her dead yet again, and she fought back the tears that welled in her eyes as she realized it just wasn't true anymore. She *wasn't* like Amira now. Brian had seen to that.

"Oh, Justine," Amira said. She rushed across the living room, sat on the arm of Justine's chair, and pulled her into a side hug, pressing her hijab-clad chin on top of her head. "There, there. I know something's wrong, but it's over now. You're here. I'm here for you. It's behind you. It can't hurt you anymore."

But it wasn't behind her, was it? It was still fresh, still looming, still raw and painful. Only that morning, she'd wished

Brian a good day as she sat on the couch, still unaccustomed to having nothing on her leg. Brian had told her to "take it easy," that she was still healing, and he wouldn't want her to make it worse. She'd smiled, but she'd long since stopped believing in his kindness. It always came with strings. There was always a price.

And love shouldn't come at a price.

That was what she kept telling herself, and it was a little easier to believe it here in Amira's warm, comfy living room. It was easier to trust in herself when Brian wasn't looming, wasn't controlling, wasn't talking for her. "Thanks," she said quietly. And all of a sudden, she realized she wasn't fighting back tears anymore. She was okay. She wasn't great. Her nose was stuffed and running, her face felt way too hot, and her outlook was still pretty grim, but she wasn't on the verge of tears anymore.

She continued to sit there, letting Amira hold her and comfort her. She had no idea how long they sat like that, just taking and offering comfort, but she could have happily stayed like that forever. When the doorbell rang, they both startled, jumping away from each other. There was a tense moment, each of them expecting the worst, then they looked at each other and the dam broke. They chuckled, releasing some much needed tension.

"That's probably the food," Amira said. She turned and first grabbed her phone from the counter, then opened the door.

Justine noticed how Amira leaned backward, looking shocked and maybe even a little outraged. "Can I help you?" she said, sounding stern in a way that surprised Justine.

She stood, wondering who was at the door. The door opened toward her, blocking the view, so she had to get behind Amira before she could see who it was.

It was Brian.

CHAPTER TWO

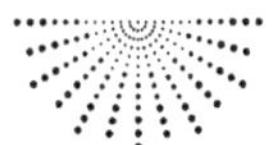

Justine was apoplectic. She couldn't move. She couldn't breathe. The world was caving in on her. He was going to take her away. She could see it in her head. He would slip past Amira, reach out and touch her on the shoulder, then gently guide her out of the apartment, probably thanking Amira and being completely charming at the same time.

The ever-building scenarios slammed into her again and again, torturing her with all the various ways he could destroy her. She was drowning in her own thoughts and losing her touch with reality, which was probably why she didn't immediately notice when Amira slammed the door and walked off in a huff. She stared at the door for a few more moments before her brain clicked into gear. Slowly and jerkily, like an old animatronic doll, she turned to face Amira, who was pacing the living room, her elbows locked and hands fisted at her sides. She was muttering something in Arabic under her breath. Justine had no idea what she was saying, but knowing Amira, it was either a prayer or a curse.

The last time she'd seen Amira like this, a man had tried to grab her ass in a bar. She'd given him an earful, then stormed off. It had taken a good five minutes to calm her down.

"Amira?"

Amira turned, her teeth clenched in anger. She visibly struggled trying to calm down. She eventually let out a breath, releasing as much of the tension as she could, repeating it again and again until she seemed to get a hold of herself once more. "Sorry, Justine." She walked over and pulled Justine into a hug. "What did he do? Tell me and I'll kick his butt. I'd rip his spleen out if you asked."

Justine pulled back, tears welling in her eyes once more. She was getting *really* tired of crying all the time. "You don't mean that. How could you possibly repent for a sin like that?"

Amira dropped her arms and stepped back, then walked to the window just beyond the couch. "Oh, I know. You have to give up the sin, regret it." She turned back to Justine, leaning against the glass. "But is it really a sin? That's one thing strange about Islam. It is a sin to run from a battle, but it is also a sin to harm your neighbor. Is this not a battle? I see the haunted look in your eyes, and I think, yes, it is."

Justine stepped forward and dropped into the closest chair, the material swallowing her up. She licked her lips, stalling.

"Please?" Amira said, touching her hands to Justine's knees.

Justine startled and looked up. Amira was kneeling before her, a look of compassion in her eyes. "He broke my leg," she said, struggling to say even that. It was only the tip of the iceberg, the final straw in a long list of grievances, but it was a start.

Amira didn't speak for several moments. "It won't be safe here. You know I'd let you stay as long as you wanted, but he already knows you're here. He'll come back, and if he's already shown he's capable of violence, he'll do it again."

"I know."

"We should call a women's shelter. You'll be safe at a place like that." Now Amira had tears welling in her eyes as well.

Justine imagined that, imagined going to a shelter, but as soon as she did, a vision of Brian standing on the other side of that door popped into her head and a yelled, "No!" fell from her lips without conscious thought. She recoiled, her heart pounding, and every part of her wanting to run. If he found her here, he could find her anywhere, right? How did he know she was at her friend's house? She hadn't talked to Amira in over a year. Could he have been following her? Tracking her internet usage? Could he hack into Amira's phone or computer?

She knew a bit about women's shelters. They were very careful about security, doing their best not to lead abusers back to the shelters, but nobody was perfect. And what if she endangered other women in the process? What if someone else's abuser found the shelter? Was that her life, then? Hiding away? Never coming up for air? Never having a normal life again?

She started shaking her head erratically, the refrain *no, no, no* echoing through her mind on a loop.

He'll never stop. Never. So long as he can reach me, he won't stop. She just knew it, could feel it in her bones, and it made her next realization that much more obvious.

I have to escape his reach.

I'll be safe if he just can't... physically... reach me.

Her eyes rounded in surprise as she came to the inevitable conclusion.

I have to leave Earth.

"Justine?"

She continued shaking her head. "It's not safe. It's not safe."

"Hey, hey, it's okay." Amira reached out and caressed Justine's cheek, encouraging her to stop shaking and just look at her. "I won't let anything happen to you. I promise. You'll be safe."

"It's not safe," Justine whispered under her breath.

Amira nodded. "We do need to do something quickly. I doubt he stuck around, but abusers aren't so easily thwarted. He'll probably be back. Let's just make sure you're not here when he returns, eh?" She smiled, clearly trying to be reassuring. "I think a women's shelter is the best choice. They're prepared for this. They specialize in these types of situations."

Justine started shaking her head again.

Amira frowned, and she sounded a little annoyed, but also concerned, when she spoke next. "Okay, then what do you want to do?"

Justine paused, her mind going blank. Both mind and body had this overpowering urge to escape, but that was where the thinking ended. She had no plan. *This* had been her plan. Conventional wisdom said she should go to the shelter, but she hated that idea. It didn't feel like safety to her, not when Brian was potentially right down the street. No matter how many precautions they took, she suspected if she stayed there, her mind would always fabricate scenarios of Brian finding her, by accident or intent.

Her mind drifted back to her thought from earlier, that if she wanted to be safe, she had to leave Earth. Was that the solution? Escape Earth? Leave Earth?

Leave Amira?

Even the thought was unbearable. How could she leave her best friend? She fantasized for maybe half a second about bringing her along when she left, but immediately remembered Amira's comments during the ad for the interstellar matchmaking agency.

And that's when the idea struck her. *Interstellar* matchmaking agency. At first, her mind completely passed over the second part, entirely focusing on the first. Interstellar. *Interstellar.* Could that be the solution? Could that be her ticket to safety? As the rest of the words settled into her brain, she started contemplating that second half. Matchmaking Agency. She'd just left a bad relationship, was still suffering from the aftermath. Could she honestly jump right into another? With someone she didn't even know?

But then, maybe that was a good thing? Maybe she could pick someone who was just right, without all the uncertainty of dating? And since they didn't know each other, he would probably expect her to be distant at first, right? Maybe this could be a fresh start, an opportunity to do things right this time?

And maybe an alien would be the perfect partner? At the moment, she couldn't imagine dating a human, but an alien? An alien wouldn't have the same culture, the same good and bad traits. An alien might be incapable of doing to her what Brian had done.

The more she thought about it, the more she liked the idea. As she sat there, she started building the fantasy even further. She would leave Earth behind. Brian wouldn't be able to follow. Even if he managed to leave Earth, how would he know where she'd gone? She would arrive on her new world and meet her "match." He would be kind and gentle. He would never say a cross word to her.

Justine smiled to herself. She could do this. She could leave Earth. The only connection she had left on this planet was Amira, and she was certain she could find ways to keep in touch. Even if it was hard, she would make it work. After all, she wouldn't have Brian controlling her every means of communication. Surely, an *alien* would be different, better.

"I want to go to Best Life," she said finally, breaking the silence.

Amira looked confused, pulling back slightly. It took

several moments before realization struck her. "The alien matching service from the ad?"

She nodded. "Yeah. Can we go?"

Amira kept looking at her funny as they drove to the agency. That was, of course, when she wasn't checking her mirrors obsessively, hunting for signs that Brian might be following.

She half expected Amira to try to talk her out of it, to try to push for the women's shelter again, but Amira held her tongue after that initial statement of surprise.

The rest of the evening had been uneventful. They'd both jumped when the doorbell rang again. This time, it was the delivery driver with their food. They'd eaten in relative silence, then eventually Amira had gone off to her room to pray and Justine had settled in for the night in her own room, trying to get lost watching TV.

The next morning, they'd woken up bright and early, feeling it was best to leave the apartment as soon as possible. They didn't want to delay and get ambushed by Brian again.

And yet, they'd have time to kill if they left first thing. The place didn't open until eight, so they went out to breakfast and wandered a shopping center for a spell.

Now, they were finally driving to the agency. Minutes ticked by as Justine stared blindly out her window at the passing cityscape, perking up when Amira pulled into a nearly empty parking lot. Excitement rushed through her as she took in her first view of the place that would change her life forever.

The excitement quickly passed, though. It was just an office building, just glass and concrete. Without the excitement driving her, every moment seemed to take forever. Picking a parking spot. Leaving and locking the car. Crossing to the front of the building. When they finally reached the double glass entry doors, she could see the building directory just beyond. Amira opened the door and ushered Justine inside.

Behind the only desk in sight, a security guard nodded in welcome, and they walked to the directory. Amira ran her hand over the long sign, presumably looking for "Best Life." She tapped the list twice when she found it, then led Justine to the elevators. As soon as they stepped in front of them, one of the elevators opened automatically. "Fourth floor," Amira said as they stepped inside, then leaned against the back railing.

The doors slid closed, and her stomach sank to the floor as the car rose. A few moments later, it stopped and the doors opened again, exposing a carpeted hallway with white walls and another directory, this one with arrows indicating where to go for each business.

There was an arrow to the right for Best Life. They turned right, continuing in silence. Each business had a small sign declaring their name next to a glass door. The sign was generic, with standardized lettering, but some of the businesses had their logos on their doors as well.

When they reached Best Life, it just had the name sign with nothing on the door. It didn't even say anything about being a matchmaking agency. Just "Best Life" in big bold letters.

Amira looked over at her as if to say, "Are you sure about this?"

Justine swallowed heavily, but pushed forward and stepped into the lobby. There were plain metal and fabric chairs, like you would see in a doctor's office, lining the walls and a single glass door across from them. Beside the door, a sign read, "Ring bell for service." It was a generic sign, probably bought online.

She crossed the room and pressed the bell. It made no sound. Was it broken or was that intentional? She turned around. Amira was still standing by the door, like she was preparing to flee.

Justine shrugged. "I guess we wait."

Amira nodded. "I guess so." She crossed to one of the chairs and sat down.

Justine settled in beside her. "I wonder how long it will be."

Amira shrugged. "There's no point wondering. It'll take however long it takes."

"How sage of you."

Amira chuckled. "Oh, I'm full of good advice." She turned to Justine. "But seriously, are you sure about this? Really sure? I don't think this is gonna solve your problems. I think you're just running. And you know how the phrase goes, 'Act in Haste, Regret in Leisure.' Are you sure you want to make this decision *now*?"

Justine shook her head. "Yes, I do. And I know I'm running. But sometimes running is the right solution. You were talking yesterday about not running away in a battle, but even Islam says it's okay in the right circumstances."

Amira nodded. "True. You're not exactly outnumbered, though."

"I might as well be. Our world isn't designed to protect people from abuse. They enable it. They make it so easy. So yes, I'm running, but I'm also starting over. I'm starting fresh. This is a new opportunity for me, a chance to move on and learn from my mistakes. I get to recreate myself without the burdens or fears of my past."

Amira shook her head. "You'll still have those fears. They'll go with you. Putting this behind you is going to take more than just creating physical distance. Promise me." She reached out, taking Justine's hands. "Promise me you'll *really* put this behind you. Promise me you'll try to trust again."

Justine was surprised. Trust? "I..."

"I know you haven't told me everything. I'm sure what you've mentioned is only the beginning. And I imagine right now that trusting anyone, especially a man, is probably gonna be hard. It's a good sign that you want a new start, but don't just try to forget what happened. It'll leak out in unexpected ways. And this new relationship you're hoping for, this new start, it'll be doomed to failure if you don't address this. Whoever he is, he isn't Brian. Don't forget that. Give him a chance, okay?"

She nodded, and Amira let go of her hands, then they both settled in to wait, staring awkwardly at the inner door next to the service bell she'd rung.

It took a few more minutes before the door finally opened, letting out a woman with long, thick, curly, vibrant red hair. Her wild hair directly contrasted the smart suit she was wearing. "How may I help you today?"

Justine straightened, self-consciously touching her much duller red hair. "I don't know how this works."

"That's quite all right. A lot of people don't." She clapped her hands together, then pressed one hand to her chest. "I'm Michelle Mackey, the owner of Best Life. Here's how the process works: you'll fill out a questionnaire, then I'll enter it into the database." She wiggled her fingers in the air like she was typing. "Then I'll contact you when you receive a match. If you like the match, we'll schedule transportation for you to go to your new home."

"We can't just do it now?" Justine asked.

Michelle opened her mouth, then snapped it closed, her eyes narrowing shrewdly. "If we have a match right away, maybe I can work it out. Let's get started with the questionnaire." She gestured with her head, then held the door open for them.

Justine, with Amira following, walked past Michelle, feeling like she was stepping into a another world.

Is this it?

Is this the moment of truth?

A small smile crossed her face as she entered the empty hallway, feeling as if destiny was calling.

And I'm gonna answer.

Michelle didn't notice it at first. She was just excited to have a new client, after all, which wasn't exactly an everyday occurrence yet. Unfortunately, the idea of having an intimate relationship with an alien was still a relatively new concept, even though an Earth ambassador had been married to an alien for decades now. Somehow, Ambassador Emma Ward's relatively public relationship had not managed to soften the natural human fear of all things "other" quite as much as Michelle would have expected.

When she'd decided to start Best Life, she'd thought it was a grand idea. Many people were fascinated by aliens, they'd had political contact with aliens for decades, and people regularly took jobs that involved traveling through space and, inevitably, working with aliens. It had seemed only logical to start a service connecting people with aliens romantically.

She'd done tons of research, found three planets in the same solar system that all had their own matching agencies, and created partnerships with them. She'd designed her questionnaire to make it easily adaptable to the other databases. It had seemed perfect.

She'd... underestimated how slowly societies changed, though. She'd thought people had overcome their old prejudices. But it had now been several months, and she'd barely had any customers. She hadn't expected things to be a raving success right off the bat, but she'd thought there would be more customers than *this*.

I suppose I underestimated the fear of the unknown.

But none of that was important right now. What *was* important was handling her new client.

And that was when it hit her. She couldn't say *what* exactly had clued her in. Maybe it was the way the woman seemed so eager to leave right away when most of her clients needed tons of time to pack up their belongings and close out their lives here on Earth. Or maybe it was the slight tremor in the woman's hands as she spoke. Or maybe it was the fact that she had brought a friend with her. No one had done that before, and Michelle wondered if she was just offering a ride or moral support.

She was holding the door open for the duo when it finally clicked in her head what detail had alerted her.

It was the eyes. She couldn't deny it; this wasn't the first time her naturally ebullient nature had blinded her to something that should have been obvious, but she still should have seen it sooner. This was something she should *always* be on the lookout for, after all.

Her new client was an abuse victim.

Michelle's protective instincts surged to the forefront. Her mind and heart filled with every tragic story she'd ever heard, and her chest puffed up with a combination of outrage and compassion. Now, in full momma bear mode, she was determined to keep this woman safe. She started building a checklist in her head of what she would need to do to get her off the planet as soon as possible. She'd have to expedite any matches, probably make a call to the individual agencies directly. That was never fun. She wasn't the best with technology, and you just couldn't avoid technology when you were calling another planet.

Then she would have to arrange transportation. Except it probably wouldn't be with her normal partners. She had an arrangement with a shipping company that made regular trips to the Tralfaire system, and they were always willing to take on passengers for a fee. She'd arranged a reduced fee with the promise that she would schedule all her off-world transportation needs through them.

But first, she needed to get her client started on the questionnaire. Nothing could happen until she had a profile in the database. Michelle pulled a tablet off the charging station by the door and placed it on the table in the middle of the room, taking it out of sleep mode. It defaulted to the questionnaire app.

The woman and her friend sat down at the table.

"This is how you'll use the app. You'll read this screen. It gives information about the service and what to expect. Then, you'll enter your personal information on the next screen. After that, each screen will be a single question. Most questions are multiple-choice or have tick boxes." She waved her hand in the air. "For the most part, we don't do free answer because it's hard to translate accurately. Anyway, after you answer each question, click the Next button in the bottom corner to advance. If you need to go back, there's a Back button in the left corner here." She pointed to an empty part of the screen where a Back button would be. "Any questions?"

The women shook their heads.

"Very well. I have a few things to take care of. I'll check on you in about fifteen minutes."

"Thanks."

Michelle nodded and walked out the door, closing it behind her. She sighed, her heart breaking for the woman. Now, she couldn't *not* see the signs. It was all little things, really. The slightest flinching when Michelle approached, a little quaver in her voice. It was right there, waiting for someone to notice. She clutched her hand to her heart and whispered, "Poor woman," under her breath, before pushing off the door and walking to her office.

Michelle closed her office door behind her and immediately went to her desk to wake her computer. She opened her matching software and clicked the button to refresh the databases. It could take a while for them to sync, and she wanted the most up-to-date version before her client finished her questionnaire. She usually only did this once a day, but this was a special circumstance.

With that taken care of, she moved on to the next item on her mental to do list and lifted her phone from its cradle. She pressed the button for one of her speed dials and waited as the phone rang. "Cox Transport. This is James speaking."

"Hi, this is Michelle Mackey with Best Life. I have a potential client that might need to be transported rather quickly. I was wondering when your next departure for the Tralfaire system might be."

"One sec. Let me check."

She could just barely hear him shuffling around on the other end as he looked up the information.

"That would be... three weeks from now."

"Oh, I was hoping for sooner."

"Is something wrong?"

"Maybe. The client expressed an interest in leaving as soon as possible. I think she's in danger."

"Okay. Let me get in contact with some people I know. Maybe I can find you something sooner. I've gotta warn you, though. It might cost a lot more than our agreement."

"I'll keep that in mind, thank you. And just know I appreciate your business."

She could practically hear the shrug in his voice. "Well, I appreciate *your* business as well."

She laughed. "What business?"

His voice grew serious. "I know it's slow right now, but a lot of businesses are slow starting out. I know mine was. I had like two jobs in the first few months. Things turned around, though. I know they will for you in time. You're cornering the market."

"Assuming I can *find* the market."

"You will."

"Well, thanks, James. I'll talk to you soon." The call disconnected, and she placed the phone back on its cradle. She sighed. "And now we wait."

Justine sat there staring down at the tablet like it was a dangerous animal waiting to strike. It was black with a lit screen covered in lettering that seemed to swim before her eyes.

"Do you want me to read it to you?" Amira asked.

Justine nodded, though she feared she might not be in the right headspace to listen. She just wanted all this to be over, to be on the other side and out of Brian's reach. She didn't want to be filling out questionnaires or reading instructions. Was it too much to ask that she just feel safe for once?

"Welcome to the Best Life Interstellar Matchmaking Agency. We specialize in connecting the people of Earth to their ideal matches, whether they are from Earth or the stars." Amira chuckled, then continued. "This questionnaire is designed to match your life goals, orientations, personality traits, and preferences to one or more individuals, with the end goal of finding your ideal life mate or mates.

"Each screen will include a question, a help text, and an

answer section. Answers are generally multiple-choice or tick boxes. Fill in all that apply.

"You can navigate through the questionnaire by using the Back and Next buttons at the bottom of the screen. Click Next to continue." Amira took a breath. "Okay, I guess we're ready to proceed." Amira tapped the screen, then continued reading from it. "Please fill out your personal information as best you can."

Amira started typing on the screen, filling out what she knew without asking. When she was done, she handed the tablet over to Justine to check the details. She looked over it and nearly burst into tears when she saw that Amira had put Justine's address as Amira's apartment. "Oh Amira," she said, covering her mouth.

Amira did a little half smile and shrugged, somehow knowing what had set her off. "It's kinda true, isn't it?"

Justine nodded, then clicked the Next button.

"Well, this just gets right into it, doesn't it?"

"What's it say?" Amira asked, leaning over Justine's shoulder.

"What are you sexually attracted to?"

"Those are some interesting options," Amira commented.

And they were. None of them were the standard options she was accustomed to, like heterosexual or homosexual. Instead, the options included: masculine, feminine, androgynous. The list went on for a while, listing traits that might inspire sexual attraction with the last option being "not applicable," which she assumed referred to asexuals. She clicked "masculine" and moved on to the next question, which was almost identical but was for romantic attraction. After that was aesthetic attraction.

"Do they really need this much information?"

Amira shrugged. "I guess they're trying to be thorough and

inclusive. Also, I imagine aliens probably don't fit cleanly into our particular boxes."

Justine thought about that. "You're probably right." She tapped Next. It had finally moved on to life goals. "Do you want kids?" She selected "Undecided."

This continued for quite a while, at times leaving her embarrassed as Amira was right there, hovering over her shoulder and watching her every answer. Sometimes, the questions were so intimate, she wanted to cover the screen. But after a few dozen screens, Amira started getting the hint and took a seat out of sight, giving Justine some privacy.

She felt like she'd been at it forever when Michelle peeked her head in to check on them. "How's everything going? You need anything?"

"We're good," Amira said. "Thanks for asking."

She turned to Justine. "What question are you on?"

"Um, it's something about housing preferences?"

Michelle nodded. "I'll check on you in another fifteen minutes." In a blink, she was gone, the door again closed.

Justine turned to Amira. "Do you think I'll be done in fifteen minutes?"

"How many questions have you done?"

"About a billion," she said, smiling sarcastically.

Amira laughed. "That many, huh?"

"I can't imagine they need to know all this."

"Well, probably the more questions they ask, the better match they can make. It's a good thing."

Justine sighed. "I suppose you're right, but that doesn't mean I have to like it."

"Well, just focus on the end result. Imagine being some-where safe with someone who is just perfect for you."

That was part of the problem; she *couldn't* imagine it. "Thanks," she said anyway. Justine smiled, but it didn't quite reach her eyes. She focused back on the questionnaire, the questions starting to bleed together, the only delineation of the passage of time being the infrequent visits from Michelle.

"What question are you on now, sweetheart?" she asked.

Justine looked down at the tablet. "Something about food preferences."

She nodded. "I'll come back in another five minutes. Yell down the hallway if you're done before then."

Justine nodded and watched as Michelle disappeared again. She turned back to the device in her hands and continued plowing through question after question.

Several minutes later, she sighed a breath of relief when the screen changed to "Thank you for completing our question-naire. We'll be with you shortly."

"Done, finally done," Justine said melodramatically as she flopped flamboyantly backward.

Amira laughed at her dramatics. "It can't be *that* bad."

She waved the tablet in the air. "Did you *see* how many questions they asked?"

She smirked. "I bet I could have done it in half the time, and with far less fussing."

"I doubt it."

Amira shrugged, still smirking, and stood. "I'll go get the lady." She opened the door, called down the hallway, and held it open while footsteps approached from the distance. A few moments later, Michelle appeared, and Amira stepped back, ushering her inside.

"All done?" she asked, a smile on her face.

Justine offered her the tablet.

"I'll get right on this." She took the tablet and clutched it to her chest. "Are you both comfortable in here?"

"Yes, thank you," Amira said while Justine nodded.

Michelle turned on her heel with an answering nod and disappeared once more.

"How long do you think she'll be gone?" Justine asked.

Amira shrugged. "Who knows?"

Michelle walked briskly down the hallway, her heels muffled by the carpet underfoot.

Once in her office, she immediately plugged the tablet into her computer, which started the data transfer. She sat down at her desk and wiggled the mouse, bringing up the desktop. In the bottom right corner, a dialog box slid on screen, saying, "Download Complete. Click to Continue." She clicked, and her matching software came up, showing the new entry on the screen.

"Justine Foley, eh? Let's see if we can't get you a match." Michelle initiated a search of the four databases, then sat back to wait. She never did this with clients waiting, and she could feel every moment as the software did its magic. She imagined those women waiting in the other room, hoping for a match, most likely hoping for an escape. Unfortunately, this was going to take a while. She usually had searches running in the background or overnight. She *never* had clients waiting in the offices and staring at the screen now was like watching paint dry.

Michelle sighed. It could have been worse, she supposed. She'd done everything she could to speed up the process when she'd commissioned the development of the software. The questionnaires were all check boxes and multiple-choice questions, resulting in specific, concrete options she could directly associate with the translated options in the partner databases. It meant matches to individual questions could do performed automatically and profiles could be paired heuristically.

Still, it always took time. There were hundreds of questions and an unfathomable number of profiles across the four databases, hers being the smallest, of course. Right now, she only had a handful of names in her database due to a combination of few clients overall and a healthy streak of luck with finding matches.

Michelle switched to checking emails while she waited, wondering at the same time if she should check in with the women. Should she offer them a drink or snack again? Would that be appropriate? Or would that be annoying, like a salesperson who just won't leave you alone to make a decision?

No wonder you have no clients.

She gritted her teeth, annoyed at the little voice that always seemed to slip in when she was at her lowest. She couldn't help that the business hadn't taken off yet. It was still early days. She hadn't even been running the agency for six months, and she'd heard nothing but positive things so far. The few people she'd placed up until now had even thanked her when she'd checked in on them. She knew this was the right direction for her life. She just needed to remind herself of that every now and then.

Michelle startled when a dialog box popped up with, "Search Complete. View Matches."

She looked down at the time. It hadn't even been ten minutes. "That was fast," she muttered as she clicked the little window.

The screen changed. Now, the profile name, "Justine Foley," was in a band across the top, with the rest of the window split into two even panels and one much narrower one. On the left, the narrow panel listed the profiles she'd matched to, each with a computer generated Similarity Score. The middle panel showed her answers and the panel on the right showed the match's answers. Each answer was ranked by color, with the most compatible in green and the least compatible in red.

The highest ranked profile, with 97% SS, was already selected by default. It was a profile from the planet Savala. Male. She started quickly scanning through the profiles, looking for any potential problems. The software pulled up the red-highlighted answers first, then dropped the green ones to the bottom as they were often less important when making an ideal match for a client.

After checking only a few of the answers for the first match, she dismissed it. This was part of the reason why reviewing matches manually was so very important. The computer could tell you where they differed, but it couldn't tell you if that difference was important. Here, at least based on her initial impression of the client, the areas where they differed would probably be a problem.

She moved on to the next one. It had 96% SS, and she immediately said, "Nope," when she saw he had a dominant personality.

The third had 94% SS, and she was starting to get worried. Ordinarily, she would take her time, go through each thoroughly, maybe even check the database in the weeks to come looking for a better match, but she suspected Justine couldn't wait that long.

There were more discrepancies with this one, but even at a glance, she could tell this would be a better match. There was a lot of yellow on the screen but no red, an indication that they differed in degrees rather than extremes. In her experience, having a lot of minor differences was better than a couple major ones. She began to relax as she scrolled through the results. The color-coded answers gradually changed from yellow to yellow-green and eventually to green.

"Maybe this will be it," she said under her breath, now

reading through each set of answers to decide if the computer analysis meshed with her own interpretations. She did it quickly, only glancing over each question before moving on. She got more impressions and general themes than anything else as she flew through the profiles. The deeper she got, the more she thought they would be a good fit.

Justine seemed fragile, in need of a listening ear and a gentle touch. He seemed laid back and flexible. He checked family oriented and supportive, but undecided about having kids. She wondered if he had a large family. That might be good for Justine, especially with her leaving her world behind.

By the time she reached the bottom of the profiles, she didn't feel she needed to check any of the other matches. This one felt right.

"Now, for the hard part."

With a keyboard command, she switched to the desktop and clicked the icon for a communications software. When the screen loaded, there were only three contacts. She clicked the first, labeled "Savala."

The screen changed to "One Moment. Connecting..."

Michelle leaned back in her seat, wondering how long the connection would take. She knew nothing about the technology, only that it cost a pretty penny and was slow as hell. It took several minutes for the screen to change. "Call connected," it said now.

"Hi, this is Michelle Mackey with the Best Life Interstellar Matchmaking Agency."

After a considerable lag, the person said, "Hello, Michelle. How can I help you today?" The lag was due to a combination of factors, including the distance and the built in translation service.

"I have a client that just finished filling out a questionnaire. She would like immediate placement, if possible. I've run her profile through the databases and got a match to a..." she pulled up her matching software, "Zayvan Akhren? My client is currently waiting in the offices for a result. I'm going to bring this profile out to her to review after this call. Is there any way you can expedite things on your end?"

"What's the rush?"

"I think she might be in danger."

"A criminal?"

"I don't think so. I don't have any information, but I suspect abuse."

"She was abused?"

"Yes."

"Okay. I have his profile on my display. I'll try to reach out to him as soon as I end this call."

"Thanks. Do you know when I can expect an answer?"

"Hard to say. I'll let you know one way or the other by the end of the day."

"Okay. Thanks."

"Goodbye."

"Bye."

Michelle hung up and switched back to the matches. She clicked the "Download to Tablet" button in the upper right corner. A moment later, a "Download Complete" dialog box popped up, and she disconnected the device. She stood, grabbed the tablet, and rushed out. A dozen or so steps later, and she was standing in front of the room she'd stashed Justine and her friend in.

Michelle knocked this time. She hadn't said when she would be returning, after all. She wouldn't want to be rude.

The door opened, and the woman in the hijab stepped out of the way to let her in.

Michelle smiled at her, then turned to Justine. "Good news. I think I may have a match for you."

"That fast?"

Michelle shrugged. "Well, ordinarily it would take a few days, maybe a few weeks, but I tried to speed things up a bit. I hope that's all right?"

"Oh," Justine blushed. "Thanks."

"No problem." Michelle stepped forward, placing the tablet in front of Justine. She turned on the display and switched the screen over to the match download. "This is the profile I picked. He's a 94% match, and I did look through the results by hand. It looks like a good fit between the two of you, but of course, you each have final say in accepting or rejecting the match.

"I've also reached out to the agency on Savala, asking them to expedite the notification process on their end as well. They promised to get me an answer by the end of the day."

"Okay," Justine said quietly.

"I should warn you. I'm doing the best I can to expedite this, but there's no guarantee we'll have a match today. We're dealing with people on another planet, and my partner agency might not be able to contact your match right away. Even if they can, he still has to look over your profile and make his own decision. Then they have to call back with an answer. There's really no fast way of doing this."

Justine nodded, looking like her eyes were glazing over.

Michelle leaned down and touched her gently on the back of her hand. "Don't worry. Everything is going to work out."

"Thanks." Justine looked down and picked up the tablet, slowly looking through the profile.

Michelle waited patiently at her shoulder, holding her breath in anticipation, praying Justine would like her choice.

It was a long wait.

Justine didn't know what to think when Michelle handed her the tablet. She was nervous and excited and just the tiniest bit scared. This was it, after all, the solution she'd settled on, the solution to all her problems.

Maybe.

With a little sigh, she dug into the information. Most of it just blurred before her eyes, her attention span already seriously strained by the questionnaire she'd just filled out.

At the top, there was his name in bold text: Zayvan. It sounded... nice. Exotic but nice. She could imagine shortening it to something like Zay, saying things like, "Hey, Zay." She wondered if it was pronounced how it looked on the screen or if she was butchering it.

After that, the questions were all familiar, the exact same ones from her questionnaire, only this time, the answers weren't always what she'd chosen. Some answers left her relieved, while others sparked her curiosity. There was no picture, so she had no idea what he looked like or if they would have any chemistry together.

But what does that matter? It's not like you're doing this for the sex.

But even if she excluded chemistry, how could she possibly *know* if this was the right man for her? How could she decide something like that without even meeting the person? Would they be good together? Or would they constantly fight? Would he be like Brian? Or would he be exactly what she needed?

Her mind ran in circles as it tried to make sense of this decision, constantly thwarting whatever progress she made with endless what-ifs. There was so much uncertainty, so much she just *couldn't* know, that it left her paralyzed.

But then again, did it really matter? Her main goal was just to leave Earth. So long as he wasn't an abusive jerk, she supposed one guy was as good as the next. Hell, for that criteria, even a woman would do. She could totally see herself living with a woman as a pair of spinsters. Had a certain appeal, actually.

Then you should have picked that on the questionnaire, stupid.

She frowned down at the tablet, continuing to peruse his answers.

Then music suddenly blared into the silent room, and Justine jerked, a high-pitched noise squeaking past her vocal cords automatically. She spun around in her seat, searching out the source.

Michelle blushed and pulled her phone from her pocket. "Sorry," she whispered, then stepped back and answered. "Michelle Mackey, Best Life Interstellar Matchmaking Agency."

Justine watched as Michelle nodded her head, saying, "uh-huh" over and over again.

"Great, that's wonderful. I'm still working out the details, but that should be fine so long as I get a response in time from my partner on Savala. All right. Thanks. Bye." She hung up and faced Justine. "Well, good news. I have transportation scheduled for ten o'clock tonight, so long as we get a confirmed match. Do you need more time with the information?"

Justine looked down at the tablet. She wanted to feel good about this choice, optimistic and hopeful even, but was there even a choice? What else was she going to do? A woman's shelter? Hope he didn't come back to Amira's apartment? Neither of those felt like options. She felt backed into a corner, and while she didn't like that feeling, she looked up anyway and said, "Looks fine."

Michelle smiled like a salesperson, clapping her hands together and saying, "Excellent." She took a deep breath. "I assume you have some preparations you need to make, so while we're waiting on a response from my partner agency, why don't you head out and do what you need to do and meet back here at say five, six o'clock?"

"Okay," Justine said, feeling even more hesitant. Preparations? What was there to prepare? She had no possessions, no purse, no luggage, no ID. Nothing. She didn't even have any money, thanks to Brian.

Amira stood up. "Justine lost her phone recently, so the number on the profile is my cell phone number. You'll get me if you call it."

Michelle renewed her smile. "That's perfectly fine." She reached behind her and grabbed a business card. "Here. In case you need to reach me."

"Thanks." Amira slipped the card into her back jeans pocket and turned to Justine. "Ready?"

Justine shrugged and stood. "I guess."

Michelle backed up out of the way. "See you soon."

As she turned toward the exit, Justine couldn't help wondering if that was true. *Would* she see her soon? Or would Brian find her and end this venture before it even got started?

As Amira ushered her longtime friend back to her car, she was plagued with a weird mix of emotions. She wanted to protect Justine, but not like this. She didn't want to let her go, to see her boarding a spaceship for some planet Amira would never see. Justine was like family to her, and the idea of never seeing her again was really messing with her head.

But at the same time, she could understand at least *some* of Justine's logic. She could understand wanting to run, wanting to escape. She could even understand thinking nowhere on

Earth was safe. While all of this was outside of her own lived experiences, she certainly had empathy.

But as she settled into the driver's seat, a sense of doom and despair blanketed her. She'd just got Justine back in her life again, and now she was losing her, possibly for good. Her hands clenched the steering wheel as she stared out at the parking lot. They'd been inside the offices for quite a while, and now the once fairly empty lot was filled with cars. With a quiet sigh, she reached to start the car, then backed out of the parking space. "Let's go get you some things for your trip."

Justine's face fell. "But I don't have any money."

A part of her wasn't surprised. After all, there had been something small and waif-like about Justine's appearance on Amira's doorstep, like an orphan begging for a meal in an old novel. She'd had the air of someone on their last leg, acutely aware that their only chance at survival was through charity. "It's fine," she said. "I'll get you set up."

Justine shook her head. "I can't let you do that."

Amira stopped and glanced at Justine before turning onto the road. "You have no toiletries, no changes of clothes. Not only will that look suspicious, it will also be a hardship, not just for you, but also for the crew of the ship. Do you really want to be begging clothes and such off of strangers?"

Justine frowned and faced forward once more.

"We can try to keep it within reason." Amira set her turn by turn directions. The *cheapest* option would be a thrift shop, but they were limited on time, and it wouldn't have everything they needed. She accepted she would be spending a pretty penny getting Justine ready to leave, but that was actually the first part of this whole adventure she could smile about. She *wanted* to get her friend ready for this next stage in her life. It felt good to do this for her, even if it meant not seeing her again.

They spent the rest of the drive in silence. Amira almost let out a breath of relief when she spotted the store and its busy parking lot. She quickly found a parking spot and led Justine inside.

The store was nothing special, a line of checkout counters to her left and displays of goods everywhere else. She didn't usually go to stores, far preferring the ease of drone deliveries, but today was an exception. Today, she was sending her friend off toward her new life, and she wanted to make sure Justine was prepared.

Amira grabbed a cart and glanced around, trying to decide where to go first. Justine needed... everything. How long would the trip be? How much would she need? She pulled the business card out of her back pocket and stared at it. Should she call and ask?

Except... did it really matter? It was bound to be a long trip. It wasn't like travel-sized products would do the trick. If she just got full-sized bottles, it was probably fine, right?

"Let's see." She leaned in, checking the first aisle on her right. Deodorant. "I guess we can start here." Moving down each aisle in sequence was as good a plan as any.

Justine started stammering. She glanced at the displays then behind her, like she was looking for something different. "I mean... I... I'm sure travel size is perfectly fine."

Amira tried not to scowl at her. "Travel size will last maybe a week. This trip is probably gonna take a lot longer than that. Pick up the full size and let me worry about the price. Okay?"

"But..."

Amira pointed a finger at her. "I mean it. Don't look at the prices. Get what you need. I'll handle the rest."

Justine shook her head. "I don't deserve you."

Amira chuckled. "Yeah, you do. I just wish we'd had more time. It kind of sucks that we haven't really spoken in so long."

She looked away and sighed. "If possible, will you try to contact me, let me know you're okay?"

"Oh, absolutely. I'll abuse your phone bills so much you'd beg me to stop."

Amira really laughed this time, holding her stomach and bending over slightly. Eventually getting her breathing back under control, she straightened and looked over at Justine. "Fair."

After that, Justine finally started putting things in the cart. Amira watched her like a hawk, making sure she wasn't just grabbing the cheapest thing on the shelves, but she seemed to take Amira's warning to heart. She watched as Justine hunted the unfamiliar aisles, looking for specific items, and from what she knew of her friend, they seemed to be products she would need. A shampoo for oily hair. A face wash for combination skin. A body wash with moisturizer because Justine had never been good at using a separate one.

After a spell, they moved out of toiletries and into clothes. Justine was more stubborn here, wanting to rush to the clearance racks first, but Amira resisted until she couldn't take Justine's pouting anymore. The clearance racks proved fruitful, though. That was the first time her friend seemed to actually get into the shopping experience, and Amira suddenly remembered how much Justine hated clothes shopping. She used to joke about preferring thrifting or clearance shopping because it was like treasure hunting. It was the only way you could get her to shop for clothes sometimes.

Justine tried on the clothes at speed, tossing the duds over the door at a pace Amira found impressive. In less than half an hour, they had a pile of clothes in the cart that would probably last Justine about a week between washings.

"Now, we just need luggage."

"Oh, this is already too much. I'm sure the shopping bags will be fine."

"Justine…" Amira said, scolding her friend once more.

"What?" she replied, sounding slightly defensive.

"We've talked about this. You need these things. You are my friend. I don't want you showing up at your new home looking like a vagabond. You wanted a fresh start. I want to give you that. I want you to meet this guy for the first time and feel like yourself. You deserve that. I want to give you that chance." Away from him.

She didn't say it. She didn't want to remind Justine of what she was running from. No. She wanted to get her looking to the future.

Justine frowned as she took in Amira's words, but eventually started searching for the luggage section.

Amira pulled out her phone and looked up luggage on the store's website. She had to change the store location, but then when she clicked a piece of luggage, it gave an aisle location next to the name. "Aisle H3."

"Where is that?"

Amira looked up from her phone. "Don't know yet, but that's where it says luggage is. Let's check the nearby aisles." It looked like toiletries and foodstuffs were on one side of the store, while automotive, tools, and toys were on the other. They were in the middle of clothing right now, but the center of the store was too big to just be clothes.

In short order, they found what they were looking for and proceeded to scour the selection for a bag that would fit everything. Justine kept leaning toward the duffels because they were cheaper, but Amira felt a proper suitcase would make things easier for her friend. And of course, Justine balked at the price tag on the one that fit all her new things.

The full-sized toiletries took up a lot of space.

Justine lifted the tag and glanced at it. "No, that's too much," she said as she turned to Amira in protest.

Amira remained firm. "You might be living out of that bag for months. This will be easier to organize." She reached for the bag, determined to just load it into the cart.

"It's too expensive." Justine pulled it away and waved her hand at the items they'd already picked out. "You've already done too much."

"Nonsense." Amira outmaneuvered her friend and dropped the suitcase in the cart over Justine's continued objections, then turned and pleaded with her. "Let me do this. This might be the last time we ever see each other."

Justine sucked in a breath, pain glimmering in her eyes, then reluctantly nodded.

Having won the battle, and feeling like she'd lost the war, Amira took up the reins of the cart and headed to the checkout counters.

It was a bittersweet moment. Justine now had everything she needed. She could leave. It reinforced in Amira's heart just how much she didn't want her to go, but there was nothing she could do. The only thing she could do was pray Justine found happiness... and wait.

<hr>

After their shopping spree, Justine followed Amira back to her car, staring at that cart full of bags the entire time. There was something about it that captured her attention in a morbid way. It kind of made her feel like a homeless person.

You are *a homeless person.*

She pushed that thought aside, trying to reassure herself that she wasn't. Amira had offered her a place. She *wasn't* homeless.

When they reached the car, they removed all the tags and loaded it all into the suitcase. It was a little heavy, but easily fit inside the trunk. It actually looked a little sad and tiny laying there on its side, a black and purple reminder of everything she'd lost. Everything she owned was in that suitcase. And she'd paid for none of it. It made her feel dirty.

She didn't tell Amira that, though.

Instead, she walked away and settled herself in the passenger seat without saying a word. She heard the trunk thump as Amira closed it, then moments later, Amira settled in beside her.

They didn't speak as they returned to the agency. On her end, she didn't know what to say. What *could* she say? She was leaving her best friend behind, and to make matters worse, she was a leach. But why was Amira silent? She glanced over at her a few times during the drive, but was unable to read her expression. Was she sad? Angry? Conflicted? Was she regretting offering to help? Did seeing the price tag on that trip make her change her mind? Was she struggling with losing a friend like Justine was?

When Amira stopped the car and pulled the parking brake, Justine finally broke the silence. "You could come with me," she blurted out.

The moment the words left her lips, she knew she'd fucked up. She didn't need to see Amira's face or hear her words or tone. She already knew what the answer would be.

"Justine, I can't."

There it was.

Amira sighed. "I don't want to lose you either, but my place is here. Earth is my home. I can't imagine leaving it. How would I know where Mecca is? How would I know which direction to pray? And I still haven't carried out my hajj. That's something I've been planning for years." She reached out, touching Justine's arm. "Listen, I know you're scared. I understand. I'm sure that's why you said that. You've always been so respectful of my beliefs. I refuse to believe you would ever intentionally ignore them now. I will be with you as long as I can, but I can't go with you. I'm sorry."

Justine dropped her head, looking down at her lap, where her hands were twisting together like a nest of snakes. "I know," she whispered. She was already sorry she'd spoken. It wasn't fair to Amira, who was probably already struggling with Justine's departure. "I'm sorry. That was wrong of me."

"It's okay," Amira said, touching her shoulder in empathy. "I know you're going through a lot. Now, why don't we go inside and see if you'll be leaving tonight?"

Justine looked up from her lap and tried to smile. "Okay."

Amira smiled back and opened her door, stepping out into the warm, now afternoon, sun. Justine followed suit, and Amira was already unloading the suitcase before Justine had closed her door.

A few minutes later and they were back in the agency's lobby, and Justine pressed the bell for service.

Would the lady have an answer already? Would she be leaving Earth today?

Justine was frustrated with the lack of answers. It was all so much waiting and worrying. When was she going to be free and safe? When could she finally start over?

The door opened, and Michelle spilled out, smiling her salesperson smile. "Welcome back." She clapped her hands together as she'd done before. "I have good news. The match is confirmed. You'll be shipping out at ten as we'd hoped."

"Excellent," Amira said, her voice thick with emotion.

Justine simply nodded, unable to look at her friend.

Michelle looked down at the packed luggage. "I see you're

all ready. I'll bring you over to the break room. It's got more comfortable seating."

They walked through the hallway again, this time passing by the room they'd been in last time. They took a left turn, then Michelle opened a door, exposing a room with a couch, a TV, and a small kitchenette.

Amira rolled the suitcase in and set it beside the sofa, then slowly spun around, taking in the area.

Which was about when a thought struck her. When was the last time Amira prayed? Was she overdue?

"Amira, you can leave me here if you need to go take care of things."

"What?" she said, looking confused.

"Prayer?"

Amira looked down at her watch. "It would be nice to pray at home, and if I leave now, I'll get there just before Duhur."

"Well then go, and maybe bring some food on your way back. We can eat junk food and watch garbage TV while we're waiting for my flight."

Amira smiled. "Just like old times." She walked toward the door and clasped Justine's shoulder. "I'll be back before you know it. *With* the requisite junk food."

"Go," Justine said, gesturing with her head.

Amira disappeared out the door and within a few minutes, she couldn't even hear her footsteps.

"Are you hungry? Do you need something to tide you over?" Michelle asked from the doorway, interrupting Justine's preoccupation.

"No, I'm fine for now." Though she hadn't eaten anything in over six hours, she definitely wasn't hungry. Life with Brian had acclimated her to skipping meals. After the injury, she'd struggled with making food for herself, eventually getting to the point where her only proper meals were breakfast and dinner with Brian. At first, she'd managed to bring some junk food like cereal and chips to the couch or bed, but Brian quickly nipped that in the bud, saying it was a bad habit. Before long, it had seemed completely normal to go most of the day without eating.

"Okay." Michelle crossed the room and picked up the remote. "This controls the TV. I have several streaming services." She powered everything up. "You can access everything from this menu." A series of boxes with streaming service logos populated the screen. "Watch whatever you like while you wait."

"Thanks."

Michelle nodded, then left her to her own devices.

Her leg was starting to hurt again from being on it for too long, so she settled on the couch and started surfing the various services, looking for something to watch.

Before she knew it, Amira was back with pizza, and they both dug into their food while rewatching an old favorite from their college days. It made her feel nostalgic and a little weepy. She yearned for the good old days, pre-Brian, when they could just be girls together, carefree and innocent. He'd taken that from her, and she simultaneously wanted to cry, which she was now beyond tired of, and hit something.

Why did good people always seem to get punished? Why did bad people just get to take without every facing any repercussions? Why did there never seem to be any justice in the world?

She stared at the screen, where a heroine was saucily declaring her victory, symbolically throwing her foe to the floor at her feet. It was cathartic and fun.

And nothing like real life.

In real life, her foe would step all over her and get away with it. Society would turn a blind eye, and some poor schmuck would be blamed for all the ills of the world. There was no justice anymore. She'd seen that personally.

They spent the evening watching episode after episode and slowly working their way through the massive pizza. At one point, they paused the TV so Amira could do her evening prayer in the corner.

Eventually, Michelle returned. "Ready to go?" she asked, peeking her head into the room.

Justine looked over at Amira. The word *no* flitted through her head. No, she wasn't ready to go, but also, her mind shied away from even the *idea* of staying. Just skimming close to that concept had her heart racing and sweat forming on her brow. She stood and nodded. Amira followed, reaching for the suitcase.

"How do we do this?" Amira asked, taking the lead once again.

Justine was grateful to Amira. She didn't think she would have managed without her. When Justine had arrived on her doorstep, she'd just wanted to run and hide. A part of her had just wanted to curl up in a ball somewhere and shiver until her mind melted into a senseless fog. Amira had been her anchor.

"Well, this whole situation is very unusual," Michelle said, turning around to talk to them as she led them down the hallway. "The matching process usually takes weeks, and I have a business arrangement with a specific transportation firm. Because of the rush, I'm working with a different company and I have to finalize some details in person, so I'll drive you to the spaceport myself."

Time seemed to accelerate and twist and jump for Justine as they continued onward. She remembered the lobby, the elevator, walking to an SUV as the sun dipped below the trees in the distance. There was a blur of travel. Trees, gray buildings, side streets, then things changed. Buildings fell away and cement started filling up the vistas.

The car turned, and Justine got her first look at a spaceship that wasn't in the air. It was massive, gray, and dirty as hell, even in the failing daylight. The shape was also not exactly what she'd expected, having grown up with the more aerodynamic designs of airplanes. It also looked... segmented... like an insect. She wondered why. What purpose did that hold?

Michelle turned the car again, and now they were approaching a big blocky building, which they stopped in front of moments later. She twisted in her seat to face Justine and smiled. "Are you ready for your new life?"

No, but what else can I do?

She nodded instead.

"Good. Come on."

Everyone exited, with Amira again grabbing the suitcase. They entered the building through a steel door. Inside, a woman waited behind a desk.

"How can I help you?" the woman asked, sitting up taller as she spoke. She had a headset on, making her look like a receptionist.

"Hi, my name's Michelle Mackey from the Best Life Interstellar Matchmaking Agency."

"That's quite a mouthful."

"Yes, I suppose it is. I have scheduled passage for one with..." She looked down at her phone. "Speedy Transit?"

"I'll let them know you've arrived." The woman looked down at her desk, doing something Justine could only guess at, before holding her hand up to her headset. "Hi, this is Stacy at the spaceport office. Your passenger has arrived." She paused. "Uh-huh." Another pause. "You're quite welcome. Goodbye." She ended the call, then looked up at them with a smile. "He'll be with you shortly."

"Thank you," Michelle said, then turned around to face her and Amira. "Ready?"

Why does she keep saying that? Of course I'm not ready. How could I be ready? How could anyone be ready to leave their entire world behind?

Justine nodded again anyway.

"I'll give you two a moment to say goodbye." Michelle walked away, striking up a conversation with the receptionist.

Justine turned to Amira. "Thanks for everything. You've been amazing. I..."

Amira suddenly lurched forward and hugged her, holding her tight without a word. They stayed that way for several minutes, with Justine awkwardly curling her hands around Amira's back in return. Her heart warmed at the show of affection, at being touched in a positive way for the first time in what felt like ages.

When the door opened, they broke apart reluctantly. Amira had tears in her eyes, threatening to fall. "I just found you again. I'm going to miss you so much. It's not fair."

"Life's not fair. And I'm gonna miss you, too." She did her darnedest not to cry, holding her emotion back, desperate not to fall apart and have Amira's last image of her being snot and tears.

A conversation went on around them as they stared at each other, dreading the moment of parting.

"Don't forget your promise," Amira said, her expression strained with the effort of holding back tears. She was clearly trying not to fall apart.

"I won't. I'll figure out a way to reach you. Somehow."

Amira nodded. "Good. That's good." She wiped her eyes, smearing a bit of black eye makeup across her cheek and finger.

"Justine?" a gruff man said, coming around her right side.

"Yes?"

"You ready?" He was big, tall, and wide, with a bushy beard that made him look like a biker.

Justine had a momentary tendril of fear, which she tamped down ruthlessly. She nodded.

"Here," Amira said, pushing the suitcase into her hand.

"Thanks." Justine rested her hand over Amira's on the handle, gripping it and knowing this was the last time she would ever touch her friend. Maybe it was the last time she would ever see her.

"Goodbye, Justine." Amira was losing her battle with composure, her voice betraying the pain she was feeling.

Justine squeezed her friend's hand even harder. "Goodbye, Amira. I'm gonna miss you so much."

Amira nodded, the tears now pouring down her face as she slipped her hand out from beneath Justine's and took a step backward. "You need to go." She sniffed. "He's leaving."

Justine nodded and turned around. The gruff man was already walking toward the door. She followed him, determined not to turn and steal one last look at the life she was leaving behind.

Hopefully, I won't regret this.

CHAPTER THREE

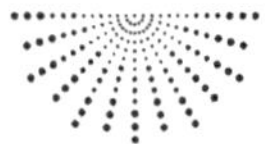

The captain, the man with the bushy beard, introduced her to the crew, but she was ashamed to admit that the introductions didn't stick. She couldn't remember a single person's name, not even his.

The entire time, her ears had been ringing so badly it was hard to focus on anything external. So, she'd quietly allowed him to show her around the ship, pointing out the galley, the bathrooms, and the private quarters. He pointed out rooms she wasn't allowed to enter and where to find anyone if she needed help. The ship was all more function than form, a lot of bare-bones metal that sent a shiver down her spine.

Finally, he showed her to her room, which resembled a closet more than anything else. She rolled her bag into a corner and turned to the captain, who was still standing in the doorway.

"Here," he said, offering her a tablet and charger. She hadn't even noticed it was there. "It belongs to that Mackey woman. Don't ask me what it's all about, but you're supposed to use it on the journey."

She accepted it, hugging it to her chest. That bit of fear earlier was returning slowly as he continued to hover, blocking her only exit.

Finally, he moved, stepping into the tiny room and crowding her.

She flinched, but he didn't seem to notice.

"The rooms are small, but kinda modular, ya' know?" He lifted the mattress, and it locked in place with a click, almost disappearing into the wall. After that, he smacked another section of wall and a desk almost fell out. A chair pulled out from underneath it. He turned to the long wall across from the now-missing bed and slapped this wall too. A display kicked on. "The TV can interface with most devices, so if you need a larger screen, you got it. We also have a number of programs saved to the ship's mainframe. You can access any of them whenever you like." He turned. "Any questions?"

She shook her head, though she felt completely out of her depths.

He nodded. "Good. We serve meals three times a day. If you miss it, you'll have to do some reheating. I'd advise catching the meals."

She nodded.

"Well," he said, clearing his throat and moving toward the hallway. "I guess that's it. Let me know if you have any questions."

"I will," she said quietly.

He nodded one last time, then left.

Finally alone, the tension slowly eased from her as she looked around at the barren room, wondering what she should do now.

Then he popped back into view. She shrieked and slammed into the back wall, which wasn't very far, but still left her breathless.

"Sorry about that. Didn't mean to startle you. Just forgot one last bit. You'll need to come up to the bridge for takeoff. It's not really safe in these little rooms at that time. Lot of g forces."

She nodded, no longer able to speak.

"Right, well, *that* is definitely everything. See you in a few."

He disappeared again, and she didn't relax until she heard his heavy footsteps slowly softening as he walked away.

After takeoff, Justine headed back to her room, wondering about the tablet. The agency woman hadn't mentioned it. What was it for?

Before heading for the bridge, she'd tucked the tablet into her suitcase, so now she put the bag on its side and unzipped it, pulling out the mysterious tablet. It looked identical to the one at the office, but when she powered it on, it didn't load a questionnaire or profile. Instead, it looked a lot like any other tablet, with icons in a grid pattern across the screen.

It was the apps loaded onto the tablet that made it different, though.

Culture

Laws & Regulations

Language

They looked to be learning apps. She clicked Language.

It opened to a welcome screen that explained the purpose of the app. At the bottom, a great big friendly button said, "Let's Get Started."

She clicked it as little butterflies took flight in her stomach.

This was it. It was time to start preparing for her new life.

She couldn't tell if she was excited or about to throw up.

During the journey, Justine devoted herself to learning on the tablet, thinking of nothing else, sometimes not even food. A couple times now, the captain had come by with a dinner tray, but each time she'd mumbled a thank you as she continued to work on her lessons. She didn't even remember him leaving.

The tiny room was both her sanctuary and her prison. Her fears and anxieties made everyone a potential threat, and she knew *none* of these people, knew nothing about their motivations or morals. Hell, even Michelle from the agency didn't know these people. She'd said this was her first time working with them. Add that to Justine's past, and she was frankly terrified of mingling with the crew, terrified of what they might do to her, even if a part of her recognized that they were probably safe to be around. Most people were. And yet, she couldn't escape the fact that she was all alone out here. Just her against the universe. No one else was looking out for her. These people could do anything they wanted to her in the black of space and who would punish them?

When thoughts like that popped up, it was hard not to think of Brian. It was exhilarating knowing he couldn't get to her, but Amira was right. That didn't mean she'd dealt with her issues. She feared everyone and everything, and throughout the journey, she often wondered if she was making the right choice. Was she going to regret this? Was she going from the frying pan to the fryer?

When those thoughts got really bad, she would pull up the copy of Zayvan's profile she'd found on her tablet, using it to remind herself of what lay ahead, of what she was looking forward to. She would reread the answers again and again, and eventually, they would help her calm down.

The rest of the time, though, she managed to keep those thoughts at bay, instead focusing on being as prepared for her new life as possible. Her fear made her obsessive, and she was convinced that if she didn't know his language like the back of her hand and understand his culture like it was her own, she would end up in an even worse situation than before. Knowledge was power, and she was determined to gain as much of it as she could in the months leading up to their arrival on Savala.

She recognized the utility of these educational programs, that they were designed to smooth the transition between one home and the next, but to her, they were a lifeline, both a distraction and a source of empowerment.

Justine spent most days sitting at that desk, back bent over the tablet as she consumed the content, never satisfied with her level of knowledge, never satisfied with her mastery of the language. Every day, she would stand up and feel her entire skeletal system crack and pop in protest at not moving for such a long period of time.

This obsession with knowledge also messed with her sleep schedule, and she often found herself leaving her room at odd hours, never realizing what time it was until she stepped out of the sensory depravation chamber her room had become. She often got up to take a shower in the middle of the night or fell asleep right as someone announced the noonday meal, her eyes no longer able to keep from blurring with exhaustion.

It became an obsession with her, trying to be prepared. It was like she was trying to build an armor, like if she just got good enough with the language, learned enough about the culture, learned enough about their world, she would finally feel safe.

"I *will* be safe," she said to herself, trying to believe it.

I have to be.

"We are approaching the planet of Savala. Please prepare for landing in two hours," the captain said over the intercom.

Justine froze, hand hovering over her tablet, and sat upright, hearing her back pop as she moved for the first time in hours.

That was stupid.

Justine rested her forehead on her hand and sighed. She'd intended to get a good night's sleep before their arrival, but that was out of the question now. She'd really wanted to make a good first impression, and she always felt her best after a shower and a solid eight hours' of rest, but she'd let her compulsion get the better of her.

Well, at least she could still get that shower. She stood, her legs protesting the unfamiliar sensation of holding her up, and grabbed her suitcase, wheeling it out through her door.

"Excuse me," a woman said as she passed by on her way to the bridge.

Justine nodded and smiled after her, feeling bad that she still hadn't learned the woman's name.

She turned in the opposite direction. The bathrooms were just a short distance down the hall, and she reached them fairly quickly. The room had three toilets and three showers. She rolled the suitcase to the middle shower stall, lifted it onto a bench, and pulled out what she needed, setting them on the designated shelves.

After quickly stripping, she stepped under the shower head, slid the door closed, and turned on the water. It poured down onto her, almost instantly providing heat and steam. She sighed as the tension she'd been living with melted away, if only for a little while. This was her favorite part of the day and, even if everything else was a mess, she made sure to make time for this. This was her happy place.

She stood there under the spray for ages, letting her skin heat, letting her cares wash away. She had no idea how long she'd been standing under the spray by the time she finally reached for the shampoo bottle, but once she did, she was quick about it, rapidly moving through washing and rinsing.

Finished, Justine turned off the water and opened the door once more. She grabbed her towel and patted herself dry, then pulled on her clothing one by one. Finally, she dried off her toiletries and put them away, rolling everything back to her room.

As she stood just inside the entrance to the room she'd lived in for the past few months, a moment of sheer terror hit her. That same question she'd been agonizing over for months assaulted her mind, this time with the force of a freight train. What if this was a great big mistake? What if he was just like Brian?

She tried to reassure herself, remind herself that she'd seen his profile. She knew what he wanted and what type of person he was.

And yet she'd thought she knew Brian as well. He hadn't started off like that. No, he'd started off sweet and caring. He'd been chivalrous, constantly making her smile. She'd felt womanly and loved when she was with him, and he always seemed to thrive on giving her the space to relax, to not have to be "on" all the time. She'd never felt like she needed to take charge with him because he was always so competent.

Justine had never expected that could be a bad thing.

She fell back against the doorjamb, her breathing a little shaky as the panic gripped her. The hard surface dug into her spine as her hands clenched on her shirt, probably stretching it out of shape.

Calm down, Justine.

He's not Brian.

He could never be Brian.

She took a slow, calming breath. "It's fine. This is a new

start. I'm putting this behind me. He doesn't have control over me anymore," she whispered.

The panic dimmed, but it left a dark stain upon her psyche in its wake. She pushed off the wall and crossed the room, gathering up the tablet so it wouldn't go flying when they started their descent to the planet. She went to put it in her suitcase, but then remembered it wasn't hers.

Justine looked down at it, and the panic almost returned. This device had been her security blanket for the last few months, a necessary crutch to keep her occupied. It had prevented her from falling apart. She knew that, and as such, she didn't want to leave it behind.

And yet, like so many other things in her life, this was outside of her control. There was no choice she could make. In fact, the only real choices she'd made in the last few years had been leaving Brian and leaving Earth.

And as she left the room and walked to the bridge, dread churned ominously in her stomach.

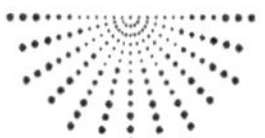

CHAPTER FOUR

Justine was on the bridge, tablet and charger clutched to her chest while harness straps kept her in her seat. From here, she could see space beyond, something she'd only had the briefest glimpses of so far.

It felt cold and vacant, like she could fall into it and never escape. From what she knew of space, that was fairly accurate. Even looking at it inspired fear in her, and it didn't start to subside until the planet of Savala came into view.

It was strange and beautiful. The only inhabited planet she was used to seeing pictures of from space was Earth, which was mostly blue and white, like a frosty blueberry, but this planet looked almost completely white, and she couldn't tell if it was cloud cover or snow.

Around her, the crew were at their stations, busily preparing to land. They were noisy, sometimes serious, but often laughing and goofing around, though she couldn't seem to concentrate enough to know what they were saying.

Gradually, the forces acting on the ship began to change. She could *feel* the planet drawing them in. They entered into some dense cloud cover, and she tensed, terrified by the lack of visibility. But the crew took it all in stride, like it was just par for the course, and she took comfort in that.

She released her death grip on the armrest and relaxed back into her seat.

Soon, they'd passed through the densest of the cloud cover, and now only trails of white clouds streaked past their view. This also allowed Justine her first gander at the surface. Somehow, it wasn't what she'd expected. From here, she mostly caught snowcapped mountains as far as the eye could see. No water. No greenery. Even the sky was a gray interspersed with white clouds.

Is this what I've signed up for?

She tried to convince herself that it was fine, that even Earth had regions with a lot of snow cover. There were entire tundras where the ground was frozen solid for a good chunk of the year.

We haven't landed yet, she reminded herself.

Her home might look entirely different.

It was going to be fine.

And yet the view didn't really relent. They did eventually fly beyond the mountains, with the peaks suddenly dropping straight into the sea, but that didn't ease her worries. After that, they flew over the water for some time as the ship continued to slow in preparation for landing.

She had no idea how fast they were going. Or how long it would take them to slow down. It did seem to be pretty fast, though. She watched as the water blurred beneath them, and briefly wondered how much of the surface was covered in it. Was it like Earth? Most of the Earth was covered in water, right?

Then finally, she spotted something shining in the distance. It both caught her attention and confused her. What could be shining in this drab environment? There wasn't even any sunlight seeping through the thick cloud cover above them.

But as they grew close, it became clearer. They were approaching a seaside city, filled with fancy structures that reflected light back and forth, making it almost twinkle in the low light. The buildings rose into the air like spires, bringing to mind a half-remembered image from a movie she'd seen once.

And as they started their final approach and the ship turning slightly to the left, she realized the buildings were all made of glass and silvery metal. Everything had the same aesthetic, like the entire city had been planned in one go rather than built over time. They slowed further and began their descent to a large, flat area to the left of the city.

We're here.

They touched down, and everyone started moving about, quickly standing and leaving the bridge.

The captain approached her before she'd even released her harness. "You ready?" he asked, and she half expected him to reach out a hand to her.

She nodded, struggled momentarily with the buckle holding her down, and stood, offering the tablet and charger to him.

He nodded in thanks, tucking them at his side, and ushered her toward the door.

She was consciously aware of him herding her off his ship, like he was eager to be rid of her. She didn't *think* she'd been a nuisance, but now she couldn't help wondering. Was he grateful she would soon be gone? Had she caused problems for him while she was onboard? She thought she'd been good, keeping to herself and studying up on her new home, but maybe she'd missed the signs just as she had with Brian.

When they reached her room, she collected her bag while

the captain waited in the hallway, making her feel self-conscious.

"Anything else?" he asked.

She shook her head. "No."

He nodded and turned to continue their journey off the ship. The hall felt long and cold as they walked together, her suitcase making obnoxious noises as she rolled it toward the exit. She was tempted to pick it up just to make it quiet, but it was still heavy, the months on board not enough to exhaust her supply of toiletries.

When they reached the door, the same door she'd used to board the ship all those months ago, she turned to the captain. "Thank you for having me."

"Thank you for being an undemanding passenger."

She smiled, her anxiety easing a bit, and turned to the door, walking toward the exit and her future.

***

Zayvan waited at the edge of the landing pad where a cargo ship had just touched down. It was... not what he'd expected. He suspected it was unlike any ship that had ever touched this concrete structure before. It was dirty, which was common enough among spaceships, but it also looked like it had seen better days. The design was lackluster at best, and he was wondering if the piecemeal appearance was a design flaw or the result of creative repairs.

When a door opened in the side of the ship, he stood up taller, suddenly getting very nervous. This was it, his chance. This woman knew nothing about him or his role in society. Her impressions of him would be colored by nothing but who he was as a person. He smiled, a little thrill of excitement rushing through him.

The excitement reminded him of the day he'd received the call from the matchmaking agency. He'd been excited when they'd informed him there was a match, even if he'd been surprised by how they'd contacted him. When he'd signed up, they'd explained exactly how the process would go, and they hadn't followed it.

Instead, they'd reached him by phone, informing him they'd been asked to expedite the match by the partnering agency.

The situation had immediately sparked his curiosity. Why did she need a match so soon? Was she trying to escape an arranged marriage? Was she in dire financial straits?

But after that initial curiosity had waned, he'd still had a decision to make, an impossible decision. Outrage had filled him. How could they do this to him? Not only did they put him on the spot, forcing him to make a life-changing decision on no notice, but he felt like there was vital information missing, information he needed.

It had been the hardest thing he'd ever done in his life.

But now all the wondering and worrying was over. She was here. She was finally here.

His match stepped off the ship with a small case at her side, and the first thing Zayvan noticed was her hair. It was one of the brightest colors he'd ever seen, and it drew his attention like a beacon. It was arranged around her face in a silky fall, and he was so enthralled with it that, before he'd even noticed, she'd already crossed the landing pad and was standing before him.

"Are you Zayvan?" she asked, her voice a soft, trembling thing that triggered as yet unrealized protective instincts in him.

"I am," he said, looking down at her with a smile. "And you must be Justine."

Because you're perfect.

Justine craned her neck to look at the man she'd been matched to. He was tall, and she had to look up to even see his chin. The way he towered over her, even at this distance, made her gut sink with dread.

And it didn't help that he was also muscular. She could see the definition in his arms and chest from here. She tried to take comfort in the more alien aspects of his appearance. He was wearing a formfitting black shirt that contrasted with his pale, blue skin tone. With the shock of dark blue hair sitting on his head, he couldn't look more alien if he tried.

Or more fitting for their current environment. Everything around them was cold and colorless, and other than his hair, he looked bleached out, like the color had been drained from him.

And yet, he didn't look sickly as a human would. His pallor looked right on him.

She didn't speak when he asked if she was Justine. In fact, she stood there, frozen to the spot. He smiled at her, and that seemed like a good thing, but she was struggling to keep her memories at bay. She could *feel* a hand on her ankle, gripping hard, though there was nothing there. All her muscles were primed and tense, as if waiting for the moment when he would try to drag her backward. Her heart raced, knowing resistance was futile.

But even as she managed to wrangle that memory into submission, Zayvan stepped forward, now looming so close she could feel his presence like an oppressive weight bearing down on her.

She squeaked, her vocal cords too tight to even let out a good, healthy scream, and fell back, landing hard on her ass. Pain radiated up from her tail bone as heat rushed to her cheeks.

Why did you do that?

You shouldn't have done that.

But it wasn't just embarrassment driving her self-flagellation, it was the knowledge that he now had leverage over her. He *knew*. Now he *knew* he could intimidate her. She'd lost that battle already, and they'd barely spoken a handful of words between the two of them.

Justine looked up from her sprawl, her hands stinging from trying to catch herself. She expected him to be looming over her, a giant monolith stretching out toward the sky. She expected him to be smirking or otherwise enjoying this knowledge he'd gained on her.

But he wasn't. He was crouched next to her, a look of concern in his eyes. "Are you all right?" he asked, his hand reaching out as if to touch her or help her.

She recoiled, cursing herself the moment she realized what she'd done.

Way to give him even more *power over you, genius.*

She cursed herself even more for making the worst first impression on the planet. Gulping down a breath, she straightened, pulling back from him at the same time.

He carefully dropped his hand to his side and settled on his haunches, watching her intently, a gentle smile on his face.

"Sorry about that," she said quietly.

"No need to apologize. I suppose it's to be expected. I *am* quite different from what you're used to, I'm sure."

She nodded eagerly, glomming onto that excuse for her behavior, and started to push herself to her feet. His entire body tensed, and she suspected he was resisting the urge to offer her a hand again, but he remained still, waiting for her. Once standing, Justine brushed off her palms and clothing, and put a hand on the handle of her suitcase, taking one last steadying breath.

Don't forget you signed up for this.

"You ready to go then?" He gestured toward the vehicle behind him, which looked vaguely like a car.

"Where are we going?"

"My family owns a cabin in the wilderness area near the city. It's quite beautiful this time of year. I thought it might be a good place to spend some time together and get to know each other, without all the drama of everyday life."

Justine paused, suddenly imagining being trapped in a cabin in the woods far from civilization with no one to save her if he turned into a psycho.

"Justine?" he said, the concern returning to his eyes.

Which was when she realized she'd taken an unconscious step away from him again. She stopped and held her ground, giving him a hesitant smile. "Sorry. I guess I'm a little overwhelmed and letting my imagination run away with me."

"Like I said, you don't have to say sorry. Would you rather stay in town? We could spend a few nights here, explore the city?"

It was kind of nice of him to offer, but the city didn't hold any more appeal than the cabin. She looked to her left, where the city that loomed over them, both intimidating and awe-inspiring. She shook her head, warming to the idea of starting off small with the cabin. Personally, she thought the city looked a bit too daunting.

Justine then locked eyes on the vehicle behind him. "Is that your car?" she said, pointing at it. It was sleek and black and would stand out like a sore thumb against the coloring of this world.

He turned around to look at it. "Not exactly."

"What, did you steal it?"

He laughed, shaking his head. "No. I'm not sure how to explain it. I sort of... checked it out? It's from a car pool."

"Oh, okay. That makes sense. Do you not have to use one very often?"

He shook his head and started moving toward the vehicle. "I spend most of my time in the city, so I'm either walking or being driven."

She nodded and followed, the suitcase handle vibrating under her hand as it rolled over the rough landing pad. When she reached the car, Zayvan opened a door and reached out his hand for her bag. She rolled it forward, and he looked puzzlingly at the handle for a moment before pressing the button to allow it to retract.

"Nice, simple design," he said as he lifted the bag into the back seat next to a soft-sided bag that must have been his.

"Thanks," she said as she turned her focus to the front door nearest her, trying to remember from her lessons on the tablet how to open doors on this planet. There was a panel with a slightly recessed edge that nearly blended into the rest of the door. She hovered her hand over it, remembering it was more or less motion sensing, but it did nothing.

"Uh, yeah, it's locked," he said, reaching forward and waving his own hand at the panel. The lock mechanism clicked twice, then the door popped open. "I can add you as an authorized user."

"Thanks." She looked over at him and smiled.

He smiled in return and walked to the opposite side of the car.

Justine pulled the door open all the way, half expecting a cramped experience, but she should have known better. She settled into the seat, and for a moment there, she felt like a child. The seat felt too large. Too wide, too long, too tall. Everything felt just a bit off from where she would expect it to be, the seat pressing where it shouldn't or controls that were just out of easy reach.

She looked over at Zayvan, who looked like the seat was molded to him. It was clearly made for his much larger frame, though as she sat there, she realized she was being a bit too critical. He was probably on the large side for the seat, his shoulders stretching past the cushioning on the backrest and several inches of thigh reaching beyond the seat. He reached out to the console in front of them, tapping to wake up the screen. She leaned forward, watching him work.

Justine smiled as she realized she could recognize and read the script on the display. There was a map screen between them on the console, and as she continued to observe, she noticed the exact same vehicle controls on her side as well. There was no steering wheel or other obvious means of controlling the vehicle, so she suspected it was automatic. "What happens in an emergency? Is there a manual control mode?" She didn't remember reading anything about these vehicles on the tablet.

He turned to her, his right hand going to the armrest, causing his arm muscles to bulge in a way that sent a thrill through her that seemed to be both fear and excitement.

I should have asked for an ID, she realized as she sat there, in a car with a complete stranger, with only the barest assurances that he was who she was supposed to meet. Additionally, he'd already admitted they were going to a cabin-in-the-woods type of situation.

Oh, I'm too dumb to live.

"There is. It drops down from the ceiling when the autopilot fails." He patted the ceiling with a dull thump-thump.

She nodded, fear overtaking the excitement. When she spoke, her voice was unusually high pitched, making her cringe. "I hate to ask, but do you have some sort of ID?"

His eyebrows rose in surprise, but he nodded, reaching into

the back seat for his bag. "Most of the time, I don't need this thing, so I guess it was a stroke of luck that we're in an area that requires it."

Justine paled. "Do I need one?" She'd left all her IDs behind when she left Brian. Now that she thought about it, she couldn't believe they'd let her leave Earth without showing so much as a single form of identification. She was so used to strict security regulations and barely being able to travel anywhere without an ID or passport. It frankly stunned her that she'd managed to leave the *planet* without one.

Can I even go back?

If things didn't work out here, and she asked the agency to return her to Earth, what would happen? Would she get stuck in customs somewhere, trying to convince them of her identity? Would she be stuck in limbo, hoping against hope that they would figure out who she was and let her through? ID verification on Earth wasn't easy nowadays, what with shifters and all. Genetic screening, multifactor IDs, fingerprint and retinal scans. It was so hard to verify someone's identity in modern times, and now she wondered if, should she return, they could *ever* confirm her identity.

And what if she had shifter genes? One of the things they'd learned over the years since discovering shifters existed was that many people in the population had the genes but either couldn't shift or just didn't know they could. Not having the gene simplified identification, but what if she had it?

"Here," he said, offering her a strangely square ID card. It had a picture of him in one corner with the Savalan script around it, providing various bits of information. She spotted his full name at the top, Zayvan Akhren, followed by a lot of information, most of which meant nothing to her.

She nodded, rubbing her thumb over the card. "Thanks," she said and passed it back to him.

"No problem."

"I don't have an ID on me, unfortunately." She looked away. "It was uh... lost. Last minute thing. No time to replace it." She chuckled to herself. "God, the process for replacing IDs in the United States is ridiculous. Takes months."

"Really?"

"Yeah, well, it's not as simple as putting a face on a card. We don't even have pictures on IDs anymore. They're not useful."

"Really?" He leaned in.

"Yeah, well, I don't know if you know this, but there are two sentient species on Earth." She held up two fingers. "Humans and shifters. Shifters can change their appearance at will and were only discovered a few decades ago. It created a bit of chaos for a while there. Back then, pretty much our entire identification system was based on photos and faces. Realizing that a face wasn't unique completely upended that system.

"Though, I guess there've always been identical twins, so the system was always pretty flawed."

He nodded, looking thoughtful, then returned the ID to his bag. "Ready to go?" he asked, turning to her once more.

"Sure."

"Okay." He removed his hand from the armrest and resumed programming the car.

A moment later, she felt the gentle vibration of the engines starting as it lifted off the ground. She gripped her armrests, looking out around her, realizing it wasn't a car at all, but some sort of compact plane. The sleekness of the vehicle suddenly made a lot more sense as she spotted the wings that now extended from the sides just below the doors.

Air rushed around the car as she watched the city fall away below them. Within minutes, they flew over the first patch of greenery she'd seen since dropping below the clouds. She stared, her jaw slightly slack as trees and meadows and maybe farmlands flew by beneath them. There were still white mountains in the distance, but everything below them, at least outside of the city, was green.

"This area was chosen for the capital city because of the environment around it. Much of the world is covered in snow and ice for most of the year, but this region is among the most temperate on the planet, making it ideal for building such a large population center."

She turned to him, leaning her back against the door so she could face him more comfortably. "Are there settlements in those snowy areas, then?"

He nodded. "Oh, absolutely. Our people have inhabited this planet for a long time. We started out in those snowy areas. Adults handle the cold pretty well, but children are a bit more vulnerable to it, which is why, as civilization advanced, we started settling in more temperate climates.

"But most of those older settlements are still around. They have their purposes." He chuckled. "Though you're *far* more likely to see dedicated bachelors taking up residence there than families."

"Interesting. Humans started the exact opposite way. We evolved in very warm climates, then migrated to colder ones as we developed more tools to handle it."

"And we ended up in the same place."

"I don't know about that. Seems to me Savalans were smarter than humans on that front. Kind of makes humans look like masochists. After all, I've lived through more than one winter storm where you could develop frostbite in just a half hour of exposure."

"What's frostbite?"

"It's..." She lifted her hand and wiggled her fingers. "Where your tissue starts to freeze. Causes damage to the cells, which can be permanent. If it's severe enough, they could have to amputate."

Zayvan gasped. "What? Your people still amputate?"

"Well, yeah. Sometimes there's no way around it. It's not common, but if a limb is damaged beyond all possibility of repair, what else can you do? And most frostbite doesn't result in loss of limb. That's pretty extreme. That's a situation where you're probably lucky to be alive."

Zayvan sat back in his seat, looking floored by the conversation. "Well, we're not going anywhere that cold. This place is on the edge of the temperate zone, so it should still be fairly comfortable, but it has a *fantastic* view of the mountains."

She looked up through the front window at the majestic peaks in the distance. They reminded her of the Rockies back home, big and snowcapped, almost looking like giant pyramids rising up from the earth. How could the view be more fantastic than this?

She had no way of keeping track of time, but it felt like she'd been traveling for a few hours when they started their descent to the cabin Zayvan had promised her.

From here, the mountains were even closer, and they were so tall, they seemed to almost disappear into the cloud cover. The car continued to descend and finally dropped below the tree line, settling in a clearing with barely so much as a bump. The engines shut off automatically, leaving them in a silence that seemed to press in on her eardrums.

She looked over at Zayvan, who was already readying to leave the car. He tapped the screen, and the entire display shut off. Then he popped the door open and stepped out into the crisp air. It wasn't cold, per se, but it was definitely cooler than the car. He walked around and opened the back door, pulling out his duffel and reaching in to grab Justine's bag as well.

Justine took a deep breath and opened her own door, finally stepping out of the car. She shivered as a gust of wind hit her. She rubbed her arms, huddling into herself against the surprisingly icy wind that seem to cut straight through her. "I thought you said it was warm here?"

He looked at her, seeming confused, then barked a word she didn't know into the crisp mountain air. She suspected it was a curse, though there hadn't been any curse words in her lessons, so she wasn't sure.

Zayvan rushed around the car, and Justine flinched as he wrapped an arm around her and hurried her into the cabin. She barely had time to react before she found herself inside. Her shivering eased slightly, but it wasn't until the heat his body was cranking out started to suffuse her own that she began to relax. She didn't know if it was just him or if every Savalan was this warm, but she wholeheartedly approved, especially in this weather.

All too quickly, Zayvan walked away, taking his warmth with him. She almost protested, but snapped her mouth closed when he grabbed a throw from the back of the couch and hurried back. "Here," he said as he wrapped it around her shoulders, rubbing them to warm her even more.

There was a chill to the blanket at first, making her realize there must not be any heat running in the cabin. Even so, between Zayvan's efforts and the blanket, she was definitely starting to warm up.

"The cabin hasn't been used in a while, so climate controls aren't turned on," he said, continuing to rub her shoulders and back through the blanket. When the shivering finally stopped, so did his hands. "Are you okay for now?"

She nodded. She currently had her face tucked against the

warmth of his neck, and she had no intention of moving anytime soon.

"Good." He pulled back, and she wanted to protest. "I'll be right back. I promise."

She frowned after him as he rushed off and out of sight. When she could no longer see him, she turned her attention to the cabin. It was pretty massive, with a big living area and a large kitchen/dining area. Zayvan had run down the only visible hallway, which she suspected must contain the bedrooms.

Considering her first impressions of the planet, she would have expected the cabin to be more cool tones. Glass, silver, blacks and grays. But it wasn't. This cabin had very clearly been designed to embrace the earthy environment surrounding it. It was an escape from the everyday life, and it seemed the design kept that in mind.

It actually reminded her a lot of cabins back on Earth, only larger. A fieldstone fireplace filled up one wall, with a couch facing it. Rugs in various places, windows looking out on the nature beyond. All the fabrics held to the same color palette, mostly in greens and browns.

No longer cold and now wondering how long he was going to take, Justine sat down on the couch, which was big and fluffy and seemed to want to consume her. It was more successful at it than the seat in the car had been, and she struggled to settle in properly.

Zayvan returned while she was still battling the blanket, which was currently trapped under her butt. He smiled, but didn't comment.

Smart bastard.

"If you like, I can make you some hal? It'll help warm you up."

"What's hal?" she asked, stopping mid struggle.

"It's a hot beverage. It's highly caffeinated, so it's a little late in the day to be drinking it, but like I said, it will help warm you up."

"Sounds perfect."

He nodded and disappeared into the kitchen, opening cabinets and pulling out contents. A few minutes later, something dinged, and he returned with two cups. He handed one to her.

The cup was similar in a lot of ways to mugs back home. It was probably ceramic, with a thick smooth feel to the material. It had a narrow base, a wide opening, and no handle, but it also didn't need one. She took a tentative sip, winced at the bitter taste, and looked down at the tan cup's contents, which were a color between green and brown.

The couch dipped slightly as Zayvan sat down next to her with his own cup. Justine looked over at him. The cup looked tiny in his hands, but it somehow humanized him in her eyes. It was such a simple thing, sipping a cup, cradling it in your hands. It seemed so normal that it actually allowed her to relax, appreciating the moment she was in.

It was so peaceful here. She could hear nothing beyond the walls of the cabin, and inside, all she heard was the humming of the air conditioning. Neither of them felt the need to break the silence.

As they continued sitting companionably side by side, Justine came to appreciate the bitter drink, her core warming little by little. Before long, she found them slowly settling so close together that they were almost cuddling. Zayvan's arm and thigh pressed against hers as the soft cushioning conspired to push them ever nearer.

When her cup was finally empty, she sighed and let her head drop to the side, resting against his shoulder.

Maybe this can work.

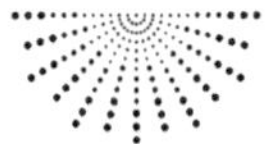

CHAPTER FIVE

Zayvan sat still as Justine, little by little, melded to his side, eventually resting her head against his shoulder. He didn't even want to breathe for fear of disturbing her. She'd seemed so fragile and skittish until now, and he feared if he moved, he would break the spell she'd fallen into.

He looked down at her. The green blanket he'd given her curled around her shoulders, highlighting her bright red hair. He couldn't help looking down at her in awe. She was so tiny. Certainly bigger than a child, but so petite it inspired him to protect and care for her, to provide her with anything her heart desired.

But it also made him realize just how much he'd let his relationship to others define him. First his family, then his brother, and now he was doing it again with her. Zayvan had been an adult for years, and yet he'd failed to really explore himself or who he was. He hadn't even *tried* to figure out who he wanted to be, not really. He'd done himself a great disservice, and now he feared Justine would be the one to pay for it.

When he'd signed up for the matching service, he'd been completely focused on finding someone who could love him for who he was inside, not a position, title, or family ties. It had been a hard thing, filling out that survey. It had forced him to think about a lot things he'd never considered before. He couldn't even remember most of the questions, and now he worried maybe he should have waited to apply. Maybe he should have figured himself out a little more before proceeding. What if he wasn't what she needed? What if he let her down? He suspected she knew a lot more about what she needed than he did, and he didn't want to fail her.

He suspected she'd been failed far too many times already.

She could just be a skittish person by nature, he supposed, or nervous in new situations, but he doubted that was the case. He'd thoroughly read the information packet they'd given him after he'd filled out his survey. He knew the process well enough to know that they hadn't followed it in this case. Instead of sending a message with her profile to be reviewed at his leisure, they'd phoned him, asking him to review her information and give them an answer by end of day.

He'd been flustered, not used to making rushed decisions. Usually, he took his time, researched the options, went over all the information in detail. It came in handy as a Royal Advisor. He'd tried to protest, to say he needed more time, but the representative had been adamant.

"I need an answer now," he'd said. "This placement can't wait."

"Why not?" he'd asked, but the man had kept his own counsel. He'd had no choice but to quickly glance over the information and give his first impression of the profile.

Was this someone he wanted to spend the rest of his life with?

Maybe if he hadn't been so lonely, he would have said no. He would have told them that this was too important a decision to make in haste. Maybe then he would have questioned things more.

But in the end, the urgency left him with the same feeling he was experiencing now.

Protectiveness.

Compassion.

Curiosity.

Empathy.

He'd agreed, and then spent the next several months poring over her profile religiously, memorizing practically every detail. It was funny how the survey worked. It gave you so much information and yet nothing at all. You could know a person's every hope and aspiration for their life, their likes and dislikes, but not the events that had formed those preferences. It was like seeing a silhouette of a person. You could see the general form, but so much was left unseen.

Before he knew it, Justine had drifted off to sleep beside him, and he swept an arm around her shoulder, pulling her in closer. One unanswered question continued to play on repeat in his mind.

Who is she really?

<hr>

Justine didn't remember going to sleep last night, but she woke up in bed, or at least in *a* bed. For a breathless moment, her mind actually thought she was back home with Brian. She half expected him to roll over and head for the bathroom as he did every morning, stomping along as if she wasn't still sleeping.

But that breath ended, and her mind started to click into gear.

I escaped. He's not here.

She started cataloging the differences to reassure herself. The ceiling was made of wood, not the textured white paint from back home. The walls were wood as well, with green curtains letting in the morning light. Back home, the walls were white, and they had navy blue blackout curtains that left the room dark.

The bed was different, too. Brian had insisted on a firm bed, and she was always overheating because he *had* to use a comforter, even in the middle of the summer. Here, her nose was actually cold, though, and it seemed the only thing keeping her warm was a quilt with leaf and vine designs on it. And the bed was soft, contouring to her form, leaving her surprisingly comfortable upon waking. Usually, even without the broken leg, she was a bit stiff in the mornings. Sometimes, she would have a kink in her neck from sleeping funky all night long.

Nothing hurts.

She lay there unmoving and wide-eyed as that realization passed through her. She wasn't stiff, achy, or in pain.

I had a good night's sleep.

She also didn't feel groggy and her eyes didn't feel heavy. For the first time in quite a while, she'd woken up well rested. Even after leaving Brian, she hadn't felt this good in the mornings. The ship bed had been a small, hard bunk, serviceable but hardly comfortable, and Amira's guest bed had been nice enough, but she'd woken all throughout the night, every stray noise triggering her fight-or-flight response.

Even the sound here was different. Through the walls, she could hear an animal calling. It sounded like a mix between a bird and a cougar, but it called again and again, and she wondered if it was excited for the dawn or calling out to someone who would never answer.

"Way to get yourself down," she said to herself, pushing

back the quilt to sit up. "This is a new start. Act like it." She tried to pump herself up with her words, but it didn't really work. The good night's sleep had helped, but the idea of leaving this room still felt a bit daunting. She stared at the closed door, wondering if Zayvan was up yet.

Zayvan.

Heat rushed to her cheeks as she remembered their less than stellar first meeting. "Really could have done that better," she muttered. But he'd been kind in spite of it all. With a little distance, she could admit he'd reacted better than she could have hoped. He'd been patient and considerate with her. For now, that was probably the best she could hope for. Thinking about it, she could almost *feel* the heat of him encompassing her as he tried to warm her up. It had been a nice moment.

Justine turned and stared at her bag, thinking of the tablet she'd had on the ship. She wished she had it now, wished she could check his profile again. She wanted to compare the profile to what she'd experienced so far. Was it accurate? Had he told the truth? A part of her *needed* to know that the profile had been accurate, that she could rely on it.

"But the profile isn't everything." The profile couldn't tell her what he looked like or what his voice sounded like. It couldn't tell her about his past or family. There were holes it couldn't fill. Were those holes big enough to cause problems, though? Was he what she'd expected based on the profile? She wasn't sure. She supposed she hadn't really created an image of him in her head. On the trip here, she'd vacillated between wanting someone meek and nonthreatening and wanting someone strong, someone who could protect her from any threat.

Except, she realized now that wanting someone big and strong was a terrible idea. She'd already proven how poorly she tended to react to anyone bigger and stronger than herself. And she knew what that strength could do. She'd suffered six months of tyranny because of that strength. So, she wasn't certain she was looking for a protector. But then again, what *was* she looking for?

She continued sitting there, reluctant to get up and face the day. What would today be like? She imagined they should start by talking and getting to know each other, but then she remembered the ride here. They'd barely said a word the entire time. She'd been too fascinated by the views and technology, and she had to admit, a little hesitant to start a conversation. After all, what could she say to an alien? What *should* she say? And would they have anything to talk about when a conversation finally began?

With all that looming over her, it was tempting to just sit in this room all day, but that wasn't exactly a long-term strategy. *Eventually*, she would have to leave, if for no other reason than to eat.

And if there was ever a time to develop a spine, it was now. She'd come all the way here, uprooted her entire life for a chance at something better. The least she could do was make that first step and not be a chicken.

With that tiny bit of gumption she'd wrestled out of her psyche, she threw back the blankets and pushed herself out of bed. Her suitcase was on a side table across from her, and she opened it, pulling out what she would need to get ready for the day. She turned around, wondering where a bathroom would be. It would be nice to start the day fresh. A shower would help her feel a bit more confident, a bit more prepared. Justine smiled when she spotted an open door on the other side of the room. She could see ceramic and glass through the doorway. She scooped up the things she'd pulled out and crossed the room, dropping everything on the counter and then loading up the shower behind her.

As she set everything up to her liking, she couldn't escape the fact that she was on an alien world. Even though the room was clearly a bathroom, none of the details were quite right. The toilet was an entirely different design, the faucet had some strange gooseneck, the shower door was curved, the lights rimmed the ceiling, and everything was just a bit too tall. It made it both alien and familiar.

Once she had everything situated the way she liked, she played with the controls until warm water poured from the ceiling. She stripped and stepped under the spray, smiling as the water caressed her skin.

She lost track of time as she washed, and she stepped out feeling refreshed and slightly optimistic. Zayvan had been pretty nice so far, accommodating in spite of his size. *This could be good*, she told herself as she pulled on some clean clothes.

When she reached the door to the hallway, she only hesitated for a moment before pushing through, not even giving herself enough time to form a complete thought in protest.

The walls here were much like in her room, wood in a warm color that felt comfortable, doors that matched the walls, and the same cold stone flooring covered in a rug. She looked both ways, realizing she might have underestimated the size of this cabin. There were closed doors running up and down the hallway, but she couldn't see the living room from here.

Which way do I go?

She stood there for far too long, hating her indecisiveness, before she heard the movements of someone coming from her left. She followed the sounds, finding Zayvan in the kitchen opening cupboards.

"Morning," she said, wrapping her arms around her middle, not knowing what to do with them.

He turned and smiled, a box in one hand. "Ha!" was

written across the box in Savalan with other characters underneath it, obviously from another alien language.

"Is hal imported?" she asked, pointing at the box.

He looked down at the hal, then chuckled and set it on the counter. "Oh, yes. It's mostly farmed on Wesa, though there are some closer exporters, I think."

Justine nodded, finding herself out of things to say yet again. She stood there, feeling like an idiot, though since Zayvan was standing there looking equally out of sorts, she supposed the feeling was mutual.

Maybe this was *a bad idea.*

She rubbed her arms, feeling self-conscious as the silence grew between them, neither of them moving or speaking.

Then Zayvan laughed. It was a rich sound, and it filled the room in such a way that she couldn't help joining in. The next thing she knew, they were both clutching their middles with tears in their eyes, bent over and leaning against the counters.

When she was completely out of breath and gasping for air, she finally stopped, but the smile didn't leave her lips.

Zayvan got himself under control several moments later. He straightened, his hand kneading his side like he had a kink there from all the laughter. He also had a smile on his face. "I haven't laughed like that in a long time."

"How long?" she said, a little breathless.

"Years, maybe since I was a kid."

The smile fell from her lips. "Now that's tragic."

He shrugged, turning away and picking up the box of hal again. He waved it at her. "Would you like a cup?"

She nodded and forced a smile back on her face. This time, it was more wry than jovial. "Sure."

He reached into a cupboard for the cups, and she watched him work, making note of where everything was. "Do you drink hal a lot?"

"Not really," he said as he put two cups on the counter and added a spoonful of hal to each. "I suppose it just made sense last night. You were clearly cold, and I figured it would warm you up."

"And now?"

He turned, cups in hand. "Social lubricant?"

She smiled as he set the cups in a countertop device. She tried to remember what it was called, but was drawing a blank.

Zayvan leaned back against the counter as the device hummed, neither of them speaking.

Damn, we really need that social lubricant, don't we?

"Do we have plans for breakfast?" she asked awkwardly.

Zayvan opened his mouth, but then snapped it shut, a pained expression on his face. "I hadn't really thought about that yet. What would you like?"

She shook her head. "I don't really know your foods."

"Oh." He looked around, finally settling on a big nearly floor-to-ceiling device that was essentially a fridge. He pulled the door open and stared inside, and the visual was so familiar, she could have laughed.

Except... Brian used to do that.

Her mood soured, and she stepped backward, finding a surface to lean against as he perused the offerings.

"I have to admit," he said, voice muffled by the fridge, "I'm not sure what's in here. When news came that you were about to arrive, I had the cabin stocked, but I didn't exactly specify what to stock it *with*." He lifted his head out of the fridge, a wry smile on his face. "I didn't think to ask." He frowned. "Do you eat meat? I read that some humans don't eat meat."

"Oh, I eat meat."

"Oh good. Meat is pretty much a staple in our diets here on Savala."

"Really?"

"Yeah." He pointed out toward the window. "Our species originated up in the mountains where vegetation is a lot more scarce. We're omnivores, but we eat more meat than anything else."

She nodded. "Humans are more balanced between meat and plants. We can develop digestive problems when we don't get enough plant-based foods."

"Understood," he said and dipped his head back into the fridge. "What flavors do you like?"

"I like sweet and savory."

"I can work with that." The device on the counter dinged as he pulled some items from the fridge.

"I'll get it," she said as she made her way across the kitchen. She stared at it for only a moment before finding the "Open" button. She pressed it and gingerly pulled out the steaming cups of hal. Turning to give him his cup, she paused with her arm outstretched. He currently had his hands full with what looked like some seasoned meat and something else that was mysteriously sloshing around in its own packaging. "Where would you like your hal?" she asked instead.

"Just put it on the counter there," he replied, pointing with an elbow.

She did and stepped back, leaning against the opposite counter and bringing the hot beverage carefully to her lips. It was just as bitter today, but it took less time for her to get used to it.

Zayvan was busily opening each package over the sink, then dropping them in pans he'd retrieved from the many cabinets.

I really need to learn this kitchen.

She smiled as she sipped and watched Zayvan work. He seemed comfortable in the kitchen, and familiar enough with where everything was that she was certain he'd been here before. He settled the pans on a range built into the countertop and in no time at all, she heard food sizzling as it cooked.

"Mmm." She lowered her cup as the cooking food started to permeate the air, giving off an aroma that had her stomach growling in approval.

"It shouldn't be too long now," he said, looking over his shoulder. "This one is diced pretty small, so it should cook quickly."

"That's fine."

He looked at her critically, like maybe he thought she was lying, but then returned to his cooking, moving a utensil around as the sizzling continued.

Putting her cup down, she asked, "Would you like me to set the table or something?"

"Sure. You can find what you need here and here." He turned and gestured at a cabinet and drawer. "There should also be some flatbread in the cabinet on the end."

"Thanks." As she pulled the dishes out, she noticed the plates were surprisingly elaborate in design. From the simplicity of the decorating so far, she'd expected a simple white or maybe green, but the dishes were white with silver and gold filigree decorating them. The pattern was identical on each, and she wondered if it meant something. Maybe a stylistic imagining of a local animal? It certainly wasn't text.

Shrugging off the mystery for now, she started setting everything on the table, which was surprisingly large for a cabin in the woods.

Maybe he has a large family. That would be nice.

She would like to feel connected again. She hadn't felt connected in a long time, not since before she met Brian, not since before her parents died.

Justine supposed it was partially their loss that had made

leaving Earth so easy. All she'd lost by leaving was a friend she had every intention of keeping in touch with.

"Oh, Zayvan?"

"Yes?" He turned to her, gripping a utensil that threatened to drip *something* onto the floor. Sunlight poured in from the window next to him, making him look surprisingly handsome and domestic.

"So, before I left, I promised a friend of mine I would keep in touch. How would I contact someone on Earth?"

He set the utensil down, the dirty end angled up over the pan. "The easiest method would probably be text-based. I'm not even sure that requires any special equipment or software on your friend's end. Voice or video is harder. There's often a major buffering problem from what I gather, but it's still doable. It requires specific software. Don't know about hardware, but I can definitely ask when we get back to the city."

"When's that gonna be? How long are we staying here?"

He scratched his ear. "I was hoping a few weeks? I don't have any specific timeline in mind. My main focus was giving us ample opportunity to get to know each other. I thought this would be the ideal place for that, and since my work is pretty flexible, I can take time off whenever I want. I figured back home, it would be easy to get lost in the day to day. Potential problems could go unaddressed and end up festering." He shook his head. "I don't want that. I want us to get to know each other and see if we're a good fit with no distractions, no complications, just two people deciding if this is the person they want to spend the rest of their lives with."

"I can see the logic in that plan."

"Good," he said with a smile as he returned his attention to the range. "Food should be up soon."

"Great." She walked back into the kitchen, retrieving her now much cooler cup of hal from the counter. She sipped it anyway, though she could tell the drink was *definitely* best served hot. It grew even more bitter as it cooled.

She eyed the device on the counter, wondering if she could reheat it. "What's this called?" she asked, getting tired of calling it a "device" in her head.

"Microrange."

She nodded, popping it open and setting her cup inside. "How long to warm this up?"

"Set it to fifteen."

"Okay, thanks." She pressed the buttons, feeling grateful she'd spent so much time on the ship learning about Savala. It was super easy to read the Savalan numbers on the buttons, and she hit the Start button with a triumphant smile. It hummed to life, though unlike with microwaves back home, there was no window to watch the contents.

Justine counted off in her head, wondering how "15" compared to seconds back on Earth. She counted to twenty before the device finally dinged. Popping it open, she sighed as her hand touched the pleasantly reheated cup.

Behind her, Zayvan laughed.

She turned and smiled at him before pulling the cup out of the microrange and taking a sip. He gave her a small smile in return before turning back around.

"Do you have a computer or tablet or something?" she asked, continuing their conversation.

"Oh, right, you probably don't have one, do you?"

"No. The agency gave me a tablet to use on the trip over, but that was just to learn about Savala, so I had to turn that in to the captain. Not to mention, it probably wouldn't have been compatible with technology here."

"True." He touched something on the counter, then lifted the pans off the range. "All done." He smiled as he triumphantly paraded to the table, setting the pans in the middle next to the flatbread. "Let's eat."

He sat down, and she settled in across from him, again feeling a little like a child in the too-big chair.

"So, what do we have this morning?"

He scratched his ear, then pointed at each item. "This is fish in a sweet and spicy marinade. That is a root vegetable seasoned with a more tart and savory sauce. And of course, that is a flatbread. Nice and boring."

"Flatbreads can be really interesting."

He shrugged. "I suppose."

"Back home, we have something called focaccia. Unlike most flatbreads, it's often cooked with a lot of spices, making it tasty on its own. Also, some flatbreads are better or worse depending on the type of flour used."

"Hm. Never thought of it that way." He shrugged. "I guess Savalans aren't big on breads, so we don't play around with them as much."

She smiled, tilting her head playfully. "Makes sense if you mostly eat meat."

"True." He reached forward, grabbing her plate. "You don't mind, do you?"

She shook her head, though her initial instinct had been to protest. She reminded herself that he knew a lot more about these foods than she did.

"I'll just give you a bit to taste." He tore off a small chunk of the flatbread, then spooned some of the fish on top. Then he added the root vegetable as a side. As he said, each was fairly small, a little more than a mouthful. "Here." He carefully settled the plate back in front of her. "Let me know what you think."

The fish was chopped into small, thin pieces and coated in a reddish sauce, which dripped off the bread a little, but was thick enough that it didn't reach the root veggies. Conversely, the root vegetables were larger dark brown chunks in a pale yellow-colored liquid that made her think of light and lemony sauces back home.

Now, how do I eat this?

The veggies were easy. She could probably just stab them with one of her utensils, but she was trying to decide between utensils and fingers for the fish and flatbread. Unsure, she watched Zayvan out of the corner of her eye to see what he would do.

While her servings were downright tiny, Zayvan's were massive. And they were mostly the fish. He laid down a piece of flatbread that took up most of his plate, piled it high with the fish, then added a small side of root veggies, almost as an afterthought.

Then, fully served, he cut into the flatbread with a knife, then used a spoon to scoop up each mouthful. She followed his example. The piece of flatbread was a little bigger than she preferred, so she cut it in half, then scooped up her own taste, settling it on her tongue experimentally.

She half expected to hate it just because it was unfamiliar, but it was pretty good. The sweet hit her first, then as she started to chew, the texture followed. The fish was light and flaky, the bread thin and reminiscent of several flatbreads back home. She chewed happily, a smile forming on her lips.

Until the heat hit, and she remembered he'd said the sauce was sweet and *spicy*. She swallowed desperately and then fanned her mouth, whimpering in distress.

"What's wrong?" He looked up, then cursed under his breath.

She was certain it was a curse this time. It sounded like the same one from earlier.

Zayvan jumped up and started frantically dashing all over

the kitchen. A few steps later, he was thrusting a cup under her chin. "Here, drink this."

She almost coughed as she tried to down it, her mouth still overwhelmed by the heat of her food. But soon enough, it started to abate, and Zayvan followed up the drink with a few pieces of flatbread he broke off and shoved in her face. "And this."

She took each and chewed them slowly now, her desperation waning. Her mouth still felt like it was on fire, but it was a contained burn.

"I'm sorry," he said as he sat back down across from her. "You didn't mention liking spicy things. I should have found something else."

"It's fine."

"It's not fine. I screwed up."

"It's not your fault," she said automatically, falling back into old habits.

He leaned forward, looking stern, which froze any further words in her throat. "But it is. You told me exactly what you liked. I should have taken that more seriously. Do you want me to make you something else?"

She blushed, feeling uncomfortable under all that intensity. "Let me try the root vegetables first."

Nodding his head, he leaned back in his seat, and she could have almost sighed in relief.

After the fish, she was a little afraid to try the other dish, but at least it wasn't supposed to be spicy. She didn't necessarily *dislike* spicy foods, but she didn't usually eat anything *that* spicy. That had been like napalm going off in her mouth.

Not wanting to use any of the utensils contaminated by the fish's sauce, she picked up her last utensil, which resembled a fork. Of all the utensils, it was the most obviously different, with only two short, curved tines instead of the usual three or four back home. She stabbed one of the chunks, lifting it to her mouth hesitantly, fully expecting another disaster. Sauce dripped off it, falling into the red smears on her plate. She licked the chunk, unsure if she wanted the entire thing in her mouth after her last experience.

She could see Zayvan looking worried on the other side of the table, and she took pity on him, finally putting the piece in her mouth. It *did* remind her of lemon-based sauces, with a bright flavor that was toned down by something similar to garlic, and some barely detected sweet undertone to finish it out. It was a lot more nuanced than the fish sauce, and she bit down, finding the veggie soft and textured like a well-cooked potato.

She continued to chew, then swallowed. For almost a whole minute, she sat there, fork resting against her lips, as she waited to see if there would be an aftertaste. Her mind kept flitting back to the spicy nightmare of the fish sauce, but nothing happened. It remained appealing, and she looked up at Zayvan and nodded encouragingly.

He sighed in relief, then stood. "I'll get you a new plate and utensils. I don't want you accidentally getting another taste of that salzé sauce." He grabbed her plate and utensils and dropped them into the sink, then returned with new ones. "Here you go."

"Thanks."

He nodded and returned to his seat, taking another bite of his food.

She served herself some more of the alien potatoes and flatbread and dug in, a smile on her face as they finished eating in companionable silence.

Oh, that was stupid. Zayvan ran a hand through his short hair as he stood over the sink. He looked over at the table, where dishes still waited to be removed. He'd eaten enthusiastically, trying to eat up the fish Justine couldn't, but there was still plenty left. It sat there as a reminder of his mistake.

I should have paid more attention.

She hadn't said she liked spicy foods. He'd just seen the sauce on the label, known it had a sweet taste, and went for it, not even thinking to ask if she would like the rest of the flavor profile.

"Don't forget she's not Savalan," he said to himself under his breath, hoping she didn't overhear. After breakfast, he'd offered to clean up while she got her things situated in her room, since she'd had no opportunity to do so yesterday. She'd been hesitant, but nodded her head and walked off.

It gave him some time to himself. He sagged for a moment before pushing off the counter and walking to retrieve the rest of the dishes.

As he walked back with the salzé fish, he contemplated just throwing it away, unable to even look at it without seeing Justine's terrible reaction to it, but that would be a waste. As he dumped the fish in a storage container and put it in the refrigerator, that image of her gasping in desperation plagued him.

"I'll do better next time," he said to himself before walking to the sink again and beginning on the dishes.

He was almost done before Justine returned from her room.

"So, any plans today?"

He straightened, shaking the soapy water from his hands. "I thought we'd just relax. We can sit out on the porch chatting with the mountains as a backdrop."

"All day?"

He shrugged. "The whole point is to get to know each other, right?"

"I suppose so. Shall we?"

Zayvan took a deep breath, trying to put his mistake behind him. No relationship was perfect, and she clearly wasn't holding it against him. Maybe some day it would be a funny story they told at parties. He grabbed a towel and dried off his hands. "Let's," he said as he offered her his arm.

They walked out of the cabin like that. He imagined walking through life with her, arm in arm, and he smiled.

***

The rest of the day went fairly well. The cabin's porch wrapped around the side, giving a beautiful view of the mountains. Zayvan had been right. It was fantastic. From here, she could see the detail not visible from the sky, and the angle made them look even bigger. The trees skirted around the lower altitudes, pointing up toward the higher peaks. Those peaks were highlighted by little glimpses of rock and the light and shadow the sun cast in those rare moments when it managed to slip past the cloud cover. There were places where it practically sparkled like precious gems and others where shading gave it contour and depth.

Also from this height, she could better see the definition between the sky and the mountains. The clouds were surprisingly thin here, so from below, they actually took on a blue or purple tone.

They sat there talking for hours, learning about each other and just enjoying the beautiful day. It certainly wasn't hot, but it wasn't cold like it had been when they'd arrived yesterday. Though mostly indirect, the sun seemed to make a difference, and she didn't need a coat or blanket.

They talked about a lot of little things, but one of the bigger things they talked about was marriage and family. Growing up,

Zayvan had watched as every last member of his family fell to loveless marriages. Even his brother, though not married yet, was arranged to marry someone he didn't even know. As he talked, Justine was quiet, both unable and unwilling to contribute to the conversation for fear of letting slip anything about her own disastrous relationship. She wasn't ready to tell him. Maybe she would never be ready, but the idea of even accidentally letting something slip constricted her throat like a vise clamping down.

She let him monopolize the conversation, happy to learn about him, to reaffirm her beliefs about the type of person he was, but then suddenly, he targeted a question directly at her. "What inspired you to leave home?"

Justine was frozen, terrified. She couldn't do it. She couldn't say it. What would he say? What would he think? She just stared at him for several long moments until both of them were so uncomfortable they each looked away, and Zayvan changed the subject.

What am I doing?

She stared off into the distance while animal noises and Zayvan's mindless words filled the air. She felt like a failure, like she'd already ruined this. It was doomed. She should just tell Zayvan to take her to the local matchmaking agency for a new placement.

"It's okay, you know," he said, breaking her out of her recriminations.

"What?" She turned, looking at him in surprise and confusion.

"It's okay. You don't have to tell me everything. Your secrets are your own, and we don't really know each other yet. I want us to be good together. I want us to be happy and hopefully love each other, but we can't have that if we don't respect each other's boundaries. Just tell me when I do or say something you're not comfortable with. I won't hold it against you, and I'll do everything I can to respect it."

"Thank you," she said, her voice barely more than a whisper.

He nodded. "Anytime."

CHAPTER SIX

The next morning, breakfast went far better. Zayvan was downright obsessive about making sure she liked every aspect of a dish before cooking it. Justine wanted to protest, but he seemed so earnest, so determined to please her, that she relented.

Still, it left a sour taste in her mouth, reminding her of the way Brian used to go over the top to please her in the early stages of their relationship. He would bring her flowers and praise her, make her feel womanly and special. She didn't honestly think Zayvan was like that, but it was like the ghost of Brian couldn't resist coming up to make her second guess every decision and judgment she made.

When Zayvan suggested a walk in the woods, her immediate instinct was to say yes.

Why did you do that? she thought to herself immediately afterward, realizing she was doing the same thing she'd been conditioned to do with Brian, going along with whatever he wanted.

Still, she didn't know how to speak up, not after Brian. Just the idea of standing up for herself seemed impossible. Hell, if Zayvan hadn't reacted so strongly to her distress when eating the fish, she probably would have gamely continued trying to eat it, no matter how much it felt like her mouth was on fire. She could imagine herself, chin tucked down to hide her tears, as she choked down the overly spicy food.

It sickened her to even think that this was what she'd become. She didn't use to be like that, wasn't always a pushover, but fear could fuck with you in truly terrible ways, changing you until you barely recognized yourself.

As she stepped out onto the porch behind Zayvan, she made the conscious decision to conquer her fears, even if she didn't know what all of them were just yet.

She stepped down the wooden steps as the sounds of nature serenaded her. The trees surrounding the cabin were not that dissimilar to the ones back home, with brown bark and green leaves. They started on a walking path with Zayvan in the lead, and Justine brushed her hand over one of the leaves. It was thicker than she expected, with no veins and a fur on it like an African Violet.

She expected Zayvan to start up a conversation right away, but he didn't and Justine's mind wandered back to her fears, more specifically, back to what to do about them. In reality, she wasn't even that sure what she was afraid of. She knew she overreacted to any indications of violence or conflict, but what else? Was there anything else? With Brian, she'd developed a habit of rarely speaking unless he specifically asked her to. His erratic behavior had left her in a state of constantly needing to anticipate his every need and emotional impulse, leaving her perpetually stressed out and anxious.

Even after she broke her leg, when he seemed to let up on her some, she'd lived in that same state of anticipation. He'd been kinder, sweeter, more doting and caring, but he'd also paired that with a propensity for controlling her every action and resource that was breathtaking in its extremity. He'd controlled every aspect of her life from that point on, taking away her cell phone and locking the Wi-Fi so she couldn't use it. Food access, communication with others, where she went, what she could do, it was all controlled by him.

She needed to believe that things would be different here. But what could she do to prove that this was different? What would it take? In reality, only time would tell if Zayvan were sincere or a predator like her ex.

And her ignorance wasn't exactly helping to move that process along because it forced Zayvan to take charge in ways that reminded her of Brian. It wasn't his fault, though. Brian had been eerily similar in the early days, and she often remembered thinking how much she'd liked his competence back then, how she could sit back and let him take charge, allowing her to truly relax. She'd loved it, loved that she could just *be* with him. Even with all that evidence, she sometimes still had a hard time believing competence could be a bad thing.

Zayvan is competent.

She shook her head, pushing herself to catch up with Zayvan, who was currently several paces in front of her. "I was thinking," she said, feeling a little out of breath. Her leg was also starting to ache from the walk, and she stumbled a little as her bad foot caught on a root.

"Whoa," Zayvan said, reaching out to steady her. "You okay?"

"Yeah, just fine." She rotated her ankle a couple times and started up again. "Anyway, I was wondering if, um, since I couldn't really bring anything like that with me, if I could have a tablet or phone or something."

He stopped and stared down at her, looking stunned. "What?"

She started wringing her hands, feeling self-conscious about even asking now. "Well, I don't exactly have money here."

He sighed and leaned forward, putting himself more on her level. "Justine. Look at me."

She looked up. There was this undecipherable expression on his face.

"I brought you here. That means it's my responsibility to provide for you and help you acclimate. I take that responsibility seriously."

Justine frowned at his wording. She didn't really *want* to be provided for. She wanted security, sure, but now that she thought about it, how could she ever feel secure when she was relying on someone else for her survival? That was where things had gone so wrong with Brian. Little by little, she'd been convinced to give up her independence, to give up control.

At the time, it had all seemed perfectly logical. She'd been working a dead-end job she didn't like and working with a broken leg would have been exceptionally hard. Plus, Brian had seemed so completely apologetic. He'd somehow convinced her it had all been a mistake, an accident, something that could have happened to anyone. They'd just been fighting, and she fell. He'd even convinced her that she'd misremembered, that he'd actually tried to save her, to catch her. It had made sense. She remembered the doctors commenting that they usually only saw spiral fractures in cases where an adult yanked and pulled a child's arm hard. One doctor had given the example of a parent pulling a kid out of oncoming traffic.

She wasn't sure exactly when she'd lost all control of her life, but giving up her job had probably been the biggest mistake she'd ever made.

If she wanted to feel secure, fearless even, that security needed to start with *her*, not someone else. She needed her own money and the assurance that she could rescue herself from a bad situation if one were to arise. Straightening her shoulders and trying to look confident, she took a deep breath and said, "Then I need a communications device and I need a job."

He smiled down at her. "A little bossy, huh?"

She blushed and ducked her head down, her heart racing in her chest.

Shit, what did I do?

"I can place an order for the phone once we get back to the cabin, and you can use mine for the time being. As for the job, I can show you how to look for work on my computer if you want, but until we know when we're going back, it might be better to wait."

She frowned, not really liking that answer, but she nodded anyway. She had to begrudgingly admit he was right. They were in the middle of nowhere, and she had no idea when they were supposed to return. She couldn't exactly line up work with an uncertain start date, now could she?

And she also had no idea what she wanted to do. She hadn't really been working her dream job back on Earth, and she couldn't say she knew what was available here, either. Did she even have any applicable skills? This was an entirely new planet. Her college degree would likely mean nothing here.

Though maybe being from Earth would have its own benefits. She didn't know much about Savala, but probably the reverse was also true for Savalans. They probably didn't know much about Earth. She could provide that knowledge, and she suspected it would come in handy in certain fields like trade, for example. Not that she knew anything about trade. She could also see it being useful in something like an embassy, like having a foreign language translator. Or maybe working for an ambassador?

But as soon as the ideas came to her, she immediately

started second guessing herself. What did she know about any of that? Justine was someone who couldn't even find a job in her own field, instead being forced to work a bunch of minimum wage jobs that had slowly sucked her soul dry. She had no work skills, no life skills, and an irrelevant degree. Brian had often said she was useless when he was peeved with her. She'd always tried to convince herself that he was just being spiteful or he didn't mean it, but it was true, wasn't it? She *was* useless.

Her steps slowed as her thoughts began to depress her, and she was soon trailing behind Zayvan once more.

What if she never found her place?

What if she was good for nothing more than taking up space?

Her leg started to ache more and more the longer they walked, but her mood was so bad, she almost reveled in it. Her limping grew more pronounced, but fortunately, Zayvan was in front of her and couldn't see it.

I'm so useless, I can't even walk.

She was quickly spiraling into a tornado of negative thoughts that fed off each other, picking away at her self-esteem until the moment of empowerment she'd experienced earlier felt miles away, and the sentiment behind that moment felt utterly disconnected from reality.

"Justine, are you all right?" Zayvan asked.

Justine froze, alarmed. For a moment, she almost thought he could read her mind, could see into the turbulent sea of her thoughts.

"Justine?"

He sounded even more concerned now, and as she looked up at him and saw that concern on his face, words slipped from her mouth unbidden. "I'm sorry."

His eyes rounded, his body tensing. "Why the kak are you sorry?!"

She flinched, her body acting without conscious control.

All the tension left Zayvan's body. When he next spoke, his voice was soft, like he was talking to a frightened child or animal. "I'm sorry for raising my voice. You were limping. Are you all right?"

It was then that Justine realized what she'd done, and she could have kicked herself. Again, she'd had an opportunity to start fresh, with nobody knowing what she'd been through. She could have started over. No pity, no questions, just defined herself however she saw fit, but she kept screwing that up. Amira's warning was coming to fruition.

I don't know how to let this go.

She had the urge to cry, but she resisted, reminding herself that she was done with crying. So, instead, she nodded. "I broke my leg about six months ago. It's technically healed, but it still hurts when I overdo it."

"Do you need me to carry you?"

Justine shook her head. "No, I'm fine. Is it faster to turn back or keep going?"

"Keep going. It's a short loop through the woods. We're already beyond the halfway point."

"Okay."

Zayvan tilted his head, looking concerned. "Are you sure you're okay to keep going?"

"Yes. I walked farther than this to my friend's house back on Earth." Never mind the fact that adrenaline and sheer terror were the only things that had kept her going on that walk, or that her leg had protested that abuse for the rest of the day.

"Okay. Do you want me to go slower?"

Justine started walking again, now hyperaware of how her

foot landed each time, knowing one wrong step could result in blinding pain. "No, I think I'm okay," she said, but still, she was watching the path closely, carefully scanning for roots and rocks.

Zayvan settled in at her shoulder, and she could feel his gaze as she walked. After a little while, she grew more confident, picking up speed. She still watched where each foot landed and how her foot and ankle aligned with the rest of her leg, but it got easier and easier to do it without thinking. It still hurt, her leg throbbing dully with the overuse, but it was at a manageable level.

"What happened to your leg?" he asked, breaking the silence they'd fallen into.

Justine stopped, her mind blanking. She didn't want to tell the truth. She didn't want to admit what had happened, what she'd *let* happen, but she also couldn't think of another scenario.

Think, damn it.

But then she realized what she was doing. She was about to lie. Not hide the truth, but actually lie. Did she really want to lie to him, a man she might spend the rest of her life with? Did she really want to start out this new part of her life on a lie? It was one thing to have some secrets, some parts of herself she wasn't ready to open up about yet, but lying?

Zayvan stood there, patiently waiting for her, clearly expecting an openness she wasn't quite capable of just yet.

So she told him what she could. "It was mostly a spiral fracture down one of the bones in my lower leg. The doctors made the decision not to operate, which I gather is unusual, but I was kind of grateful. The idea of surgery terrified me."

He nodded. "I can't imagine a break so bad it required surgery. Surgery is done so rarely on Savala."

Justine smiled teasingly at him. "Is medicine that much more advanced here?"

"Oh, I have no idea. I read the information packet they gave me on Earth and humans, but I somehow doubt it was very comprehensive. Then again, I'm not sure anything they provided could have been."

"You're probably right. Earth isn't very consistent. Too many cultures, governments, religions and so much more. Everything is so fractured and divided, it would be hard to make one statement that covers every group."

"What's it like being from such a diverse planet?"

She thought of the wars, the discrimination, the ideological fights. "Hell."

"What's that?"

She looked over at him, realizing she'd spoken in English from the confused look on his face. She also realized didn't know any word in Savalan that fit what she wanted to say. "Hell's a concept on Earth, religious. It's an idea that some hold that people who are bad in life are punished in the afterlife. It's supposed to be brutal. It's often used in vernacular when you're saying something is intolerable to experience." She sighed and chuckled. "It's not really that useful in this situation, though, is it? Doesn't exactly tell you what you want to know."

Zayvan looked thoughtful. "No, I guess it doesn't."

Justine nodded. "Okay, so, the question. What's it like being on a diverse planet? Um, well, it constantly pits groups against each other, either in verbal discourse or in physical altercations. Even only a few decades ago, the government in my country was taking shifters from their homes and dumping them in these... camps." She'd never seen one of the camps and knew nothing about them. Her mind brought up pictures of the concentration camps of World War II, but she hoped to hell it was nothing like that. At least, she'd never heard of the shifters being treated that way.

But of course, that didn't mean it didn't happen. Governments were known for their secrets, and sometimes those secrets were horrifying.

"That's..." He didn't finish his sentence.

He didn't have to. What was there to say? Justine didn't want to continue that conversation any more than he did. She started walking again, and thankfully, the cabin was now in sight. She could finally get off her feet.

***

Someone had hurt her.

That thought was foremost in Zayvan's mind on the last leg of their walk. He was outraged by the very idea, but it was clear as day, especially after seeing her reaction to him raising his voice. He supposed he should have seen it earlier. She frequently flinched or startled, and she'd fallen to the ground and squeaked when they'd first met, like the very appearance of him was enough to unsettle her.

At the time, he'd dismissed it as her just seeing an alien for the first time, which he imagined could be a harrowing experience for someone so petite, but now he knew better. He was almost certain her leg injury had been the result of some form of abuse.

"I'm going to go to my room and place a call to my brother," he said as they stepped back into the cabin. "When I'm done, I'll show you how to use the phone, and you can pick out your own, okay?"

"Sure," she said, nodding along, but as she looked helplessly around the entry, he realized she would literally have nothing to do. There were no entertainment devices in this cabin, a place intended entirely for family trips. There were games in the closet, but she wouldn't know how to play any of them.

"I tell you what," he said as he crossed the room to the

closet, which almost blended in with the wood grain on the walls. "You sit on the couch, and I'll get out some games. Take a look through them and maybe read the rules and decide which ones you'd like to try."

She smiled, and he realized just how small she seemed with that hesitant expression crossing her face.

He opened the closet, looking inside at the spare blankets on one shelf and stacks of games on the one below it. He frowned at the selection. There were too many to just take all of them out, so he picked a few that seemed the easiest to learn from scratch and closed the door.

Justine was on the couch, rubbing her leg and making him feel even more guilty.

I wish she'd told me.

And yet he suspected he knew why she hadn't. With how skittish he was increasingly realizing she was, admitting weakness or speaking up for herself was probably hard.

Then you'll just have to encourage her.

He smiled as he settled the games on the small table in front of the couch, liking the idea of reforming her, so to speak. "Do you need anything for your leg?"

"No, it's fine," she said, continuing to rub it.

He was tempted to ask her again, but decided against it. Getting her to come out of her shell and recover from her ordeal would be a process, and certainly not something he could accomplish in a day. He nodded and walked away, slipping into his room.

The room, which had been his since he was a kid and hadn't changed a bit, was decorated in faded blue. His little "treasures," which he'd found in the woods growing up, held pride of place on his dresser while pictures of grevians covered the walls. Grevians were the largest predators on Savala and well adapted to the cold mountainous regions here. They had big, sharp claws, fangs, a long powerful body, a long tail, and a thick build. Zayvan knew from his childhood obsession that their thick build was mostly fat to keep them warm in the cold temperatures, that their white coat was actually clear, and that they had black skin under that clear fur to help absorb heat from the sun. He wasn't a child anymore, but he still admired them to this day, so he'd never bothered taking the pictures down.

Zayvan closed the door behind him and pulled out his phone before crossing the room to sit on the bed. Waking the phone, he selected his brother from the contacts and brought it up to his ear, waiting for his much busier sibling to answer.

"Zayvan!"

"Hey, Rekhem. Are you lost without me?"

Rekhem laughed. "Not even close. Maybe I don't need you after all."

"Oh, you need me. Just wait for the first major crisis."

"I hope that never happens."

So did Zayvan. He joked, but his brother was fortunate to have never needed to be that kind of leader. He'd inherited a role that largely took care of itself. Their parents had done a good job, people had loved them, and they were greatly missed.

"Well, why did you call, brother? How are things with your match?"

Zayvan took a moment to gather his thoughts before speaking. "It's hard to say. She seems nice enough. A little quiet, skittish. I think something bad happened to her."

Then he remembered the speed at which the match was made and started putting the pieces together. "I think she was running from someone who hurt her. I think that's why they rushed the match."

"What makes you think that?"

"Little things. The way she acts. Even raising my voice startled her."

"You raised your voice to her? You? Mild-mannered Zayvan?"

Oh, his brother was never going to let him live this down. "She kept saying sorry. She actually apologized after I asked her if she was okay."

He could imagine the gears in his brother's mind spinning as he tried to work out her logic. Zayvan couldn't figure it out either. He wished he hadn't spoken that way to her, but the repeated apologies were fraying his nerves.

"That *is* strange. What do you think happened to her?"

He started to mention the broken leg, but then realized he knew nothing about that incident. In fact, Justine had managed to skate past massive portions of her life in their conversations so far. She'd talked about family, friends, growing up, school, jobs she'd hated, but nothing about her previous partners, nothing about how she got hurt, nothing to indicate why she seemed so fragile and scared. "I can only speculate at this point."

"Do you need advice?"

"I don't know. I guess I just needed to talk about it. I don't know what I was expecting. You know how vague those profiles are, but I don't think I was prepared." He chuckled humorlessly to himself. "I had months, but I definitely wasn't prepared."

"Zayvan, you were never truly going to be prepared. You were meeting a complete stranger at our private launchpad. What's more, she's not even Savalan, so you don't even have the benefit of common cultures to rely on. This was always going to be unexplored territory. Has there ever been a match between a human and a Savalan before?"

"I don't know. I didn't think to ask."

"Well, I imagine they would have told you if there had been.

They might have even encouraged you to get together with that previous match for pointers." Rekhem paused, giving this far more thought than he would usually expect from his more take-charge brother. "I tell you what. Take all the time you want. I don't need you right now and clearly she does, so I want you to do whatever it takes to make this relationship work, okay?"

"Rekhem," he protested.

"No, I mean it. That's an order."

Zayvan held his tongue, knowing his brother wasn't likely to change his mind. He never did when he got like this. "Are you sure?"

"Absolutely. She needs you, brother. Take good care of her."

He nodded even though his brother couldn't see him and then dropped the phone to his lap after Rekhem ended the call, not even bothering to say goodbye.

Justine watched Zayvan disappear down the hall, her gaze taking in his form in a way she hadn't before. He was big, massive, really, and that should terrify her, but it didn't anymore.

Today, he was wearing a lightweight t-shirt that melded to his form, highlighting everything to its best advantage. The shirt itself was plain, just a simple blue in a deeper shade than his skin, but the muscle definition behind it made the shirt look impressive.

She stared at that shirt, at the clearly defined back muscles that shifted constantly beneath it as he walked. They drew her eye down his body, caressing his butt and giving little hints at the thighs beneath the looser fabric of his pants.

She sighed when he turned, slipping out of sight and into one of the rooms. "What the hell are you thinking, Justine?" She could admit that while she definitely admired his form, a form she would have drooled over in the pre-Brian days, she suspected her reaction would be very different if that fantastic shirt suddenly came off, even for completely non-sexual reasons.

This is how you got into this situation in the first place.

Though she supposed that wasn't entirely true. It had taken far more than just a hot body to entice her with Brian. He'd wooed her, and she'd lapped it up like crazy, unfortunately. Looking back, she cringed a bit at how she'd acted around him in the early days. But she'd been young, and young didn't often translate to "makes good decisions."

Justine turned around, forcing the afterimage of Zayvan's impressive body out of mind to focus on the games he'd laid out instead. She knew none of them, games not being one of the topics included in her studies. The packaging reminded her a lot of the games back home. Different shapes, fonts, and languages, of course, but there was a similar feel to them. Most of them had boxes in shapes that seemed to lump them into specific categories, and she wondered if there were standardized box sizes for the industry.

She sorted and stacked them by shape, then examined them one by one. It wasn't the easiest thing in the world. She was still really new to reading Savalan, so she was slow as she read each box, and she was just as likely to nix a game because she struggled with the wording as she was because she didn't like the concept.

By the time Zayvan came back, she was leaning toward a game with one of the smallest rule books among them, figuring it would probably be easiest to learn. The concept on the back of the box seemed fine enough, just a card game, and she liked card games.

"Did you pick something?" he asked as he leaned over the couch, hovering above her head.

Justine was surprised when she didn't panic, when the action didn't startle her or send her heart racing with fear. She rolled her shoulders and tried to pass it off as normal rather than monumental. She lifted the box in her hand, offering it up to him. "This one."

He took it and smiled. "This was a favorite of ours when me and my brother were kids." He leaned forward, showing her the box. "See this?" It was a corner that looked half crushed. "Rekhem threw the box at me and missed, hitting the wall. Mom was livid and took all the games away for the rest of the trip."

Zayvan straightened and walked around the couch, sitting next to Justine. He set the game box down on the table, then leaned to pull his phone out of his pocket. With a finger movement, he woke the screen. "Let's get you that phone I promised."

"Would it get delivered here?"

"Yup." He navigated through several screens, images that looked familiar and utterly alien coming and going as he navigated to his destination. "Here. This is the same manufacturer as my phone." He handed her the phone.

It was sleek, but massive. A smooth device that didn't really fit in her hand. She looked over at his hands where they rested in his lap and wondered at their size. If they held hands, his would probably swallow hers entirely. She turned back to the phone, awkwardly holding it in one hand while she started to scroll with a single finger.

Justine frowned down at the screen, feeling overwhelmed by the information there. She had no idea what she was looking at. She wasn't the *least* tech savvy person on Earth, but this was completely beyond her. Nothing, not even the dimensions, made any sense to her. She looked over and up at Zayvan, offering him back the phone. "Is there one smaller than this? One that will fit my hand better?"

He took it back and started searching. "Looks like they have two models. This one," he said, lifting the phone so she could see the screen, "is for children. It's um..." He looked around himself, though what he was looking for, she wasn't sure. He settled on a game box. "It's probably about up to here and here." He indicated the dimensions on the box.

Justine took the box, comparing what he'd shown to the size of her hand. It would probably be an okay size. She looked back up at Zayvan's screen. That model came in a variety of colors, each comparably bright and almost garish. It also looked a little more durable, like the children's tablets back home.

Her immediate thought was how she would stand out holding such a phone. Would people laugh at her, call her a child? Or would it just make her already alien appearance that much more obvious? Brighter, bolder, more difficult to hide? She reached up, touching her red hair and suddenly feeling self-conscious about it. Red hair, already rare on Earth, was probably going to make her stand out that much more on Savala. Those phone colors just made her realize how different she truly was here.

She hadn't even considered that before making this decision, but it was true, wasn't it? She was an outsider, a freak. No one else on this planet would look like her. And she was so much smaller, meaning everything from furniture to cars to clothes would be outsized for her. Even something as simple and straightforward as picking out a phone involved a reminder of how different she was here.

Zayvan scrolled again, pulling up another model. This one

was clearly not geared for children, without the bumpers on the edges or the bright colors. It was subdued in tone like so much of this world had been so far. He showed her on the box how large he thought the phone would be. It was definitely larger than the child phone, but not by too much. "This is the smallest adult phone they have." He looked awkwardly down at her hand then back up again. "I could try to look up some other manufacturers?"

She doubted another manufacturer would be any better, and at least getting one of these would mean Zayvan could more easily teach her how to use it.

But looking down at the still fairly massive phone on the screen, she started to wonder just how big Savalan women were. Did Savalans have sexual dimorphism like humans did? Were women bigger or smaller? There was no specific reason for the women to be smaller, was there? Maybe she was going to be mistaken for a child for the rest of her life.

She frowned down at the screen. At first, she had been looking forward to getting her own phone, but now she just wanted to pick something and be done with it. Maybe it would have been different if they were in a store, picking up models and feeling them out, talking about the different features excitedly, but like this, she just felt like the entire process was hopeless, like there was no chance she was going to find something that would be perfect for her. Everything was going to be too big and not her style.

"Let's just go with that," she said, pointing at the screen.

"Are you sure? We can keep looking."

She shrugged. "It's fine. Just go with that."

"Okay," Zayvan said, sounding hesitant. "What color do you want?" He handed her back the phone.

She looked at each, tapping the different versions, swiping left and right to spin the image around. Each was metallic and subdued, with a few being basic metal colors like black, silver, gray, bronze, etc. Others were clearly not metal colors but still metallic and definitely not as bright as the child phones. They had practically every color in the rainbow, and Justine stopped continuously swiping when she came to the purple one. It was striking, the way the light hit it, making it almost mesmerizing. She could imagine holding it in her hand, carrying it around with her. "This one," she said, offering Zayvan his phone back.

"Okay, I'll get that ordered." He stood and started messing with his phone as he walked toward the kitchen.

Justine wasn't sure exactly what he was doing. Maybe he was placing an order on the website, but a few moments later, he reached the fridge and pocketed his phone. "What do you like to eat when playing games?" he asked as his hand reached for the door.

"Most gaming foods on Earth are crispy and salty."

He thought for a moment. "Crispy and salty. I can do that." He changed direction, going for the cabinet the flatbread had been in. He reached up and pulled a bag off the top shelf, then opened it and dumped some into a bowl. "Let's play on the table." He motioned to the spot where they'd eaten their last two meals.

Justine nodded and grabbed the game she'd picked, crossing the room. She was a little less confident, though, when she sat down with the game and tried to figure out how to set it up. She could understand the words, even if she had to sound out some of them, but her mind was struggling to convert them into directions she could follow.

"Here," Zayvan said as he set a bottle and two glasses on the table.

She looked up, noticing he must have already made a second trip as the bowl of snacks was sitting in the middle of the table. She handed him the instructions.

He smiled. "I meant the deck. I've pretty much memorized the instructions by now."

"Oh, sorry."

"Don't say sorry."

"Sorry."

He silently raised his eyebrows at her, and she snapped her mouth shut. He reached out and picked up the deck, starting to shuffle it and deal out cards. "The game is pretty simple, and I suspect that's part of what makes it so fun. You can just relax and enjoy rather than trying to come up with complicated strategies or keep up with complex scoring systems." After that, he poured them each a drink, sliding hers in front of her. "Careful, it's alcoholic."

"Okay," she said, taking a tentative taste. It was sweet, and she smiled at him, appreciating what she suspected was a thoughtful gesture on his part. He'd remembered what she liked. It gave her a little tingly feeling to know he'd been so considerate. And also because he'd been careful to let her know it was alcoholic. He wasn't trying to get her drunk.

They played open handed for the first round, with Zayvan explaining the rules and showing her what the best strategy was and what to avoid doing. It felt good, normal, like happy little moments from before everything had gone to hell. She remembered playing card games with her family. Parents, grandparents, aunts and uncles. It had always been a good time. Being together had been more important than winning the game, and they'd spent the time laughing and talking and catching up. Games were the social lubricant of her childhood, and somehow she'd forgotten that.

As they moved beyond the first round, switching to hiding their cards, Justine couldn't help smiling, sometimes even laughing. When she had a good hand, her entire body would sing with excitement. She sipped carefully at the wine and found the snacks quite enjoyable. She wasn't sure what they were, but they were nearly paper thin and just salty enough, with a little something else she couldn't quite identify. Still, she found her hand moving to the bowl over and over, and Zayvan had to get up multiple times to refill it.

The bottle of wine, too, slowly emptied, and they both lost track of time.

Eventually, Zayvan set his hand down, looked over at the window, and laughed. "It's dark out."

She looked over herself, shocked that so much time had passed with them just sitting there playing round after round. "Wow. Time flies, huh?"

He turned back to her and paused for a moment before smiling. "Indeed."

Justine smiled back, her heart warmed by the expression on his face. "Do you think we should stop?"

His smile grew crooked. "Only if you want to."

Be still, my stupid heart.

Then her stomach growled, and she laughed. "I guess that answers that question."

He nodded, chuckling quietly. "I'll get dinner started."

Justine watched as he walked away from the table, again taken in by his masculine form. He was perfect, and she hoped to hell there were no surprises in their future, because she could very easily find herself loving a man like him.

CHAPTER SEVEN

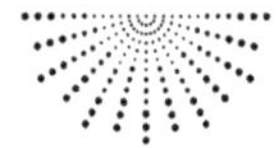

For the past few weeks, things had been going well, Zayvan thought. The two of them had relaxed into a routine together.

Within a few days of arriving, Justine had started insisting on helping with cooking and meal prep. She was full of questions, asking about what each ingredient tasted like, how to cook it, what its texture was like, and so much more. She forgot things constantly, having to ask the same question multiple times before it stuck in her head, which resulted in her saying sorry more than a few times.

The word was starting to really piss him off. He wanted to be patient with her, but there were only so many times in a day you could hear the word "sorry" without wanting to snap at someone. The fact that she did it automatically just irked him even more. She didn't mean to, and he understood that, tried to be accommodating, but it wasn't easy. He just wanted to get past this. He wanted *her* to get past this.

Maybe I should take her to a mental health professional?

It wasn't the first time he'd had that thought, either. He was sure there was some sort of trauma to blame, but he didn't want to push her on it. He wanted to give her the space to deal with it in her own way. She just didn't know or trust him enough yet to be open about everything.

He sighed as he sat on the porch, checking his phone for messages. This was what they tended to do after breakfast. Justine's phone had arrived the day after he'd ordered it, and she liked to spend this time writing a message to her friend, Amira, and familiarizing herself with the phone.

The first time she'd received a message back, she'd honestly squealed and jumped up and down in her excitement.

It was also the first time she'd hugged him. He'd been surprised by the action. Certainly, he hadn't expected it. Immediately after, she'd broken away from him and pulled up the message, reading it aloud. He'd loved seeing her so excited and happy. And getting to hear the message she'd received from her friend had made him feel like a part of her life.

After that first message, every day seemed to include some moments where she was griping about how long it took messages to travel back and forth between Savala and Earth. There was nothing he could do about it, so he just listened patiently as she voiced her complaints.

But that was only a small portion of their time. In truth, most of the time passed quickly and without conflict. He couldn't believe it had been weeks since he first met her. As Justine would put it, the time was flying by, and he couldn't be happier. Visions of domestic bliss passed through his head as he pulled up the weather on his phone, wondering what today would bring. In his head, he imagined the future. He saw them smiling over meals, cuddling on the couch, and laughing with friends and family.

Zayvan smiled down at the phone when he saw the forecast. It was already feeling like a nice day to him, but he'd come to learn that the best way to judge the weather for Justine was to check the temperature on the app. He'd been paying careful attention the last few weeks, noting when she thought it was chilly and checking the temperature to see what it was. It often felt fine to him, but he wanted her to be comfortable.

Today was looking to be a mighty fine day, with the temperature set to hit a point that he suspected Justine would find very comfortable. It was also supposed to be an unusually sunny day, with the forecast indicating the cloud cover would be especially thin in their area in the early afternoon.

Zayvan stood, pocketing the phone, and started making plans in his head for an afternoon picnic. They hadn't done that before, but it looked like the weather would be perfect for it, and he really hoped it would please her.

He entered the cabin excitedly. "I'm preparing a picnic!" he declared.

Justine, sitting on the couch, looked up from her purple phone. "But we just ate."

He laughed. "Not now. I was thinking for the midday meal."

"Oh."

Zayvan paused, the door still held partially open in his hand. "Do you not like picnics?"

"I don't dislike them. I just don't usually eat that early."

Looking back, he realized she really didn't. She would eat the midday meal, but she often approached it like she didn't know what to do with it. He pulled out his phone again and rechecked the weather. "We could have an early dinner as a picnic? Would that be better?"

She thought about it and nodded. "Sure."

"Excellent." He closed the door behind him. "Do you want to help me pick the menu?"

Justine stood and pocketed her phone. "I'd love to."

When Zayvan started packing up for the picnic later that day, Justine was actually nervous. Butterflies were flying like mad in her stomach as she watched. He was methodical with his movements, and she found his size no longer bothered her in any way. Sure, he was big and tall, but he was *hers*, and she was finally starting to believe that. They weren't strangers anymore, and she was really beginning to feel as if she knew him.

They often spent the evenings talking about their lives. Zayvan would describe what it was like growing up on Savala, his brother and their relationship, what he did for a living. She felt like she could paint a complete picture of it in her head, and she couldn't wait to see it all herself. She wondered if Rekhem would like her and what she would think of him in return. Would she end up with a large extended family that accepted her as one of their own or a bunch of in-laws who barely tolerated her and talked about her behind her back?

Justine was sort of ready for this little hiatus here at the cabin to be over. She really appreciated the peace and the time it had given them to get to know each other. It had allowed her to get over some of her fears with little or no pressure from Zayvan or their surroundings.

"Okay, let's go," Zayvan said, hefting the large bag over his shoulder and pulling her out of her musings.

"Are you sure you've got that? It looks heavy."

"It's fine. Besides, you've got that leg that's still recovering. Let it heal."

She looked down at her leg, wondering if it would *ever* heal. The doctors had said the fibula had bowed because it hadn't broken along with the tibia, and that wouldn't go away no matter how much she took it easy. She just needed to get used to it. She needed to learn to live with it. "Okay," she said as she looked up and nodded.

Zayvan shifted the bag and walked to the door, pulling it open and gesturing for her to proceed him in a way that made her smile.

"Thank you."

"Any time, my lady," he said, returning her smile.

When she walked out the door, it immediately hit her how nice it was outside. She didn't even need her jacket for once. Stepping out of the way so Zayvan could exit and close the door, she pulled off her jacket and tied it around her waist.

They walked down the steps together, then Zayvan offered her an arm. She wrapped her arm in his, the height difference making it a little awkward, but still, she appreciated the romantic gesture. So much of their time together had just been getting to know each other, building familiarity and friendship, that these little overtures today really made her hopeful. They were moving forward. This was really happening. This could actually work. They could build a life together, and she was really excited about it.

Justine had gone into this without even considering what it meant in the long run. The idea of a romantic relationship, a real partnership, had seemed so alien that she'd barely given it any thought. All she'd thought of was getting away and maybe, just maybe, feeling safe with someone again. Safety had been her main concern. Not love, not romance, certainly not sex.

And yet she found the idea of sex entering her mind more and more of late. She hadn't had sex since before she broke her leg, and she kept wondering what it would be like with Zayvan. She'd certainly never been with an alien before, and she wondered if he had the same parts as humans. Would it be better? Worse? Would they even fit together?

She suspected they *must* fit together somehow, or why

bother with the matchmaking agency? Since sex was important for a vast majority of people on Earth, not mentioning any issues in that department would be deceptive as hell, so she figured it must be fine.

But was she really ready for sex with him? They'd never even kissed, and the most intimate they'd been so far had been a few hugs she'd thrown at him when she was excited and cuddling sessions on the couch in the evenings, all of which felt great. Justine loved being physically close to him. She missed that. It was something she'd lost with Brian. Near the end, every time he was close, all she could feel was fear, and she was so relieved she didn't feel that with Zayvan. He went out of his way to ensure she didn't feel afraid, and just thinking about it made her eyes tear up a little.

She wiped the tears away, hoping Zayvan didn't see, and sighed, returning her focus to where she was walking. This was only the second walk they'd gone on together, and this trail was much nicer. It was wide, smooth, and free of rocks and roots. Trees rose up on either side, but none of the branches were low enough for her to touch, making her think they'd probably been trimmed back.

And after only a few more minutes, they stepped out into a meadow. The standard animal noises were present, but so was the sound of water rushing over rocks. She looked over at Zayvan. "Is there a stream or something?"

He grinned down at her, then guided her through the meadow.

The meadow was pretty, with surprisingly colorful flowers topping the long, knee-high stalks. A gentle breeze caused them to sway ever so slightly back and forth.

Soon enough, she spotted a gap in the flowers, and they stepped out onto a beach covered in dark earth. Before them, a small creek ran past, disappearing into the trees on either side.

Zayvan put the bag on the ground and began setting up.

Once he laid out a blanket, Justine sat down and started helping, pulling out their food and laying it out on the sheet.

After the last item was set out, Zayvan sat down close at her side, their arms nearly touching as they loaded plates with food. Zayvan poured them both cups of wine, and she tapped their cups together. "Cheers," she said before taking a sip, a shy smile on her lips.

Justine probably didn't need the wine. She was already feeling pretty good, but it just felt right. Feeling high on life, all her problems seemed far away and forgotten. She trusted Zayvan and wanted to trust him even more.

Throughout the late afternoon, they mostly sat in silence, eating and drinking with silly expressions on their faces. She felt like a teenager again, like she was on a first date with her crush.

And suddenly she wanted to kiss him.

She wasn't sure if it was the alcohol or her own budding feelings, but suddenly, it was all she could think about. What would his lips feel like? Would they be soft? Firm?

She was breathless as the thoughts spiraled around in her mind, ramping her up to take action.

"Zayvan?" she said, her mind now focusing on his size as a problem to be solved instead of something to be feared.

"Yes?" He looked down at her, giving her his full attention.

She crooked a finger at him.

"What is it?" he whispered as he leaned forward, a small smile on his face, like he was curious to know what she wanted.

She reached out a hand, curling it around the back of his neck. His hair was short there, both soft and a little prickly at the same time. She pulled, bringing his face even closer, and took a deep breath before pressing her lips to his.

He gasped, and she leaned in, pressing her advantage. He

didn't at first respond, and her anxieties began to sneak in at the corners of her mind. She started to pull away, but then she heard the light thump of something falling, and his hands were suddenly curled around her ears and the back of her head. He pulled her in and intensified the kiss.

Justine lost complete track of time, and when their lips finally broke apart, her heart was racing, her breaths ragged, and they were each glued to each other, clinging together as if their lives depended on it. She laughed, and they fell over, with Justine now half resting on top of him. Her entire body buzzed, and she couldn't help but notice his warm, muscular body pressed against her own. She pulled back a little, smiling down at him, and touched her lips in awe. "I've never felt like that before."

He curled his hands around her, lazily running them back and forth. "I don't think I have either."

"I think we should do that again."

His smile grew. "Oh, definitely." He sat up so their lips were breaths away. "Have to make sure it wasn't a fluke."

She silently chuckled as a big-assed grin stretched her lips tight, her gaze now glued to his lips. "Can't have that," she whispered before leaning in to kiss him again.

There was this charged quality to the air between them after those kisses. Zayvan kept looking at her, unable to help himself. All his fantasies to that point had been domestic, maybe a little romantic, but now he couldn't stop thinking about her in a sexual context. The kiss had put it there, forefront in his mind, and now it wouldn't leave.

He supposed part of the reason he hadn't really thought of her that way until now was because she was a different species.

She looked different, very different, from Savalans. There was no denying that fact. And yet, he supposed, in the grand scheme of things, she wasn't *that* alien in appearance. He'd met his fair share of aliens in his work, and some looked so different from Savalans, it was hard to believe they were sentient.

With Justine, it was her size that had thrown him the most. She was so small that the first phone he'd suggested to her had been a child's phone. Looking back at it now, he cringed at that move. She had a smaller frame overall than Savalan women, and there *were* Savalan children that were taller than her, especially boys. He sighed. Without the hair and skin color, she *would* sort of look like a Savalan youth.

Not that he had any capacity to see her as a youth right now. Instead, he wanted to run his hands through that fantastic mass of red hair, to kiss those lush lips that only grew more irresistible after kissing. He wanted to run his hands over that curvaceous form that reinforced the fact that she was all woman. He wondered what her skin would feel like under all that clothing she liked to wear. Because the weather was a bit cold for her, she'd never so much as worn a short-sleeved shirt since arriving here, leaving the feel of her naked skin still a mystery to him.

It was driving him mad.

After returning from the picnic, they'd fallen back into their normal routine. They'd washed the dishes and put away leftovers. Then Justine had picked out a game to play, but neither of them seemed to be in the right headspace for it. They were both making stupid, obvious mistakes, and often had to remind each other to start their turn.

Probably, a game had been a bad idea, but he didn't know what else to do. His mind was consumed with things he was sure would be terrible ideas.

She's not ready.

He had to remind himself that they'd only just kissed for the first time today. She would need time. After all, she'd needed time for everything else, hadn't she?

Then Justine suddenly lowered her cards and placed them face down on the table. "I think I want you," she said out of the blue.

Zayvan wasn't sure he was hearing that correctly, or maybe it was a translation issue. Maybe she thought she was saying something else. "You... want me."

She was taking deep breaths as she nodded her head, her gaze never leaving his. It was intense, and she even shivered a little.

Is she cold?

But... no. That look she was giving him didn't say, "I'm cold." It was a look he knew all too well from when he used to date, from back when he'd naively believed a Savalan woman could separate him from his title. "You... want sex?"

She nodded three times, looking a little eager as she continued to breathe deeply.

Zayvan didn't know what to do. He felt paralyzed and unprepared, like a callow youth. Was this really happening?

He stood, as if on autopilot, and offered a hand to her. She took it, and he led her down the hallway to his room, his mind still unable to believe this was happening. It seemed too much, too soon, but he couldn't imagine trying to stop or slow down.

He pushed open the door and stepped back, letting her take the lead.

She peeked inside. "It's nice," she said, then took that first step forward, her head pivoting as she took in his room.

He waited, afraid to pressure her or scare her.

She turned around and smiled. "Are you coming in?"

"Only if you want me to." His own smile was lopsided and hesitant.

She nodded. "I do. Come here."

She motioned him forward, and he stepped into the room, quickly closing the gap and looming over her. He didn't like that, afraid it would bother her, but she just reached up to run her hands over his exposed skin. Her soft fingers and palms ghosted over his arms, across his clad shoulders and up his neck, stopping at his chin, which was as far as she could comfortably reach with him standing.

He closed his eyes, reveling in the feel of her gently caressing him, the movements slow and sensual. He did nothing but stand there for several moments, just letting her do whatever she wanted to him.

"Sit," she said, pushing against his chest.

He opened his eyes, stepped back, and sat down on the edge of the bed. Now Justine loomed over him, her ample chest at eye level. He looked up at her. She had this soft expression on her face. He couldn't decipher it, but it warmed his heart. He reached up, caressing her cheek. She leaned into the touch, her hair brushing against his fingertips as she moved.

"Show me what you want," he said, looking up at her, suddenly desperate to please her.

She reached down and tugged at his shirt.

He obliged immediately, yanking it up over his head and dropping it on the floor. Her hands touched the newly exposed skin a moment later. It felt like silk caressing his skin, and he reveled in it for a while, just enjoying being touched. It felt almost like a spiritual moment, with Justine hovering over him, her hands ghosting over his body in a way that was both sexual and not. She was touching nothing overtly erogenous, and yet he couldn't deny there was something special about it.

He reached out, looping his arms around her waist and pulling her closer. She smiled down at him, her hands shifting to his shoulders, then his neck, then his hair, where they wove in and held on, firmly massaging his scalp in a way that had him forgetting what he was doing as he groaned in pleasure.

Her smile grew, and he started rubbing his hands up and down her back, slipping them underneath her shirt. She leaned into the touch, pressing her back into his hands as if encouraging him to do more.

Continuing up her back, his fingers touched an undergarment. He traced over it, feeling a hard clasp. He played with it, wondering how it worked. Then the material gave, exposing more skin to his exploring touch. "What next?" he whispered into her shirt, right over her breasts.

She didn't respond immediately, and he looked up. She took several deep breaths before releasing her hold on his hair and reaching down. The material confining his hands lifted up, exposing the undergarment beneath. It was loose and gaping, obviously because he'd opened the clasp on the back. Two straps held it up now, with material covering each breast. He'd never seen such a garment before, and it suddenly occurred to him that humans had larger breasts than Savalans, large enough to require this garment. He shifted position, pulling a hand away from her back to touch the silky material. The flesh behind it was soft, and he wanted to explore more. He looked up at her, asking for permission with his eyes.

Justine hesitated, and he wondered if this would be the end of their play. Was this as far as she was willing to go today? If so, that was okay. Today had been a revelation, and they'd gone a lot farther than he'd expected. He would be content. He was about to say so when she shifted her shoulders, letting the garment fall down her arms. For a moment, it still covered her breasts. She touched the material, as if uncertain if she wanted to really remove it, and Zayvan was again about to tell her she didn't have to, when she closed her eyes and pulled it off, dropping it to the floor.

She stood there, a little tense and awkward, for several long heartbeats, and while he was tempted to touch, he resisted, waiting for her to relax.

"May I?" he asked.

Her eyes were still closed, but she let out a long, audible breath and nodded.

He very carefully ran the backs of his fingers over the sides of the pretty peaks, watching her face closely for a reaction. She tensed momentarily and gasped when he first made contact, but then relaxed into his touch, her body leaning even closer to him than before. The skin was silky soft, only growing softer as it approached the color change at the tip.

His other arm, which had still been behind her back, came forward to join in, exploring her breasts' unique shape and experimenting with various touches.

Justine was restless, shifting constantly as he continued to touch her in this clearly intimate place. Her hands went back to his scalp, massaging more firmly this time, and he groaned, his breath wafting over her exposed skin.

This continued until he noticed his pant leg growing wet. He looked down and realized Justine had been straddling one of his legs, rubbing herself against it with her restless movements.

She's aroused, he thought to himself, surprised. Savalan women required more direct stimulation to get to this point. He glanced up at her face, noticing now how her head was thrown back, her mouth gaping open in pleasure.

She wasn't making a sound.

Zayvan moved, cupping the sides of her face with his hands, and kissed her. Her breath puffed into his mouth, and it was only a moment before her tongue plunged in as well. They dueled for control over the kiss, and before he knew it, they were tumbling onto the bed, limbs tangled together. He pulled back, breathing hard. "Tell me what you want."

"You," she said breathlessly. "I want you."

"You have me. Tell me what you want."

She chewed on her lip, and Zayvan leaned in, nipping it before pulling back and waiting.

Justine's hand skimmed down his body, sliding and caressing, and finally settling over the uncomfortable bulge in his pants. "This," she said with a squeeze that had him struggling for control. "I want this."

He leaned down and kissed her forehead, suddenly struck by an inexplicable moment of tenderness. "Then *that* you will have."

He leaned back and slipped off the bed, kicking off his shoes and removing his pants. They pooled at his ankles, and he stepped out of them as Justine shimmied out of her own, pulling off an undergarment at the same time. She shoved them to the side when she was free of them, and Zayvan climbed back onto the bed and crawled toward her. Now hovering above her, his hands pressed into the bed on either side of her arms. "Is this okay?"

She nodded.

He leaned down and took her mouth in another kiss. Justine moaned into it, arching up into the press of his body above her.

"Do it," she whispered against his lips. "Please."

Zayvan nodded his head, pulling back from the kiss. He reached down to line himself up as Justine spread her legs, wrapping them around his waist. When he got close, he was again surprised, pleasantly surprised, by the wetness already there. He pressed that advantage, pushing forward with a moan as her body began to swallow him up. The pressure was intense and pleasure immediately ran through his body and up his spine. He had to stop, finding it difficult to take a breath. Her body rippled around him, and he shivered.

"More," she whispered into his ear.

He continued, trying desperately to contain his ardor as their bodies pressed closer and closer together, and he sank deeper and deeper.

Justine gasped, and he stopped, looking down at her in concern. "Are you okay?" he asked, even though his body was screaming at him to keep going or give up entirely.

She nodded eagerly. Her breath shivered out of her, a little smile crossing her face. "Feels real good."

He smiled, relieved. "Good. Want more?"

She panted. "God, yes."

He pressed forward, groaning in excitement when he bottomed out.

When he stopped to revel in the feeling, she snapped at him, "Move, damn it!"

He nearly growled as he pulled back. The return happened at lightning speed, and Justine squealed in pleasure. He began a rapid pace that had his heart pounding and his body screaming *move, move, move*. Justine was squirming underneath him, a constant litany of unintelligible sounds escaping her lips, and he prayed he was pushing her higher and higher toward her peak. He knew almost nothing about human pleasure, and his brain had essentially devolved into an animalistic instinct that was conspiring to drive him to completion.

His body was singing, begging him to finish, but a small part of his rational brain, maybe only a couple brain cells, was still firing, insisting he hold off, that he wait for her.

After a while, he started saying, "Please, please, please," as if he were begging her to climax. His body was screaming for release, consuming every ounce of his being with the need.

Then her body seized, locking up, her mouth wide open,

her pleasure locked in her throat. He couldn't take it anymore and came, all the tension he'd held in his body suddenly releasing in a wave of pleasure that left him boneless.

He collapsed, barely having the wherewithal to roll off of her as his vision dimmed momentarily.

When he came back to himself, he was holding her tight to his chest, both of them breathing heavily, their sweat-slick skin sticking to each other. "Please tell me you came," he said as his heart rate started to slow.

She nodded against his chest. "Shit yes, I came."

"Good, cause I don't think I have another round in me."

Justine laughed against his chest, seemingly too exhausted to lift her head. "I don't think I do either."

"Good," he said as he leaned down and kissed her temple.

She nodded again, shifting a little to get more comfortable. She fell asleep quickly and, to his surprise, he found himself following her into sleep moments later, the comforting weight and warmth of Justine's body keeping him company in his dreams.

CHAPTER EIGHT

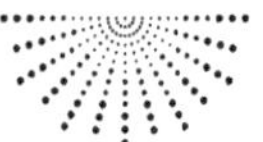

Justine woke the next morning feeling boneless and well rested. She rolled onto her back and stretched, realizing when her arm brushed against something that she wasn't in the bed she'd slept in since reaching Savala.

She looked over and smiled when she spotted Zayvan there, sound asleep.

He looks adorable.

She rolled onto her side to watch him, bringing up a fist to rest under her chin. Dim light from the early morning was peeking through the window, and it was quiet, the animals not yet awake. This was the earliest she'd woken up since coming here, and she didn't want to get out of bed. The bedding was comfortable and laying there with Zayvan at her side was almost magical. It made her heart warm with some undefinable emotion, something that left her wondering if she was going to smile or cry.

Either way, she was happy, so very happy. She was here with

a man she was starting to love. He was kind and considerate, and she really thought she could trust him. Going in, she never really expected to trust again, but Zayvan made her believe she could. He made her believe not every man was like Brian, that not every man cared only about himself. He didn't treat her like an accessory, but like a partner. Zayvan gave her what she needed to stand on her own rather than taking those things away to ensure she couldn't. She had no doubt he would help her find a job once they returned to his home. She truly believed that.

I can't wait to tell Amira.

Then Zayvan started moving, and Justine's heart leaped with excitement. She pushed herself up on her elbow, eager for him to wake.

He opened his eyes, and she smiled. "Morning, sleepyhead."

"Hi," he said with a smile.

Justine didn't know what else to say, so she just leaned in and cuddled up next to him, throwing an arm over his chest. She sighed into his neck, and he laughed, shifting position to pull her even closer.

"No regrets?" he asked.

She shook her head. "Not even close."

"Good."

They stayed that way for a while, enjoying the intimacy, neither of them eager to start the day. *This* was why they were here, to get closer. They didn't feel the need to say a word, just idly touching and listening as the animals finally woke up outside, calling out their morning songs.

Then the door slammed open, and men in black tactical gear barged into the room.

Justine screamed, scrambling to pull the blankets over her naked form. The people filled the room, pouring in like a flood, as Zayvan sat up, barking, "What's the meaning of this?" at the top of his lungs.

Justine was moving farther back on the bed, putting Zayvan between her and the intruders as best she could, not that it helped. She pulled the blanket a little higher against her shoulders, feeling naked in a way that even clothing couldn't fix.

One of the intruders, someone with a splash of color on their uniform, stepped forward. "Apologies, Your Highness. It was an emergency. We need you to return to the palace."

Zayvan swore, then hung his head, took a deep breath, and straightened his shoulders. The move was remarkable, making her laid back Zayvan suddenly have an authoritative air that sent a chill down her spine. "Very well." He waved his hand. "Leave the room. We'll need to pack, but we'll be along shortly."

The people filed out quickly and closed the door behind them.

Justine looked up at Zayvan, feeling very afraid. "Zayvan, what's going on?"

He sighed and turned to her. She wished he didn't look so guilty. Her stomach turned ominously.

"We have to go home."

"Home?" Her voice was barely even a whisper at this point.

"Yes. Home."

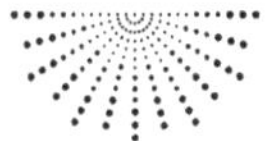

CHAPTER NINE

Justine stared at Zayvan in shock as he calmly got up and started packing. She felt like she was watching a stranger. She clutched the blankets to her chest as she sat there in bed, too shocked to move.

The silence was maddening. They had to go "home," but suddenly, she didn't want to. She didn't know this man she was seeing now. This was not the Zayvan she'd met and started falling in love with.

He zipped up his bag and turned to her. "You should get dressed and pack."

"What's going on, Zayvan?" She felt vulnerable as she asked, and a single question kept running through her head.

Who are you?

She didn't say it, was afraid to say it.

I trusted you.

Nothing made sense. She didn't know what to think, what to feel. Up until now, she'd been building this idea in her head of who Zayvan was, and now she was wondering if everything had been a lie.

She felt betrayed, like someone had pulled the rug out from under her.

"Justine?" he asked, taking a step forward.

"It's fine," she said, her voice just a little too high. "Do what you need to do. I'll be out in a moment." She continued clutching the blankets to her, unwilling to expose herself to this man even though he'd already seen everything. It seemed somehow profane now rather than the beautiful experience it had been only last night.

He nodded and picked up his bag. "I'll just put this in the vehicle."

She watched as he turned his back on her and left the room, the door clicking shut behind him.

Justine let out a breath of relief and dropped the blanket to her waist. "What am I gonna do?" She pushed the blankets back and stepped out of bed, collecting her clothing from the floor and donning them one by one. Her cheeks burned hot, realizing those people would be a witness to her walk of shame, even if it was only across the hall.

Fully clothed, she peeked her head out of the bedroom door, looking down the hallway to check if anyone was watching. She could hear some people in the living room. They were talking and moving about, but she couldn't make out what they were saying. Her Savalan just wasn't good enough for eavesdropping yet.

In a mad dash, she rushed across the hall, slipping into her own room and slamming the door behind her. Once safely ensconced within, she leaned against the door, trying to get a hold of herself. "You can do this." Except, she still wasn't exactly sure what *this* was. Why did those people barge in here? Who were they? And why did Zayvan seem to take this entire situation in stride, like it was perfectly normal for a bunch of people in body armor to invade your bedroom first thing in the morning?

Frustrated with the entire situation, she pushed off the door and crossed the room in a huff. "One thing at a time. Just pack up and leave the cabin. There's time enough for questions on the way back." She crossed the room. Her suitcase was sitting on the dresser, currently partially filled with dirty clothes. She stuffed the dirty clothes into a separate compartment and began transferring the rest of her belongings to the suitcase, first pulling things out of drawers, then collecting them from the bathroom.

After only a couple minutes, she was zipping everything she owned inside that one suitcase. It was sort of depressing, realizing she was yet again being forced to leave somewhere through the actions of someone else.

She resisted the urge to question why this was happening as she lifted the bag and set it on the floor, extending the handle. The trip out of the room, through the hallway and living room, and outside was completed in a haze.

"Here," Zayvan said, rushing up to take her bag.

Her hand flexed on the handle momentarily as he reached for it, as if some part of her was hesitant to let him have it. She looked down, slowly loosening her grip and watching as he took it away and loaded it into the back of the car.

That was when she saw the other vehicles parked in front of the cabin. Two giant, black monstrosities were wedged on either side of the car they'd arrived in, reminding her, for some weird reason, of the SWAT trucks back home. They really had nothing in common except being huge, black, a bit boxy, and having white symbols on the sides. They weren't letters, though. They were something else. She stared at one of the symbols as she stepped down off the porch and crossed to the car. Curly, ornate lines sat in stark contract to the black vehicle, a seemingly abstract design her brain couldn't interpret with its human upbringing.

She was tempted to insist on riding in one of those vehicles rather than with Zayvan, but she supposed the devil she knew was better than the devil she didn't. She walked to the car and with a sigh, she opened the door and settled inside, feeling just as small as she had that first day. It was like none of the last few weeks had happened.

If anything, it felt like they were worse off than they'd been that first day. At least back then, there'd been no baggage to deal with between them. Now, she sat there, staring out the front window, contemplating her situation, wondering if she shouldn't just cut her losses and start over.

But starting over wasn't any more appealing than staying put, and she couldn't help the questions that kept roiling through her brain on repeat.

Who is this man?

What has he been lying about?

What have I gotten myself into?

***

Zayvan was frustrated as they made their way back to the capital city. He'd never expected them to be interrupted like that. Only the day before, his brother had continued insisting he should stay away as long as he needed.

So seeing those Royal Guards storming into his room while he was still lounging in bed had been quite a shock. He looked over at Justine, and for the first time, he realized how much more of a shock this must have been for *her*. She was staring out the side window, her shoulders tense and jaw protruding stubbornly. Every once in a while, he thought he saw her tremble a bit.

He wanted to explain, to tell her about the parts of himself he'd kept from her while they were getting to know each other. He wanted to explain why he'd done it, why he hadn't told her, but he couldn't seem to find the right words, leaving only the gentle hum of the engine to break the silence.

Zayvan told himself that she wasn't ready to speak just yet, probably still shocked by the ridiculous entrance those guards had made into his bedroom while they were still both extremely naked. He still couldn't believe they'd done that. They hadn't even called out before entering, instead just storming inside like the room was on fire.

He'd even confronted them about it while Justine was packing, but they'd insisted they were following protocol. If that really *was* the protocol, he couldn't really blame them for what they did, but he also didn't have to like it.

Just thinking about that conversation brought to mind the news they'd shared shortly afterward, leaving him feeling queasy once more. He pushed it from his mind, unable or unwilling to face that truth right now.

And yet, what else was he going to focus on? Justine was rightfully ignoring him, and he didn't know what to say to make it better. So instead, the silence between them grew deeper and stronger, until even the idea of speech seemed impossible.

With a sigh, he looked out his own side window, hoping the trip would be over soon.

It wasn't until they arrived "home" that it finally clicked what was going on here and what he'd lied about.

Justine was staring out the side window, as she had the entire trip, when the car started its descent toward a large ornate building. It was a sprawling structure with several stories and wings jutting out in every direction. The city she remembered from her arrival on Savala sprawled around it, a mess of glass and metal that shimmered and stretched toward the sky, both breathtaking and somehow obscene.

And yet as they grew closer, she noticed that, while the building was made from the same materials as the city, the metal here was more sculpted, the glass more etched. Not a single surface was simple or plain.

Even the space they touched down on had intricate swirls flowing over it, clearly designed to be admired from above. Zayvan turned off the car, and Justine got out on her own, pulling open the back door to retrieve her suitcase without his help.

She stood there waiting, hands resting on the suitcase handle, as an attendant of some sort rushed out of the building and slipped into the car, taking it away to be parked elsewhere.

"Shall we?" Zayvan said, offering her an arm.

Instead of taking it, she gestured with a hand for him to lead the way.

His arm dropped, disappointment on his face, and he nodded, walking toward the door.

The inside was just as ornate as the outside. It felt cold and impersonal, and a chill ran through her that had nothing to do with the temperature. Sound carried, and their footsteps almost echoed against the marble floors. In the distance, she could hear movement and voices.

She stopped in her tracks, suddenly remembering something she'd heard when those people had stormed into Zayvan's room. Palace. They'd said palace. Return to the palace. She looked over at Zayvan, who was still walking, moving farther and farther away from her in more ways than one.

"Why are we here?" she asked, her voice unusually loud in the empty corridor.

Zayvan stopped and turned around, his arm clutching his bag to his side. "What?"

"Why are we here?" She was more insistent this time, her voice firmer.

"There's a crisis. They needed me to come back."

She shook her head. He still wasn't answering the question. He still wasn't giving her the information she *needed*. She frowned, starting to get mad. "No, why are we *here*?"

He looked confused. "I don't understand."

She shook her head, disgusted with the entire situation. "Here, this place." She pointed a finger at the floor. "Why are we here? What is this place to you?"

He looked around as if seeing it for the first time, then looked back at her. "It's home."

She shook her head and rolled her eyes. "No, Zayvan. You're not listening. Just tell me. Why are we here? What is this place?"

She could see the moment it clicked in his head, but there was also a moment of hesitancy and maybe even fear in his eyes before he finally spoke. "It's the Savta Palace. This is my home. I've lived here my entire life."

She didn't speak, just silently condemning him with her eyes as he continued trying to weasel his way out of answering.

He sighed. "I'm a member of the Royal Family. My brother is Crown Prince." With that bomb dropped, he turned and walked away, not even bothering to make sure she was following.

Justine was shocked, unable to move for several moments, but then she remembered those people calling him Your Highness. It had probably been rambling around the back of her mind unnoticed the entire flight here, so the shock didn't last long.

I should have expected that.

The palace, the raid, the "Your Highness" she'd been too overwhelmed to process on the spot. It was all so obvious now. She looked up. Zayvan was growing farther and farther away with every second she hesitated. She quickly got moving again, following him to wherever their destination might be, not wanting to be left behind.

After turning down several hallways, Justine was hopelessly lost, and she pulled out her phone, wondering if she could find a map of this place somewhere. Zayvan was still within sight, but she didn't like relying on him, especially now.

Finally, he stopped in front of a set of double doors. He raised his hand to a panel like the one on the car, and the lock clicked as it disengaged. He pushed the door open and turned to her. "The door should work for you, too. I asked the Guard to update this lock when I updated the one on the car."

Justine nodded, and he slipped inside, letting her follow or not as she saw fit. She stood there for several long moments as the door started to slide shut. Right as it was about to close completely, she stuck out her foot, then pushed through.

The space looked nothing like what she'd expected. A part of her had assumed, or maybe hoped, that it would look exactly like his room back in the cabin, but this was just as cold and unwelcoming as the rest of the palace, forcing her to wonder who the *real* Zayvan was. Was it the man she'd met in the cabin or this "prince" she was meeting only now?

As she stood there, feeling increasingly heartbroken, she desperately hoped she really *did* know who he was deep down, that he'd shown his true colors back at the cabin and this was all windowdressing, but she had a hard time believing. Her trust had been broken too many times, and she was afraid it wouldn't even matter who he was anymore, that it was already too late.

She stepped into the room, taking in the fancy furniture and cold, distant decorating style.

Do I even know him at all?

He returned to the main area from somewhere at the back of the apartments, and she asked, "Where am I staying?"

He looked surprised for a moment before his entire form sagged a little, and he nodded his head. "Through here." He moved off to the side, leading her to a small bedroom. It was well kept, with a bed dressed in white, and furniture that was just as ornate as the rest of the building. It left her feeling like their situation was hopeless, and she contemplated calling up the local matchmaking agency and requesting a new match.

Anything's better than this.

She stepped into the room, rolling her suitcase to the end of the bed and admitting to herself that she was seriously exaggerating with that last thought. She would rather be here than back with Brian, but this also wasn't the new start she'd been hoping for.

"Those doors lead to a walk-in closet and attached bath. The apartments have a full kitchen, but you can also call the palace kitchens and order a meal brought up." He pointed at a phone on the nightstand. "I... I wish I could stay, but there's pressing business I need to attend to."

She stared at his receding back, shocked that he would just dump her here and leave. Though at this point, nothing should surprise her anymore. At the doorway, he paused and looked back. "I'm sorry," he said, then left. The front door clicked a few moments later, leaving Justine all by herself in this empty and unfamiliar apartment.

She sat down on the bed and looked around. "Now what?"

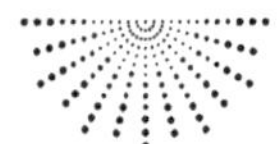

CHAPTER TEN

Justine barely saw Zayvan at all over the next few days. He was rarely in his apartments, and she wasn't sure if that was normal, a result of the "crisis" that had interrupted their getaway, or if he was trying to avoid her.

What had that crisis been, anyway? Zayvan never said. Instead, she was left to her own devices, in the dark and struggling to make sense of her new reality on her own.

Her mind drifted longingly to the agency tablet she'd been forced to relinquish. It had included tons of information on the government of Savala, and while she'd poured over it religiously on the trip here, she suddenly felt woefully unequipped to deal with her new situation. So instead, she sat down on the couch in the foyer and pulled out her phone. The couch was hard and uncomfortable, but then again, so was the bed. It all stood in stark contrast to the comfort and luxury she'd felt back at the cabin.

She rearranged the pillows and cushions, hoping to get more comfortable, before giving up and focusing on finding answers. A quick search started filling in the blanks in Zayvan's story. Rekhem, Zayvan's brother, was the Crown Prince of Savala. He held almost all the power in their government, and Zayvan was one of his advisors.

But try as she might, she couldn't find any information on the "crisis," leaving her a bit frustrated.

Thwarted, she moved on to learning as much as she could about Rekhem and Zayvan. Rekhem was easier to find information on. He was gregarious and well-loved among the people of Savala, a "ruler of the people" as one source called him, a leader who was more prone to sending votes to the people themselves than sending votes to Congress. She also quickly learned that he was unmarried, but engaged. The woman had been picked by his parents, and it seemed as if, according to the more tabloidy sources, he had been actively avoiding the marriage.

She still couldn't quite grasp the idea of Zayvan being a prince, though. She had this idea in her head of princes being these untouchable entities, barely even people. They were symbols, idols. Even when she tried to force herself to see them as real people, she still had a hard time equating the two concepts in her mind. She thought of the working royals of the UK and more nebulous figures from other European countries, people she only ever heard of in passing and without any personal details attached. Even the better known UK royalty, though, seemed nothing like Zayvan. Zayvan was down to earth, laid back, generous and kind. She had yet to see him once put appearances over other, more important, matters.

Which was nothing like how she perceived royalty back on Earth. To her, at least, Earth royals were separate. They were figureheads. They were always proper, always perfectly dressed and perfectly coiffed. They didn't play games around a table, relax in a cabin in the woods, or wear comfortable clothing.

So how could she take that image she'd cultivated over the last few weeks and fit it in with the idea of him as a prince? What did that even *mean* on Savala?

And why didn't he tell me?

She put down her phone in disgust and stood, beginning to pace the room and nearly stomping her way across it. The marble floors made a satisfying cracking noise with each step, encouraging her to let her emotions out on it. "Gah!" she yelled, stomping her foot and throwing her arms to her sides. "Why! Why didn't you tell me?"

More than anything, that was the part she just couldn't get over. They'd had *sex,* and yet he hadn't bothered to tell her. "By the way, I'm a prince," she said mockingly to the empty room. "See? It's not that hard." She didn't care if he was a prince. If anything, the idea of living a public life left her feeling nauseous. She'd never been the type to fantasize about being a princess. She'd always felt sorry for real princesses and the way they had to live. It wasn't *anything* like the fairy tales. Maybe it would have been different in the past, like in the Middle Ages when life was hard for all but the richest of people, but things were different now. Nowadays, being a princess was a life of sacrifice, of having your every decision judged by not only your family, but your entire country. One misstep could have you ruthlessly attacked by the media. Your choices were limited. You couldn't do anything that wasn't seen as proper, even if that was what you wanted to do more than anything else in the world. Your life wasn't your own.

Was that the life she'd signed up for?

Which just brought her right back to the question at the heart of everything. Why hadn't he told her? He'd lied by omission. He'd taken away her opportunity to choose. He'd hidden vital information from her. Maybe she would have kept her distance if she'd known. Maybe she would have asked for another match.

Now, it almost felt like it was too late. She felt trapped, like she couldn't back out, and that scared her. She was stuck between two realities she couldn't possibly hope to reconcile. On the one side, there was the Zayvan she'd met back in the cabin, the man she'd started to fall in love with. She so desperately wanted him back, but sometimes you can't go back.

Which brought her to the other side. On that side was Zayvan the Prince. Here, those weeks were but an illusion, an illusion designed to reel her in and imprison her. It brought to mind the early days with Brian, but she didn't want to think about Brian. She didn't want to feel betrayed. She didn't want to question her judgment. She didn't want to look back at their time together and think it had all been a mirage carefully orchestrated to hurt her.

Fool me once, shame on you. Fool me twice, shame on me, right?

The whole situation was bringing up a lot of memories and feelings she would have much rather left buried, all of them focused on Brian.

Things hadn't always been bad with him. In fact, in the beginning, they'd been fantastic. He'd been generous, often making these grandiose gestures that made her smile, her heart soaring in her chest. It had been like that a lot during their initial courting. He would take her out on fancy dinners or to romantic venues like botanical gardens and stuff. He would give her little tokens of his affection, seemingly just because he felt like it. No special occasion required. During the quiet times, they might cuddle up on the couch watching a movie, and he often complimented her in offhand ways. She never remembered a single moment where there was anything negative to say about him back then.

Eventually, they moved in together, and life continued on like that, with Justine not suspecting a thing. Looking back, she couldn't really say when everything changed. It was insidious, really. Little moments she would never remember afterward except as maybe impressions. The first thing she really noticed was the little ambiguous comments he would make. At first, the comment might even feel complimentary, but then, like a bad aftertaste, she would notice an alternative way it could be interpreted, something a lot more critical, leaving her wondering what he really meant. Was she just imagining this other meaning? Was she being overly sensitive? It left her questioning her every thought and sometimes he played into this uncertainty, especially when she called him out on his wording. It was like he could read her mind as he spoke the very thoughts that were keeping her so off-kilter.

He also started expressing opinions about friends he didn't get along with, venting frustrations when time was tight or chores didn't get done. It should have been a red flag, but if anything, she'd thought this was a good thing. They were settling in together, moving beyond the honeymoon phase where they thought the other could do no wrong. She knew no relationship was perfect and that a relationship with *no* conflict would probably self-destruct eventually.

So she started working harder at their relationship, trying to talk through the small problems of everyday life. She didn't notice right away that the effort was one-sided. She didn't notice that every time a grievance was voiced, *she* was the one to bend. With each argument, she would bend more and more. She didn't notice that *she* didn't voice any of those grievances. It was always him. As such, she fell into a pattern of always trying to please him, rather than the two of them trying to find a compromise together.

And because she'd been so blind to all of this, the fight that broke her leg had come as a complete surprise. It had been building for weeks, maybe even months, yet she'd been kidding herself, somehow convinced that they were just going through a rough patch.

There had been a few verbal fights by that point, each leaving her more shaken than the last. The violence had been inevitable. All the classic signs of an abuser had been there, but she'd been too close to see it. She'd thought she'd been too smart and too strong, that it could never happen to her. She'd thought someone as opinionated, as independent, as her couldn't *possibly* fall victim to abuse like that.

She'd been wrong.

No, no one was safe from someone like that. She'd always heard abusers could somehow suss out who were the easy targets, the weak ones, the victims, but she now knew they didn't need to hunt out the vulnerable. Even the strongest could fall victim if they were manipulated just right. Everyone had a weakness somewhere, after all.

The process was imperceptible and slow. From the outside, it might be easy to see, but from within? You were just too close to realize what was really going on. And even when you did notice, you made excuses, because anything was better than dealing with the problem and admitting you'd been had.

Justine sat back down, feeling depressed. "Am I doing it all over again? Is he just another Brian?" She thought she'd been smart. She thought the questionnaire results would have given her the clues she needed to avoid disaster.

With a heavy sigh, she leaned back and stared up at the ceiling, which was adorned in intricate swirls of gold and silver relief. It reminded her all the more of why she was so upset.

Frustrated and unable to sit still anymore, she pushed off the couch and onto her feet, but she just couldn't escape it. The reminders were everywhere. Every surface was the same, fancy and expensive and ostentatious. "This is not the man I met," she grumbled under her breath, pocketing her phone and crossing the room.

The apartments felt claustrophobic now, so she pushed the doors open and stepped into the hall. It was empty, just as it had been the last time she'd seen it. She wanted to see *people*, people other than Zayvan. She wanted normal people, people who weren't royal and had no ulterior motives.

The problem was, she still didn't know her way around the palace. She'd been so wrapped up in her own drama, she hadn't even bothered to leave the apartments. She'd sulked and stormed and raged, but she hadn't explored. Even the idea of leaving had seemed overwhelming, and a small part of her had held out this faint hope that if she was there when Zayvan returned, maybe he could make it all go away. If she gave him a chance, maybe he could explain.

"That's a pipe dream," she muttered to herself as she tried to start mapping her surroundings in her head. It was surprisingly easy. Since this was a palace and, presumably, the center of their government, she'd kind of expected a maze, something to confuse invaders, but she soon picked up on the architectural patterning. It was subtle, almost subconscious, but easy to follow.

It wasn't until she reached the junction of two wings that it completely clicked what she was picking up on, though. From here, she could see the distinct difference between the decor of the two wings. The designs on the walls and floors and the color choices made were all intended to make navigation easier.

When she looked down into the other wing, she could distinctly see what made the design so simple to follow. The shapes were the densest closest to the center, gradually thinning as they disappeared at the vanishing point. She looked back and saw the same scenario behind her, but with different shapes.

Turning back forward, she faced the new corridor. It was somehow distinct from the wings, and she knew she'd arrived at the heart of the palace. Another hall or two, and she started seeing people. She jerked backward when she saw the first one. He was a pale, green-skinned man even taller and broader than Zayvan. Just being this close sent a little tendril of fear through her, and she frowned, irritated with herself.

Why am I always so damned afraid?

She *knew* most big men meant her no harm, but she couldn't shake the knowledge that they could also break her like a twig at a moment's notice. *But capacity doesn't equal intention,* she reminded herself. She just needed to get her logical brain to convince the rest of her of that.

Within moments, he was gone from sight, having not even noticed her standing there. Another hall or so, and a constant flow of people started streaming past. Every one of them was taller than her. Some by only a few inches, but many, especially the men, were tall enough to give her a complex. She stayed close to the wall, suddenly wondering why she'd thought this excursion was a good idea. She wasn't even interacting with anyone. Countless opportunities to strike up a conversation or ask a question passed her by, and she watched, frozen by indecision or something more insidious.

Maybe I'm not ready for this.

She'd forgotten that she hadn't really interacted with more than one person at a time in months, far too many months. The only people she'd talked to since breaking her leg had been Brian, Amira, Zayvan, the lady at the agency, and the captain. She hadn't even talked to her doctors, instead merely nodding as Brian dictated the direction of her care.

Eventually, she found her way to what seemed to be a

break room or cafeteria. She stepped inside, immediately comforted by the fact that at least *this* room didn't look completely and utterly ridiculous and over the top. The room was mostly empty, with a couple people sitting and chatting with food between them at a far table and a couple more standing behind a serving area at the back wall.

Justine stepped toward the back, wondering what food was available. She'd been ordering from room service since she still wasn't confident enough to cook on her own, and there was no way she was cooking or eating with Zayvan right now. But now she wondered if that food was coming from here.

"Good morning," she said as she took in the display of food.

"How can I help you?" the woman asked. She had light purple skin, long dark hair, and a frown that could win awards.

"I'm afraid I'm not terribly familiar with your food yet. What have you got?" She stared down at the dishes. There were several colorful options, and she immediately spotted a red dish that reminded her of her first meal on Savala. She shuddered.

"Oh oh, wait, are you a human?" the other person behind the counter said. Their skin had more of an orangey tone to it, and it was the closest to human skin tone she'd seen since coming here. They had short, spiky hair and a build that left Justine wondering if they were a man or woman or something else entirely.

"Um, yes?" she said, not quite knowing how to react to such a question.

"I've heard of you!" they said, pointing at Justine then turning to their coworker. "You remember, right? It's been all the talk. The human woman in Prince Zayvan's apartments."

Justine winced, hating the reminder of Zayvan's status and, by association, her complete obliviousness to it.

They turned back to Justine. "You've been the talk of the

palace. Everyone's been wondering about you." They leaned forward, putting their elbows on the glass barrier between them. "So, what's the story? How did you come to meet the prince? What's your relationship? Why are you staying in his apartments? What are you doing on Savala?"

Justine was suddenly embarrassed. She didn't want to tell this total stranger about her life and choices. And she wasn't sure how to explain their relationship. What could she say? Were they dating? Engaged? Was using a matchmaking service a normal practice here on Savala? It certainly wasn't on Earth.

They frowned self-deprecatingly. "Am I prying? I'm prying, aren't I? I'm sorry." They slouched backward as the purple-skinned woman turned to them and glared. "I guess I'm just looking for good news."

"More like a distraction," the woman sniped.

They turned to their coworker. "Is that so wrong? The Crown Prince's disappearance has thrown everyone in the palace for a loop."

"Wait, what?" Justine said, reeling in shock.

Both the cafeteria workers turned to her in surprise.

"The Crown Prince is missing?" she asked faintly.

"Well, yeah," the orange-skinned one said, rolling their eyes. "It's practically the only thing people are talking about... except for you, of course."

Zayvan stared at the wall, barely seeing his office as he spent a rare moment in silence and solitude. Returning home had triggered a constant flow of activity. He'd been involved in countless strategy meetings over the last few days with the Royal Guard and military, trying to decide how to recover his brother. And every time he left one of those meetings, it seemed the advisors wanted a piece of him. The team of advisors his brother relied on, his coworkers, had started breathing down his neck the moment he returned.

He understood, he really did. You couldn't spend your life working for the government without understanding what an event like this meant. They had to plan for the possibility that Rekhem would never come back, that Zayvan would have to take over. He shuddered at the thought. He'd never wanted his brother's job. Sometimes, he'd wondered if he even wanted to be an advisor, but he enjoyed working with his brother. They'd always got along great, and Zayvan had just sort of fallen into the role.

But without his brother, none of this held any appeal to him. He didn't want to rule. He didn't want the responsibility. And he certainly didn't want to be pressured about his life choices. Rekhem had weathered it well, graciously accepting the arranged marriage their parents had planned for him, but procrastinating the marriage itself again and again and again, also with a surprising amount of grace. His brother had been engaged since he reached the age of majority, and yet Zayvan couldn't honestly imagine his brother as a married man, let alone with kids.

He often teased his brother, asking him when he was going to make Zayvan an uncle. It was a constant refrain from the other advisors, insisting that Rekhem *needed* to marry and *needed* to have heirs. Rekhem always laughed it off, saying there was plenty of time for that. In private, Rekhem often vented about it, insisting it wasn't that big a deal. He had plenty of family. What did it matter if he himself had a direct heir?

Now, all that fussing was being directed at Zayvan. And having Justine here was only making it worse. At least most of the time, Rekhem's fiance was nowhere in sight. She attended social events, but since the Savalan Royal Family wasn't big on hosting them, she was rarely in the picture.

Justine, on the other hand, was right here, in his apartments, and the other advisors wouldn't let him forget it. "When are you marrying her?" they would say. "You should think about children. The monarchy needs an heir." He didn't even know if he *wanted* children, and from what he remembered of Justine's profile, she was of a similar mind. They hadn't discussed it, and there was no way he was going to let the advisors pressure her on something so important. So far, he'd been determined to keep her as far away from them as possible.

Unfortunately, that meant he hadn't so much as talked to her since returning. And he knew he needed to. There was a rift between them now, one he was afraid he couldn't fix. He'd never been this deep with a woman, and he was convinced he was screwing it up.

You are *screwing it up.*

He dropped his face against his desk, his hard head connecting with a loud thump. "I have to talk to her," he muttered to himself.

Because if he didn't, he would *definitely* lose her.

Zayvan left his offices early that night, determined to talk to Justine.

It was evening and the sun had not set yet, its warm light creating patterns of light and shadow in the silent hallways as he approached his apartments. He stopped when he reached the double doors, his hand hovering near the lock panel but not activating it.

He hadn't seen Justine since returning to the palace. Each night, she was already in bed by the time he got back, and she was still asleep when he had to leave. It was exhausting just thinking about it, but now he suspected he'd been letting it happen rather than deal with their problems.

He remembered how her voice had barely risen above a whisper back in his room after the guards had left, how she'd stayed in that bed the entire time he'd packed, and how she'd remained huddled under those blankets even as he'd walked out the door.

What would he find beyond these doors now? A part of him feared she would be gone, that maybe she'd been gone this entire time. Or maybe she would be fed up with him, just waiting for him to return to tell him she was leaving.

Why are you doing this to yourself?

He pressed his hand against the door, taking several deep breaths as he realized he was doing the same thing he often warned his much more volatile brother against.

You don't know what's in her mind, not unless you ask.

He stood up straight again, holding his head high, and started doing what he always did—work through the scenarios. The first scenario was simple. Was she here? That was binary, yes or no. If she was, she could be avoiding him, refusing to talk. She could be angry and just want to yell at him. She could even be violent, though he had a hard time imagining that.

If she wasn't here, she could just be wandering the palace, familiarizing herself with her new home. She could be lost. That thought struck him in a visceral way. Or she could have left him. That was the thought he didn't want to consider, but it plagued him none-the-less. He was the only thing holding her here, and he'd been nowhere in sight. There was nothing stopping her from calling up the agency and requesting a new match, especially with how he'd treated her the last few days.

That possibility hit him hard, and he rushed to unlock the

door, pushing inside and scanning the foyer, desperate for any sign of her. "Justine?" he yelled, hoping for an answer.

She slipped out of her room, and the panic receded. He nearly sagged with relief.

The relief was short-lived, though, as she didn't say anything, just hovering at the doorway, watching him with uncertain eyes.

"I'm sorry I've been so busy. I should have made more time for you. I'm sure this is all a huge shock." He stepped forward, his hands reaching out to her automatically.

She tensed and took a step back.

"Justine?"

This wasn't the woman he'd come to know. This was the woman he'd met *weeks* ago on that launchpad. It was like all the intervening time hadn't happened.

"I'm sorry. This wasn't what I'd planned."

"And what did you plan?" Justine asked angrily.

He scoffed. "Well, we certainly weren't supposed to be interrupted by a bunch of Royal Guards in tactical gear."

She scowled at his flippant tone.

"Sorry. Why don't we sit?" he said, gesturing at the couch in the foyer.

She didn't move at first, so he crossed the room, letting the doors slide closed behind him, and sat down.

Justine waited for a few moments before stepping out of her room, but she didn't sit on the couch with him, instead sitting cautiously on the edge of one of the chairs facing it. She leaned forward, forearms crossing her thighs, not saying a word.

He sighed. "As I said, my intention was to tell you everything while we were at the cabin. I was going to tell you about my title and who my brother was. I just wanted to make sure we'd be a good match first." He shook his head. The plan had been to go slow, test the waters, but she'd been so skittish at first, and he'd ended up going a lot slower. Still, he'd absolutely planned to tell her before coming here. "I never imagined Rekhem would get kidnapped."

Her expression and posture softened, and he held out hope.

"When they barged in like that, I knew something was terribly wrong. I guess I just fell into that same mode I always do in a crisis. I just started focusing on what needed to be done and how to fix it. I knew we needed to leave, we needed to pack. Looking back, I know I should have explained. I should have comforted you. I guess I'm just used to being alone. I apologize for that."

"You're right, you should have. I was shocked and confused, and you just stood up, going through the motions like some kind of robot." She leaned forward, a strange fervor in her eyes. "I *needed* you and you were just *not there*." She scoffed, rolling her eyes to the ceiling. "Stupid me. I just wanted you to *explain* and make it all better. I kept thinking there had to be a good explanation, but I was fooling myself. It didn't matter what the explanation was!"

That brief hope withered away to nothing, and his stomach sank as her rant continued.

"The truth is, you *lied* to me. You purposefully hid stuff about yourself that I damn well needed to know. You should have told me from day one that you were a prince. That was important need-to-know information, and you withheld it from me." She stood, getting even more animated with each word. "You let us have *sex* without me knowing. How could you *do* that? What type of person *are* you? I thought I knew you, but I didn't really know you at all, did I?"

"You *do* know me," Zayvan insisted, finding himself on his feet as well. "I told you who I was. I told you everything that really matters. The rest is just details."

"It's not just details!" she yelled as she invaded his personal space, leaning into her words. "Being a prince is not just details! Being royalty is not just details! Your brother is the most powerful person on this planet, but you made it seem like you just *worked* for him."

"It's not that big a deal."

"It *is* a big deal. It's a *huge* deal. Why can't you see that?"

"Why can't you see that being a prince isn't who I am?"

"It *is* who you are!"

"No, it's not!" he yelled.

A silence settled over the room, and he could almost hear his yelled words echoing between them. Zayvan was shocked stupid at the realization that he'd actually *yelled* at her. *Again.* He never yelled. He was always the calm, rational one.

But as the surprise waned, a more devastating reality settled in. He looked down at Justine, who was now trembling, and when he reached out to comfort her, she recoiled away from him. Her eyes were big and glistening with unshed tears. He lowered his hands, stepping back to give her space.

"I want you to leave," she whispered.

"Justine, I'm sorry. I shouldn't have raised my voice like that."

"I want you to leave. Please leave. Please go," she said, her voice getting firmer and more rushed with each word. He could see the panic growing in her eyes, and he hated that he'd put it there.

"Okay, I'll leave. I'll go. I'm sorry. I'm so sorry," he said, backing away until he reached the doors.

He slipped into the hallway without a sound, feeling like the worst kind of monster, those unshed tears in her eyes tearing him up inside.

CHAPTER ELEVEN

Justine broke into gasps and tears when the door clicked closed behind him. Anguished cries filled the room as she fell to her knees. She punched the couch in front of her, yelling over and over and over again.

This was supposed to be a new start, a better life. This was supposed to be different. Why couldn't she just be happy? Why couldn't things just be better? She wanted to call him back, to yell at him some more until he finally got it through his thick skull why she felt so betrayed.

Eventually, though, the emotions that had powered her through that fight drained away, and she collapsed against the couch, exhausted. The cushions were hard against her flushed face, and she just stayed there, staring blindly into the distance, her mind not really settling on any given thought as her limbs trembled with fatigue.

I didn't even mention feeling betrayed, she thought eventually. The thought was like a lightbulb going off. She sat up slowly and wiped her cheeks, finally seeing her surroundings. The overly fancy room seemed alien to her once again, even though she'd started to get used to it over the last few days. The pale couch with silver and gold filagree seemed untouchable. The busy walls felt tacky. The ceilings too bright and distracting. She hated it all. It was too much, just too much, and it made her head hurt.

She rubbed her arms, then pulled herself to her feet. The room felt too big and empty in the wake of their fight. There was no life here, and she shivered, wishing Zayvan were back. She missed his warmth, his kindness. "I shouldn't have yelled at him like that."

At first, her mind recoiled at those words, her immediate instinct telling her that she was falling back into old patterns, but as she walked to her bedroom, she realized nothing between the two of them was anything like her relationship with Brian. Even during their fight, Zayvan did nothing more than defend himself verbally. Sure, he yelled, but he had to build up a lot of steam before it came to that. And he immediately apologized.

He apologized, but he didn't say anything about me yelling at him the entire time.

Suddenly, she felt like a complete asshole.

Justine sighed. "I fucked up." She remembered all the relationship advice she'd watched or read back on Earth and cringed at her own behavior. She and Zayvan absolutely had problems, but yelling wasn't going to solve it, and she damn well knew it.

Can we even survive this?

She had no idea, but at least if their relationship died, she didn't think it would be because of Brian. Zayvan was a good man, a better man, and the pain she was feeling now was of a very different sort to what she'd felt with Brian. She still felt betrayed, lied to, but not manipulated or controlled. Zayvan would never intentionally try to hurt her.

Justine sighed and lay down on her bed, kicking her shoes off and pulling the blankets over her shoulders without bothering to get changed first. It was early to go to bed, but she didn't care. She was physically and emotionally exhausted, and she just wanted to escape her problems for a few hours.

Renewed tears filled her eyes as she lay there feeling fatalistic.

"Why couldn't he have just told me?" she whispered under her breath as she closed her eyes, praying for oblivion.

Zayvan woke with a groan, almost every part of him protesting his decision to sleep on the small, hard couch in his office last night. He thought mournfully of all the beds in his apartments, most of them empty. But Justine had asked him to leave, and he'd respected her wishes. What else could he do?

He sat up, rubbing his eyes and scuffing his hair as his mind slowly came to awareness. His hair felt a little greasy as it always did in the mornings, and he thought about heading home to take a shower, but he wasn't sure if Justine would welcome him back yet. She hadn't given a time limit on her demand, and now he wondered what he should do. He supposed he could go about business as usual. There were bound to be countless meetings on his agenda, but his heart just wasn't in it.

Even the meetings geared toward finding his brother failed to hold his interest. There were entire teams of professionals currently investigating and searching, but he was just a figurehead, a person "required" at the meetings. He brought almost nothing to the table. He so desperately wanted to find his brother, but he also couldn't help wondering if he was just getting in the way of the *real* efforts.

His heart clenched, and he put a hand to his chest. Fear and worry for his brother hit him hard, surprising him with their intensity.

What if he dies?

What if he's already dead?

What if we never find him?

What if he's never the same?

It could be days or weeks or months before Rekhem was found. Or maybe he would never be found.

Zayvan stood and started pacing his office. The room was small and cramped due to all the furniture and books, but that only drove him to walk faster. His long legs devoured the short distance, and instead of calming the emotionally charged energy running through him, the pacing only made him feel more helpless.

He stopped and stared out the window. It looked out over the palace gardens, with the cityscape rising behind it. Millions of people lived there. So many places to hide. How could they ever find him? "Where are you, brother?" With no hope of an answer, he closed his eyes, turned away, and rested his back against the smooth glass. He let the cold seep into him little by little until he imagined it freezing him to the bone.

"Why can't I fix any of my problems?" He'd been Rekhem's advisor for years, always having a smart answer for whatever quandary his brother might be facing, and yet now, when he needed it most, that wisdom evaded him. No one knew what had happened to his brother. The Royal Guard were scrambling to not only find Rekhem, but cover their own asses. Everyone was pointing fingers, insisting they couldn't have seen it coming or that someone else was clearly to blame. It was a nightmare.

Zayvan didn't know or care who's fault it was. He just wanted his brother back.

And the situation with Justine just made it all worse. Zayvan missed their closeness, but he couldn't seem to get his act together long enough to repair their relationship. He *needed* her right now, needed someone to talk to, someone to draw comfort and strength from, but he had no one.

He felt like he was reaching for the impossible, like no one in his family was ever destined for a love match, for a true partnership. It felt like every time he tried to reach for her, she just slipped farther and farther from his grasp.

He sighed. "I need a drink."

Justine woke up feeling like shit. Her shirt was twisted around her torso, restricting her movement, her pants were digging into her, and her head was pounding from the crying fest last night.

When did I fall asleep?

She groaned, pushed herself upright, and readjusted her shirt. The apartments were eerily quiet.

Which was strange, because every morning here had been quiet, but today was different. It felt oppressive, like the space could somehow *feel* the fact that he'd been missing all night.

Where did he sleep?

She wondered why she even cared. She'd kicked him out, after all. But she *did* care, damn it.

You can't feel betrayed if you don't care.

Justine sighed, then lethargically changed into fresh clothes, not bothering to take a shower, comb her hair, or any of that other stuff she would normally do in the morning. She just didn't give a shit today.

As she stepped into the foyer, she was confronted by the wrongness of the space. Every time she stepped into this room, it felt worse than the time before. Now, it represented their fight, the echoes of those unkind words reverberating through her psyche.

Justine shook her head. "I can't do this today. I just can't."

She stormed out of the apartments. Her shoes clapped against the marble flooring as she took turn after turn, searching for a way out, the sound chasing her down the seemingly infinite hallways. She didn't find one, though she eventually made her way back to the cafeteria. It was busier than last time. Many of the tables had people at them, and their voices filled the space in a way that just made her want to run away even more.

She walked up to the counter, but had to wait in line behind a rainbow of people. Literally. She couldn't remember how many colors there were in the rainbow, but it looked like all of them were represented here. She waited impatiently until it was her turn and internally groaned when it was the grumpy one from yesterday. "Hi, again," she said, trying to force a smile on her face. Her lips seemed to twitch constantly, like her muscles refused to perform the action. "I'm looking for a way outside. I was wondering if you could point me in the right direction. I've been cooped up for days."

A compassionate expression slipped onto the other woman's face, surprising Justine. "Sure, sweetie. Right through there." She leaned over the glass and pointed at a set of French doors. They looked out on a patio with tables and hedges beyond.

Justine smiled at her in earnest now. "Thanks. I really appreciate it."

The woman nodded, then turned to the next person, a frown forming automatically on her face.

Justine stepped back and crossed to the doors. When she pushed through them, it was like a weight had been lifted from her. The patio was empty, and it looked out over some really fancy gardens that stretched out as far as the eye could see. "Wow."

The gardens drew her in, compelling her to start walking, and as soon as she slipped between the hedges, more of that tension drained away. Though she was on an alien world, the gardens reminded her of visiting botanical gardens back on Earth. It was the first time she'd felt even remotely at home since coming to the palace, and it made her realize just how *alien* everything in the palace was. Back at the cabin, the most alien thing had been Zayvan, and it hadn't taken her long to stop noticing.

Everything else was different, but not in any way that screamed "alien world." The food had just tasted like food, with different colors and textures, but it was like trying something new on Earth. It could have just as easily been food from a culture she'd never tried before. It didn't once scream *alien* to her.

And the cabin had been like any cabin back on Earth, the woods like any forest back on Earth, the mountains like any mountain back on Earth. Back there, it had been easy to overlook the fact that she wasn't on Earth anymore. The differences weren't enough to leave her feeling out of place. She could see herself traveling somewhere new on Earth and seeing trees she'd never seen before. She could see herself traveling on Earth and staying in a cabin just like that. It felt so normal.

But the palace wasn't normal. Maybe if she'd been rich or royal herself? Maybe then it wouldn't have been so alien? But she wasn't rich. She wasn't poor, but she wasn't rich either. She'd lived a life where walls were plain, floors were wood or carpet or vinyl, and furniture was geared toward comfort rather than appearances. It was practical, basic, no fuss. You made it your own with little touches that added personality to the space.

And maybe that was the problem. Those apartments didn't feel like they held anyone's personality. They felt like a show-piece, something fancy to show off your wealth. It made her question everything she thought she knew about Zayvan. Again. The room back at the cabin felt like him, like the man she'd met and come to care about. But those apartments spoke of a very different man, one she wasn't sure she could ever love.

"Captain Veshuu?" a guardsman said over the comms.

"Yes?" Pazran responded. He was sitting in his office, staring down at paper after paper, trying to figure out where they'd gone wrong. It was his responsibility, after all, as Captain of the Royal Guard, to ensure that things like this never happened.

How the kak did the Crown Prince get kidnapped?

What was worse, there had been no communications from the kidnappers. There were no clues. It was like the man had disappeared into thin air. The disappearance had been so well orchestrated, they had nothing to go by, which had them bickering amongst themselves and passing blame back and forth instead of doing what really mattered... finding the prince.

"A man claiming to be your brother is here."

"You checked his ID?" They'd cracked down on security since the kidnapping, and now no one could enter without ID verification and a valid reason to be there. Pazran trusted no one.

"Yup. Ochran Veshuu according to the ID."

"I'll meet him at the gate."

"Understood, sir."

The comm cut out as Pazran stood and rapidly made his way from his office to the gate. It was a quick trip made faster by his long legs and rapid stride. People hurried out of his way, eager to avoid being trampled. Within moments, he stepped out of the palace and onto the grounds. Before him, a long flat area of short green ground cover stretched out to the walls in the distance, broken up by the main circular driveway and two straight footpaths on each side.

Pazran took one of the footpaths, his attention trained on the guard station in the wall ahead of him. It was a warm day, and the standard uniform made it feel all the warmer, a trickle of sweat forming along his spine as he jogged to his destination.

When he reached the guard station, he knocked. The door popped open almost instantly, and the guard manning it nodded his head in greeting. "Captain."

"Private. My brother?"

He pointed at a man waiting impatiently on the other side of the guard station, visible through the reinforced glass. It was definitely Ochran, bad attitude and all.

Pazran frowned, but said, "Let him through."

"Yes, sir." The guardsman rushed back to his station and pressed a button, unlocking the pedestrian gate. A small door popped open in the wall, and his brother stepped through moments later.

"Was that really necessary?" Ochran said.

"Yes, it was. Security's been tightened. I'm sorry. No exceptions."

Ochran's expression immediately changed, growing compassionate. "I'm sorry. I know things have been bad the last few days." He chuckled and wrapped an arm around Pazran. "That's why I'm here, actually. I figured you could use a break from all this, even if it was just for a little while."

"I have work to do, Ochran. A lot of work."

"And you can take a break. You work *really* hard, Pazran. I know you. And I also know you always take on *way* too much of the burden yourself. But it wasn't your fault." He shook his head. "I don't know what happened, but I know it's not your fault. Give yourself a little forgiveness and the grace to step away for a bit. It might help, give you some necessary distance from the problem."

Pazran sighed. "Maybe you're right."

"Of course I am. I'm always right." Ochran smirked as he patted Pazran on the shoulder. "Now, why don't we go get something from the cafeteria and catch up? I haven't seen you in ages."

He smiled, grateful to his brother for once. They didn't always see eye to eye, but Ochran was a good person and a good brother. They talked and caught up, never mentioning the kidnapping, while they made their way to the cafeteria, and before he even realized it, they were sitting and picking at their trays while they spent more time talking than eating.

After a while, Ochran stood up and asked, "Where's the bathroom? This hal is running straight through me."

"Through there," Pazran said, pointing him in the right direction.

Ochran nodded and stepped away from the table. "Thanks. I'll be right back."

Pazran returned to his food. It was a little cold now, but the spicy sauce still managed to warm his tongue and insides in a pleasing way. He dipped some flatbread into the sauce and sopped it up, humming to himself as the zing hit his tongue once again.

When his tray was finally empty, streaks of red smeared all over the surface from wiping up the last of the salzé, he realized his brother was taking an awful long time in the bathroom. He turned around in his seat, scanning the cafeteria for Ochran, but didn't spot him.

I hope he's feeling okay, he thought as he stood. He grabbed his tray and deposited it to be cleaned, then made his way to the bathroom and pushed open the door. "Ochran?" he said, but there was no response. He stepped inside, letting the door swing shut behind him. "Ochran, are you okay?"

The bathroom consisted of sinks on the right and fully enclosed stalls on the left. He touched each of the stalls as he passed, the doors easily swinging inward, clearly unoccupied. One by one, his fingers pressed against open doors, confirming each stall was empty, until he reached the last one. He stood there, his hand holding the door open, his mind at first unable or unwilling to believe what he was seeing.

Then his training kicked in, and he pulled out his comm, pressing the button that contacted the entire guard. "Attention, guard. This is Captain Veshuu. We have an unchaperoned male guest on the grounds. Skin tone green, brown hair, green eyes..."

Once finished with the announcement, he dropped the comm to his side and stared at the empty bathroom, feeling baffled.

Brother, what are you doing?

The gardens were doing Justine a world of good. Getting away for a while had given her some time to think about her situation. It had given her some much needed perspective and a little closure. Hopefully, the next time she saw Zayvan, she could talk to him without screaming her head off at him. And she had a vague idea about writing him a letter, hoping that a written format would allow her the time to thoughtfully and more rationally tell him how she felt. It might prevent tempers from getting the better of them and ensure she got her message across, unlike last time. Of course, there was no telling if she and Zayvan would be a good fit in the end, but that didn't mean they shouldn't try, and now she felt like she had a path forward.

Making her way back through the gardens, she started planning out that letter. Of course, she needed to tell him about her feelings of betrayal, but what else? She'd talked about getting a job while they were at the cabin, but she hadn't thought about it since arriving at the palace. She should start on that once she got back to the apartments. Having a job would make her feel more secure. It would also give her something to do, which would give her less time to overthink things.

Plus, she'd been without a job since breaking her leg. It would be yet another way to break away from the control Brian had asserted over her life in those last months.

She wrung her hands as she continued walking. "What else can I do?" She thought about all the things that seemed to be wrong in her life right now. She felt adrift, out of place. Her relationship with Zayvan was on the rocks.

"So, how do I fix that?" she said to herself, stopping and staring at a particularly beautiful flower. It had a huge white and purple blossom that was larger than her hand, and its petals reached out to the sky like it was trying to trap something. She smiled down at it, brushing her fingers along the silky soft surface. "How do I fix it?" she playfully asked the flower. She bit her lip, trying to think. "Well, everything I've ever read said communication is key. We need to talk and not with hurt feelings." She shook her head gently. "Considering how the last conversation went, we definitely need structure. We *might* need a third party."

Justine straightened and started walking again. "Maybe I need to jot down a list of topics to cover in the letter." She pulled out her phone and pulled up an empty document, titling it "Things to Discuss with Zayvan."

"One, feelings of betrayal, obviously. Two, a job. Zayvan

said he was going to show me how to look for work here, but he still hasn't done that. Three, the decor. I really fucking hate the decor in our apartments." She sighed, remembering how seeing it had made her question if she knew Zayvan at all. "I need to ask him how he feels about it. Maybe he didn't decorate it. Maybe he's not even allowed to. It's not like he owns the place. Maybe there's some Savalan policy that all rooms in the palace need to be decorated a certain way." She shrugged. "I wouldn't know, and I'm never going to know if I don't ask. And maybe it'll lead to the more important conversation, one about who he truly is as a person. I need to know that. I need to know if he's the man I thought he was."

Justine sighed, suddenly feeling miserable. "I *really* want him to be who I thought he was," she said, her voice thick with emotion. "Please let him be that."

"Let him be what?" a masculine voice said, coming from right behind her.

Justine startled, shrieking and leaping to the side. Before her stood a burly man with pastel green skin, short brown hair, and dark eyes that seemed inscrutable. She tensed immediately, her fight-or-flight response kicking in automatically.

Stop that.

She forced herself to relax. He was a bit bulkier in build than the other Savalans she'd met so far, but not by a ton. By this planet's standards, he was pretty average. If she was going to live here, she needed to recalibrate her brain, because if she freaked out over every muscular man on Savala, she would have a heart attack before she was thirty.

"I'm sorry." She inwardly cringed, imagining Zayvan scolding her for apologizing yet again. "I thought I was alone, and I'm still not used to some of the differences between humans and Savalans."

"That's okay." He tilted his head. "What species are you? You're not from this solar system."

"I'm guessing you don't work here, huh?" she said with a crooked smile.

"Nope. Came to visit my brother for lunch. He works too hard."

"Well, then it sounds like you're a good brother for encouraging him to take a break."

He nodded in agreement.

But then something occurred to her. Justine looked around, but they were completely isolated and alone, the hedges creating both a visual and sound barrier. She turned back to him. "Where's your brother?"

She didn't even have time to breathe as he pounced, latching onto her mouth at the same time he tried to restrain her. She fought back, her limbs swinging, kicking, punching, grasping as she tried to break free. He held onto her mouth with one hand while another looped across her middle, making it hard to take in a deep breath.

Her screams were muffled, but felt deafening in her ears. Every time her fighting limbs made contact, pain flared more and more, punishing her for fighting back.

"Stop struggling," he whisper yelled.

"Never," she mumbled into his hand, wondering if she could bite it. She tried, but her teeth wouldn't gain purchase.

Then she swung at him with her bad leg, connecting with far too much force. The pain was intense, her vision whited out. She lost track of time for a moment, then a weird lassitude flowed through her and the battle was lost. All her limbs went limp. She tried, but couldn't move, and her mind was too sluggish to care.

Wah? her brain managed to get out before she lost consciousness.

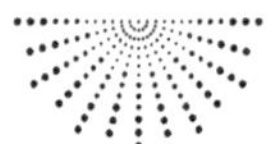

CHAPTER TWELVE

Justine woke up with another pounding headache and wondered if she'd cried herself to sleep again. She groaned, her hands going to her head as she rolled over, but something wasn't right. She couldn't place it at first, her head too fuzzy to process more than pain and misery.

But then it clicked.

I'm not in my bed.

She jerked upright, then immediately regretted it, her headache amplifying. She groaned again as her brain throbbed in protest, sharp knives slicing through her skull until, eyes closed, it finally settled into a dull pounding pain.

Even with eyes closed, though, she could now recognize what was wrong.

I don't know where I am.

The room was cooler, the mattress harder, and the blankets rougher and thinner. The bed creaked with each movement she made, and she had the vague sense that, in spite of her being much smaller than the average Savalan, it wasn't quite stable under her weight.

Finally, she carefully opened her eyes. The first thing she saw was the man from the garden. "You drugged me," she slurred, her mouth feeling weirdly swollen and fuzzy as the words tumbled out.

He shrugged nonchalantly. "You struggled. I didn't expect that much of a fight."

And yet he'd brought drugs to subdue her. "Why?" she continued, keeping her voice low, hoping it wouldn't make the headache worse.

He shrugged again. "Plan B."

"Plan B?" she shrieked, then winced as her head flared in pain. She clutched her temples and closed her eyes until the pain receded, then looked up and glared at him. "What the hell is Plan B?"

Instead of answering, he stood, and her heart lurched in her chest. She recoiled backward, slamming into a cold, rough wall. It dug into her spine through her shirt and light jacket, but she didn't care. A part of her felt smaller and smaller with each step he took, burrowing deep until it could find a safe place, somewhere no one could reach.

He leaned down, his entire form looming over her. "Be a good girl, and you might get out of this alive, okay?"

She nodded, and he straightened, turning his back on her and crossing to the other side of the room. He sat back down, completely ignoring her and pulling out something to read.

Justine sat there, paralyzed, as he just relaxed into his seat like they were just chilling. There was something about the whole situation that was simultaneously surreal and also familiar. She felt floaty, and her mind pulled up countless memories of her time with Brian, times when she sat there in terror, pretending everything was fine, while her tormentor went about business as usual.

It was the same. It was exactly the same. Her mind was

screaming warnings at her even as she grew lightheaded and feared she might snap, never to recover.

I'm back where I started.

Her mind even began playing tricks on her, trying to convince her that this was just a dream, that she'd never left Earth, that this was really Brian in front of her, that she couldn't make him angry. It made no sense and perfect sense, all at the same time.

Do what he says.

She sat upright, even though her every muscle trembled and the coarse stone pressed even harder into her back.

Smile.

Pretend everything's fine.

If you convince him, he won't get angry.

If you're convincing, you'll be safe.

Zayvan was pacing outside his apartments, trying to decide how to approach Justine. What could he say that would make things better? That question had consumed him all day, leaving room for nothing else.

So when his last meeting was canceled, he took it as a sign. He left his office, hoping he and Justine could somehow manage a calmer conversation, one that didn't end in yelling.

You're never gonna find the perfect words, Zayvan.

He stopped his pacing, scanned his hand, and entered the foyer. The lights came on automatically as he stepped into the empty space. *Maybe she's in her room?* "Justine?" he called as he looked over at her bedroom. But even from the doorway, he could see that the room was dark as well.

"Justine?" he called again, making his way slowly through

the various rooms, checking each space thoroughly. But each room was dark.

When he'd made a full circuit, he stopped in the foyer, not knowing where to look next. Where could she be?

But then he got an idea. He rushed across the room and picked up the phone.

"Palace switchboard."

"Has Justine called asking for any assistance today?"

"Let me see…" The clacking of keys carried over the phone. "No, there haven't been any calls from your line today. One moment." The noises continued. "I don't have any requests under that name in the database today, either."

He sighed and pressed the handset harder against his ear before relaxing and changing gears. "Can you connect me with the Captain of the Guard?"

"One moment, please."

He nodded, even though she couldn't see him.

"Captain Veshuu."

"This is Prince Zayvan. I'm currently looking for my…" he paused, unsure what to call her. Matchmaking wasn't terribly uncommon on Savala, but it was usually between Savalans or other people from this solar system. There were certain expectations, certain milestones you tended to hit. It seemed like he and Justine had regressed rather than moving forward, and he was hesitant to give a name to their relationship without talking to her first.

Which you can't do because you can't find her.

"… guest, Justine. She is not in our apartments."

Captain Veshuu didn't immediately speak, his silence causing dread to churn in Zayvan's stomach. "Do you know when she was last seen?"

"No. We haven't talked since last night."

"Does she have a phone on her?"

"Hold on. Let me check." He rested the handset on the side table and rushed over to Justine's room. A charging pad sat on the dresser, currently unoccupied, and while there were some clothes discarded in a pile in the corner, there was nothing else sitting out. He quickly checked the pile for any hard objects, then rushed back to the phone. "I don't see it, so I'm assuming it's with her."

"Good. Can you give me the code?"

He blurted out her contact details, his feet restless beneath him.

"Okay, please wait."

Zayvan was put on hold, and he felt like cursing. He was starting to get worried. Not only was the Savta Palace a big place, but there had recently been a kidnapping from the grounds. And while he'd been assured that they'd increased security since then, it didn't stop him from worrying.

If it can happen once, it can happen again.

Time dragged on as he continued to wait on hold, praying nothing was wrong, praying they would track down her phone and tell him she was just wandering the palace or something.

"How long can this take?" he muttered to himself as he started to pace in front of the side table, the phone's impossibly short cord restricting his movements. Logically, he knew it probably hadn't been that long, but it felt like an eternity, each moment stretching longer and longer as his runaway thoughts distorted reality.

His mind was warring against itself, both refusing to believe anything bad could happen and tormenting him with everything bad that possibly *could* happen.

"It'll be fine. She'll be fine," he said to himself again and again, trying to keep calm. "You're probably just freaking out because Rekhem is missing. You're overreacting. She's fine."

"Your Highness?" Veshuu said, finally taking him off hold.

"Yes?" His voice was unnaturally high and tight.

"We found her phone."

He couldn't speak. He couldn't move.

We found her phone.

"Where is she?"

"We don't know."

CHAPTER THIRTEEN

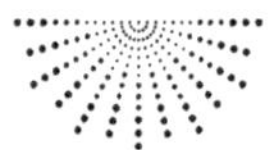

Justine wasn't sure when things had changed. She wasn't sure how much time had gone by or what she'd been thinking or doing. She only knew when her thoughts were finally clear.

It wasn't even a gradual thing. She didn't remember a "surfacing from the depths of her thoughts." She didn't notice herself slowly coming to terms with anything or getting a grip on her emotions. It was like one moment there was a black hole and the next she was clear. She had no other way to describe it.

She was grateful, though. It gave her the chance to really process what was going on. She started by taking in her environment for the first time. In the distance, she could hear water dripping, which made her realize just how cold and damp this room was. She shivered and wrapped her arms around herself to brace against the inhospitable environment. The light was dim, but she realized she must have been here for a while, because her eyes had already adjusted to the dark.

The walls were made of stone, roughly cut and unlike

anything she'd seen since coming to Savala. Even the cabin had been of better quality construction than this.

The air held a musty scent, reminding her of old buildings and mold, and the humidity was nearly suffocating. The entire experience made her think of old dungeons, and she shivered all over again.

There has to be a way out, she thought, looking for a door or an opening.

She found it behind her captor. It looked like thick, old wood, dark with wear and swollen with damp. Her captor sat with his head bent, his eyes struggling to stay open.

How do I get out of here?

She didn't want to move, concerned he might hear and jerk to wakefulness. She remembered the bed creaking beneath her when she'd first woken up. It would serve as the perfect alarm clock for the bastard.

So how do I get out of here?

That was the question. There was no point asking herself *if* she was getting out. That was a path toward madness, and she'd already lost enough time to that specific condition. She had no intention of making it worse.

Even so, the fear and anxiety were still there, an unwelcome parting gift from her past. She couldn't escape them. Maybe they would always be there, but for the first time, the specter of Brian didn't have the same power over her. She'd broken down and fallen apart, but she felt like she could pull herself together again in spite of her past. Her mind conjured up the fabled phoenix, rising from its own ashes. It was an inspirational image, and she liked it, deciding she would run with it.

"I'm a phoenix," she mouthed silently. *I even have the hair for it.* A smile crossed her face, which only grew bigger as she imagined herself as the phoenix, rising from the ashes of her decimated life, soaring big and bright and beautiful, a flaming orange, red, and gold beacon that streaked through the sky, awe-inspiring and beautiful.

As she came back to reality, she had to force away the smile. She wanted to keep smiling, but this wasn't a time for smiles. This was a time for soaring, for rising from the ashes. She couldn't *shine*, though, until she could see the skies. That meant finding freedom.

And how are you going to do that?

That was the question, wasn't it? How was she going to get out of here? There was a big, burly man between her and the only door. That way held her only option for escape. If she wanted out, she needed to get past him.

Brute force is out.

She wasn't an idiot. She knew she would never win a contest of strength against this guy. He'd already proven himself once, and he hadn't even taken her by surprise. A little martial arts or self-defense training would have gone a long way in this situation, but those weren't skills she had and there was no point dwelling on it. Maybe she could address that after she escaped, but until then, she just needed to focus on what skills she *did* have.

Could sneaking out work? She would need to get off the bed without making a sound, which would definitely be hard, then sneak past him and open the door without his knowledge. Could she do it? She stared at the intervening distance, at the door she could barely see in the poorly lit room, and shook her head. She would need a closer look at that door to know for sure. That would mean taking a big risk with no guaranteed chance of success.

Not a good idea.

What else?

The only other option she could think of was manipulating him, but what did she know about manipulating people?

A lot. Brian did it to you for years.

Justine froze, her eyes wide with realization. Her mind raced over all the times Brian had manipulated her, messing with her head and destroying her self-esteem. Could she use her own traumas to her advantage? Could she manipulate this man into releasing her?

Even the idea of it made her sick to her stomach, that phoenix image dulling in her mind's eye. But survivors couldn't always be choosy about how they had to survive, and as she looked over at the man who'd taken her, she resigned herself to a course of action that was looking more and more inevitable.

She took a moment to shore up her courage, then said, "What's your name?" as she shifted on the bed.

His head jerked up. "Wah?" He looked around, seeming confused.

"I said, 'What's your name?'"

He scowled, looking more defensive than tough, as his gaze finally settled on her. "That's none of your business."

"Isn't it?"

"It's not."

"Hm." She looked away, trying to pretend he was below her notice. "Pity."

Out of the corner of her eye, she noticed him tense. "What do you mean 'pity'?"

Justine looked back at him, trying to pull off the perfect expression and afraid she would fail epically. Did he see it? Did he see the lack of fear she was trying to show him? The slight disdain? "Yes, pity. I thought maybe you were someone of significance. I guess you're just a hired thug."

He bristled, standing up from his seat. "I'm not a hired

thug. I'll have you know I was involved in the planning of this coup from the beginning."

She arched an eyebrow, hoping it showed disbelief, but suddenly, she started to worry that it might come off differently to an alien.

"I did," he said, pointing a finger at his chest. "I was the one that said we needed a plan B in the first place." He laughed, the sound disturbingly sinister, making her wish she'd kept her mouth shut. "I knew that bastard wouldn't give in so easily. Self-righteous prick. Just the fact that he'd avoided his arranged marriage for so long should have said as much, but the others couldn't see it. No, they kept pushing." He pointed at Justine again and again in emphasis. "Pushing and pushing and expecting a different result. What did they think was going to happen? Did they think he was just going to give in when they had no real leverage?" He threw his hands out to the side, a smirk spreading on his face. "Of course not!" He pointed again. "That's why you're here. You're leverage."

"Leverage? What do you want from him?"

"Power," he leaned in, the word popping on his lips.

"How?"

His smirk grew. "We make him do what we want. If he doesn't, we kill you. If we decide he'll never relent, we kill you both and go after the brother. There are a lot of members of the Royal Family out there, and we have all the time in the world."

Justine shivered at the ruthlessness of the man before her. But unfortunately, nothing he said surprised her. You couldn't live on Earth your entire life and not accept that people could be monsters. You just had to deal with the monsters when they showed up.

And this particular monster had a problem, one he didn't even realize he had. And the solution would serve her purposes nicely. She shook her head at her captor. "It sounds to me like you're having a hard time motivating him, and I'm not surprised. Did bringing me here change anything at all?"

He silently fumed.

"Oh, come on now. Why would he do *anything* you asked? Because of some vague threat?" She rolled her eyes. "You haven't even proven to him you'll follow through. Why would he believe you? You've already shown him you have poor moral character."

"Poor moral character?" he said in outrage. "You think *I*," he pointed at himself, "have poor moral character? Me, who's done everything I can for the betterment of my people? I've watched Savala deteriorate under the oppressive structures of the monarchy. They're not willing to do what's necessary to bring our people back to their former glory." He waved angrily at the wall. "That batak won't even marry like he's supposed to. Our entire government is dependent on the two vote system, which *requires* two monarchs, yet he won't do it. He refuses again and again and again." Each time he said "again," he flung his hand at the wall, little bits of spittle leaving his mouth. He turned back to her, calming slightly. "That's why we had to do this." He shook his head. "He left us no choice."

"We?"

He nodded. "The Silent Majority."

Justine tried to control her expression as he said that. There was something inherently delusional about believing that most people thought like you did, but just weren't willing to admit it. She fought hard to make her expression curious rather than expressing some of the other emotions running through her mind. "Is that... a movement? A group?"

He nodded again, his chest puffing up with pride. "We're working to make a better Savala."

"That's an admirable goal. Beyond this," she waved at the cell, "do you have plans on how to do that?"

"Oh yes," he said with a small, creepy smile. "We're going to end the monarchy."

Justine thought for a moment, wondering how kidnapping the Crown Prince would accomplish that. As he'd already said, there were a lot of members of the Royal Family. Killing him would just change who became king. So what was their plan? How were they going to do it? "Are you... going to force him to dissolve the monarchy?"

His smile grew, becoming downright maniacal. "That's the plan. We marry him to one of our own, then make him a puppet for our machinations. Once we have full control, we'll increase power to congress until the monarchy is nothing but a figurehead."

Like the United Kingdom. "But how will you get him to willingly give up control like that? From the sound of it, your compatriots aren't having a lot of luck in that department?"

He frowned and grumbled something unintelligible under his breath. "As I said, he has a lot of family, a lot of potential targets for leverage. Most of them don't live in the palace. They have normal lives. That means no guards and no privileges. They're just ordinary folk. Getting to them would be easy."

Justine shivered at his words and tone. It was so cold-blooded. "And how do you ensure that whoever you plant on the throne doesn't grow attached to that power? What if they turn against you?"

"Then we kill her. There are no traitors in the Silent Majority."

"As it should be," she whispered while trying to control her emotions. Their movement was so brutally ruthless and seemed to care nothing for the people it claimed to be fighting for.

After that, several long moments passed in silence while Justine tried to decide how to proceed. This line of conversation wasn't really getting her anywhere. At best, it was humanizing her in her captor's eyes, making her sympathetic and likable. Maybe she could get him to see her as a potential ally if she played her cards right, but how long was that going to take?

Then something occurred to her. "I understand using me to try to force the Crown Prince's hand. I can certainly play my part, but it just occurred to me that you never answered the question of how that would work. I mean, if he doesn't know I'm here, if he doesn't see what happens to me, why would he believe you? Wouldn't visual proof and proximity serve as a better motivator?" The plan started forming even as she said the words. Somewhere nearby, there was a potential ally in this bastard's hands.

"You're right, of course. I believe the plan currently is to throw your lifeless corpse in with him if he continues to be uncooperative."

Justine blanched, but inwardly congratulated herself when she quickly recovered. "Well, that won't do. And I don't just mean because I, personally, don't want to die. I mean, when you have one trump card under your control, it's best not to overplay your hand." She leaned forward conspiratorially. "Wouldn't you rather he cooperate *before* it gets to that? After all, while you might be able to get more hostages, it still requires additional work and potential exposure. Better to maximize those assets you *have*."

"What are you suggesting?"

She looked away, pretending she had to think about it. "Visibility is key. If you want to make him cooperate, the best thing you can do is make your threats very visible and very real. I would suggest bringing me to him. Make the threats right in front of his face. Show real consequences for disobedience." She leaned back, trying to pull off a confident, almost smug appearance. "Now, don't get me wrong, especially early on, you shouldn't overdo it. Often, the threat of violence is far more effective than actually committing it."

"Oh?"

"It's a well-established truth back home. There's a long history of practicing torture on my planet, but generally speaking, torture doesn't work. When it does, it's usually because the victim is inexperienced and easily manipulated, and even then, any cooperation can't be trusted. If you're looking for information, for example, it's rarely ever accurate. The most effective practices always involve developing a rapport with the captive, often by controlling their environment and experiences, through threats of violence, and, under very rare circumstances, by committing *actual* acts of violence. You have to show you're willing to follow through if they go against you, but you also have to reward obedience. Once a certain standard is established, threats of violence are far more effective than the violence itself. "

"Hm." He rubbed his chin. "You may have a point." He stared at her thoughtfully for several moments before speaking again. "Thank you. I'll be back. I'm going to discuss this with the others."

Justine watched as he left, then rushed the door as soon as it clicked closed. She checked the handle, but it didn't budge. The hinges weren't on this side either, and when she slammed bodily into the door, she did nothing but send pain shooting up her arm and shoulder.

"Damn it," she said through gritted teeth before stepping back. "Genius, Justine. What the hell did that accomplish?"

She turned away from the door with a sigh and started crossing back to the bed, but then stopped midway. "Wait a minute." She looked back at the door. "He's going to talk to the others? Does that mean the Crown Prince is *here*?"

I'm gonna die down here.

Rekhem was panting from exhaustion after his most recent attempt to break his bonds, which had done nothing more than rub his wrists raw and nearly throw his shoulder out of socket. He wished he could say he'd made some progress, but the rope felt just as tight as before.

In another corner of the large, dimly lit room, several of his captors were huddled together, talking. He strained to hear, but the words came back to him muddled, and he bowed his head in defeat.

I'm never getting out of here.

He'd come to accept that fact, but he so desperately wished it weren't true. And not just because he didn't want to die. He knew what would happen when he died. Succession would go to Zayvan, and more than anything, he didn't want that for his brother. Zayvan was a strong man, a good man, but he was not built for leadership. Rekhem feared it would slowly wear him down, and he would do anything to protect him from that fate.

Unfortunately, he was out of options. He'd been down here a long time, and he'd given up hope that he would be rescued. If the Royal Guard hadn't found him yet...

Mid musing, one of his captors marched in from the hallway, his steps loud and echoing off the walls. Rekhem looked up and blanched.

It's her.

The man was pushing someone ahead of him. She was tiny, much smaller than a Savalan adult, with bright red hair that mostly covered her face and a skin tone you wouldn't find anywhere in this solar system.

That's gotta be Justine, Zayvan's match.

His entire body went cold as the man behind Justine

shoved her forward. She lost her balance but stayed on her feet, catching herself after a couple stumbling steps.

The man sauntered forward, grabbing the back of Justine's neck and forcing her to her knees in front of Rekhem, directly in his line of sight. Their captor leaned forward, looming over Justine's tiny form, an evil grin stretching his lips. "Now, Your Highness, I'd like to continue our conversation from earlier."

Justine whimpered, and Rekhem realized the man was squeezing with that hand on her neck, digging his fingers into her flesh. He bit his lip, forcing himself not to react.

"As I was trying to point out, actions have consequences. Though, it seems that maybe I didn't make myself clear enough, so I thought I would bring some visual aides to help you understand what I mean."

No.

No, they couldn't. They wouldn't. His mind went back to the phone call with his brother. Zayvan had said he thought someone had hurt her. She was skittish, constantly saying sorry. He looked down at her now, being put in yet another bad situation because of *him*. Her life was being threatened because of *him*.

Zayvan will never forgive me if something happens to her.

Their captor reached down, grabbed Justine's hand, and placed it on the floor. She squirmed and resisted, but then he ground his hand down into her neck and shoulders, nearly bending her in half. She stopped fighting. Then he put his foot on her hand, and Rekhem knew the moment he pressed down.

She tried to get away, pulling desperately, then gasping and crying out when it got to be too much.

Their captor stared Rekhem down with a malicious intensity that spoke of his resolve. "There are a lot of small bones in that hand. How much pressure do you think it would take to break all of them? For that matter, how much effort do you think it would take to break every bone in her body? Like I said last time, Your Highness, I've got all the time in the world. Do you?" He pressed down harder, and Justine's movements grew more frantic. Her cries became higher in pitch, and she started trying to dislodge him. She hit his shoe again and again while shoving into his leg with her whole body, but he didn't budge.

An image of the future stretched out before him, becoming crystal clear. They were going to bring her here every day, maybe several times a day, and hurt her. Again and again, they would hurt her.

Every time he refused them, Justine would pay the price.

Rekhem thought of his brother, Zayvan, who'd been lonely for so long. He thought back to when he'd been matched, how conflicted he'd been, nervous in a way Rekhem had never seen before. He thought about how happy and eager Zayvan had been as he'd waited for her to arrive.

I can't take that away from him. I just can't.

I'm so sorry, Zayvan.

It's all my fault.

Tears started to leak from his eyes. "Stop." He sniffed. "Don't. Please stop."

Their captor's foot lifted. He caught a glimpse of her hand, red and swollen from the abuse, and his heart twisted in his chest. "You'll do it?" He started to press his foot down again, the threat clear.

Rekhem nodded. "Just don't hurt her," he whispered as the first tear reached his chin. "You can't hurt her."

Zayvan paced back and forth as people filtered into the small meeting room in the Royal Guard Headquarters. He felt every muscle tensing, his jaw almost painful as he gritted his teeth.

There was an odd energy to the room, each person looking at him like he was a wounded grevian, unpredictable and likely to lash out at a moment's notice.

He couldn't say it was an inaccurate analogy. He felt out of control, like a man on the verge of losing his mind. It took everything he had to keep himself from running from the room and just blindly barreling through the halls of the palace, screaming Justine's name at the top of his lungs. His logical mind had just enough control to keep him in the room, but it was a near thing.

Zayvan scoffed and turned away, staring out the window that made up one wall of the room. His mind couldn't quite make sense of what he was seeing, the architecture and greenery blending together as he stood there. *Where are they?* Somewhere out there, everyone he cared about was in danger. How could this be happening? *Why* was it happening? What had he ever done to deserve such torture?

Around him, the sound of many people moving about and chatting drifted to his ears. He heard chairs scrape against the floor as people sat down, readying for the meeting. All of it rubbed his nerves raw because it was just so *normal.* His world was falling apart. Nothing was normal. How could they just be chatting? How could they just be sedately walking through the room, pulling out chairs and sitting without a fuss? It wasn't *natural.* It felt so *wrong.* Where was the anger? Where was the yelling, the fear? Why wasn't anyone in a rush? Why wasn't anyone demanding action?

The whole situation was intolerable. More than anything else, he just wanted to *do* something. He needed to be out there, looking for them. Just standing here doing nothing was driving him mad.

There's nothing you can do, he reminded himself.

But that fact itself was also intolerable. He knew it was

true, knew he needed patience and a steady resolve, but it made his mind and nerves feel stretched thin. And if something didn't change soon, he would snap.

Someone touched his shoulder, and some fight-or-flight reflex kicked in. He nearly swung out with a fist, but stopped himself, his arm already raised, when he realized it was only Captain Veshuu. His behavior embarrassed him when Veshuu only stared back at him with an expressionless visage, like he either had complete faith that Zayvan would never hurt him or he was so dedicated to the monarchy that he would willingly allow himself to get hit for no reason at all.

Zayvan dropped his hand and pulled his arms behind his back, not fully trusting himself anymore.

"We're ready to start the meeting," Veshuu said, giving him a respectful nod.

"Proceed," Zayvan said with an answering nod.

Veshuu turned around and addressed the group, most of whom had now grown silent and were seated around the table. "Thank you for coming. Most of you already know why we're here. Justine Foley, matched to our Prince Zayvan, was kidnapped today. We are fortunate that security was tightened after the recent abduction of the Crown Prince, so surveillance was able to collect enough information to trace the exact path the culprit took with her."

Zayvan zoned out a little as Veshuu started planning out the rescue. He droned on for some time, calling out names, then assigning them to specific teams. He was reassured by the fact that they knew where Justine was. They would find her. They would bring her back. It was going to be okay. *She* was going to be okay.

But when Veshuu finally moved to dismiss the group, Zayvan realized he'd never been mentioned.

I can't stay behind.

Just the idea was unthinkable. It would drive him mad sitting around the palace, waiting for word on whether Justine was alive or dead, harmed or untouched.

Unable to help himself, he surged to his feet. "I'm coming too."

Veshuu looked over his shoulder at him, giving him an expression that verged on a glare. "I don't think that's a good idea, Your Highness."

Zayvan stepped up. "I think it is. She doesn't know any of you. She'll have no reason to trust you."

She has no reason to trust you either, remember?

"You're too emotionally invested," Veshuu said, his stance growing stiffer.

"I don't care."

Veshuu frowned and opened his mouth, looking like he was about to object, but his mouth snapped shut instead. He shook his head, grumbled something unintelligible, then looked up again to speak. "You're with me. You stay with me at all times. You stay out of harm's way at all times. You do exactly what I say. Do you understand?"

He nodded and followed the Captain of the Guard as he left the room. They were the last to exit. Zayvan chaffed as they entered the staging room. Veshuu calmly pulled out weapons and body armor. Many of the others were already gone, heading off to their designated assignments.

Veshuu handed him equipment, then started donning his own. Zayvan put down the weapon and holster and lifted the body armor. It was little more than a thick vest, and he quickly found the fasteners and pulled it over his head. It was surprisingly easy to move in, and he picked up the holster next.

This, at least, he knew a little something about. He, like the rest of the Royal Family, was required to train in weapons handling. It was a safety concern, especially for those who lived in the palace, as weapons were always close at hand, and the single best way to have a tragic accident was lack of training.

He slid the gun into the holster and clipped it in place, then looked up at the Captain, who was currently checking his wrist comm, and waited.

Seemingly done with his comm, Veshuu lowered his wrist, looked up, and nodded. "Let's go."

Zayvan caressed the butt of his gun as he followed him out. They passed through several hallways until they stepped out into the gardens.

"This way," Veshuu said, waving his hand discretely.

They crept through the hedges, and for the first time in his life, the gardens took on an ominous tone. He realized how easy it would be for someone to hide here, to pop out of nowhere. The vegetation dampened sound, making their footsteps almost completely silent. His back twinged slightly at the stooped posture, but he didn't protest.

I'm getting her back.

That thought consumed his mind as they made turn after turn, finally coming upon a disguised maintenance grate. It was large, about the size of the average Savalan male, making it easy to enter for pretty much everyone. Beyond, darkness consumed the space almost immediately. He could only see a short distance, maybe the length of an arm. The light seeping through the grate exposed a harsh stone facade, utilitarian and stark. He'd never seen anything like it on the palace grounds, where almost every surface was ornately decorated or carved. Even servant and maintenance areas were more ornate than this.

Veshuu pulled out an actual key and pushed back the leaves and vines on the right-hand side, which exposed an old-fashioned lock that had seen better days. The metal was rusted, and the lock creaked and groaned as it released. He pulled the lock off and set it aside, then pulled out his gun.

Zayvan followed Veshuu's example and pulled out his own gun. There was something reassuring about holding that firm, cold metal in his hands.

Veshuu pushed the grate open. Zayvan tensed, expecting the grate to protest, just as the lock had, but it was perfectly quiet. They slipped into the gloom, and there was an immediate change, like a curtain falling over them, as a chill settled in. It wasn't oppressively cold, but it made him worry about Justine all the more.

She can't handle the cold.

He sped up, an urgency hitting him, even though he knew a few more moments would make little difference. He couldn't help himself, eventually stepping on Veshuu's foot and bumping into him full-bodied.

Veshuu turned and glared at him.

Zayvan stepped back and muttered, "Sorry," under his breath. Seemingly appeased, Veshuu turned back around and continued on into the darkness. Zayvan could barely see a thing. *What the hell am I doing here?* He'd never really done anything like this in his life, and he couldn't help wondering if Veshuu could see more than he could, or if he was more accustomed to working in such conditions.

At least the dim light from the entrance continued to give just enough illumination to see where they were going, aided by the fact that the passage neither curved nor turned.

Every step was measured as they continued forward, with Zayvan cringing every time he set his foot down and it made more noise than he expected. Conversely, Veshuu seemed to slip through the hall like a wraith. If the man hadn't been visible right there in front of him, he might have questioned if he was even there at all.

Then he heard something that echoed down the hall around him, and he stiffened. *What was that?* Veshuu continued onward, completely ignoring the sound, with his gun raised at shoulder level, and Zayvan followed suit, trying to take comfort from his example.

After a while, it felt like his mind started playing tricks on him. Sounds erupted that seemed to come from everywhere and nowhere. Shuffling footsteps. Indistinct voices. Scraping sounds.

The farther they traveled, the more the cold air rested damp and clammy on his skin, which was so tacky his fingers stuck to the grip and trigger guard. The corridor seemed to go on forever, and he was starting to wonder if they would ever get there. Was she even here? Veshuu had mentioned surveillance, but what if the kidnapper had only passed through this area with her, coming out the other side unnoticed?

He swallowed heavily, then Veshuu held up a hand, indicating they should stop. Zayvan tensed, anticipation swirling in his gut.

Veshuu motioned to the right, and Zayvan shifted his focus, now just barely noticing a door there. He stepped in front of Zayvan and, gun hand still raised, pulled it open. Zayvan could see nothing but the flickering light that blinked on automatically when the door opened. A gentle hum of machinery slipped from the room.

"Anything?" he whispered.

"No."

Zayvan nodded as Veshuu stepped back out of the room, closing it silently behind him. He waved them forward and a few steps later, they finally reached a junction. Zayvan hovered just behind Veshuu, peeking around the corner, expecting an even gloomier corridor. Except here, track lighting lined the walls in either direction. It was still dim, and none of the light bled into the hallway they were in, but at least they wouldn't be in perfect darkness.

"What is this place?" he asked.

"Maintenance corridor."

Zayvan rolled his eyes at the man. "I can *see* that. I'm not an idiot."

Veshuu pointed at the ceiling, where Zayvan could see a bunch of long, thin lines running in parallel. "Infrastructure for the palace. We're in an access tunnel." He pointed in one direction. "That runs to the city center." Then he pointed in the other direction. "That runs underneath the palace, then up into the walls and maintenance areas."

Zayvan nodded, finally understanding where he was. The palace didn't have its own independent supply of utilities, so it relied on the city for those. And for security reasons, most people didn't even know these tunnels existed, let alone *where* they were or how to access them. Even *he* didn't know before this, though he suspected that was more out of lack of interest than anything else.

"Which way do we go?"

Veshuu didn't speak, he just turned left, toward the palace.

There was an immediate difference between this passage and the one before it. For one, because the light was all around them and not just at their backs, it was a lot easier to see. As he glanced behind himself, he realized that was intentional. By not illuminating the previous corridor, it prevented light leakage. Add in the shrubbery covering the grate, and the entrance would be nearly impossible to find if you didn't already know it was there. A person would have to stumble upon it, and they still might not find it.

"How did they end up in here?" he asked, suddenly realizing the insanity of the kidnapper choosing *this* place to hide in. How did he find it? How did he get in? That lock had looked like it hadn't been touched in ages.

Veshuu stopped and dropped his gun to his side. His shoulders slumped. "I told him."

"What?"

Veshuu turned and glared at him, silently scolding Zayvan for speaking too loudly and possibly giving away their location.

He looked both ways, then turned to Zayvan fully. "He's my brother, okay? And before you say anything, I didn't tell him where the entrances were or how to access them. I only told him they existed. It was in passing a long time ago. It never occurred to me that I couldn't trust him." The corners of his mouth rose in a sneer. "Clearly, I was wrong."

Zayvan felt sorry for him and touched his shoulder in sympathy. He, himself, had an excellent relationship with his own brother, but not everyone was so lucky. He wondered what Veshuu's brother was like. Had Veshuu been blind to his brother's faults? Or did the man put up a facade to hide who he truly was in his heart of hearts?

He released the other man's shoulder, and they continued on, leaving Zayvan to his thoughts once more. What were the other teams doing? Had they found her yet? Or her captor? How long were these tunnels? How many times did they split off?

They stopped at the second junction, turning left yet again. Now, no semblance of daylight remained, the space solely illuminated by the track lighting on the walls. They stopped at another door. Veshuu slowly opened it, his gun aiming into the space as yet another light flickered to life. This room was different. There was no hum coming from it, and from his spot over Veshuu's shoulder, it looked empty.

"What is this?"

"Defunct."

"Defunct what?"

"The palace was built on the grounds of a much older castle. The tunnels beneath the castle were repurposed, but that left most of the rooms down here vacant." His head tilted back and forth as he scanned the space. "This looks like it was probably a storage room." He closed the door. "There are also cells in here somewhere, though the maps don't differentiate."

Zayvan nodded. He knew about the old castle. While the palace had been here for generations, everyone knew of the mysterious castle that had preceded it. By the time they'd chosen this place for the palace and capital city, the castle had been nothing but ruins. They knew not what it had looked like or who had resided there. Most of his people, until fairly recently, had lived up in the mountains where their species originated. They were well adapted to the cold, harsh climate and for thousands of years, they'd seen no reason to move.

Which was maybe why he'd always wondered about the castle when he was growing up. Why had some of his people come down the mountains? Why had they settled on the coast? While it had been a practical decision in modern times, it wouldn't have been in ancient ones. This area had taken generations to cultivate. The land had been harsh and nearly completely infertile this close to the coast. Without modern technology, they would never have been able to convert the surrounding areas to farmland. Without technology, they would not have been able to cope with the various dangers that existed here.

So how did they do it? How did they scrape out a living from the infertile soil? How did they avoid the jaws of the beasts here that could swallow a man whole?

He shook himself, realizing what he was doing. He was distracting himself, his mind scrambling for an escape from everything that was happening. It was dangerous, especially now, and he pushed himself to focus.

Justine needs me.

It was strange how he could go so long without thinking of her. And yet the moment he did, it was like he was being strangled, his lungs unable to pull in a breath. The feeling was so intense, he nearly doubled over, but he couldn't.

She needs me.

They stopped at another door. This one looked different. He couldn't say how, though. The track lighting cast strange shadows that twisted the shape of things, making it hard to discern anything but vague impressions from their surroundings.

"A cell," Veshuu said, this time pressing his ear to the door.

He expects something behind it.

"How many cells are down here?" he whispered.

"Don't know. Like I said, the maps don't say."

Right. Veshuu *had* said that. "How many *could* there be?"

"Dozens, though it's probably nowhere near that much. Food storage would have been more important to the castle denizens."

Zayvan nodded, and Veshuu stepped back. He had a gleam in his eye as he looked over his shoulder at Zayvan. Somehow knowing they would find *something* on the other side of this door, Zayvan raised his gun in preparation.

Veshuu reached for the door to pull it open, but it didn't budge. There was a dull thud as it clunked against the doorframe.

His chest swelled with anticipation. "Is that a good sign?" he whispered.

"Maybe," Veshuu replied in kind.

Zayvan looked at the door. It didn't have a panel next to it to unlock. *Does it work on a key lock? Does it still have the same lock it did back when a castle rested above?*

Veshuu examined the door and lock mechanism. "It doesn't appear to be stuck. The door is moving in the frame, so it isn't swelled shut."

Bang, bang, bang.

They both tensed, staring at the door, waiting. Zayvan's hand flexed on his gun.

Moments ticked by as silence consumed them. Had they imagined it? Was it some spirit trapped here for centuries?

Bang, bang, bang.

Veshuu knelt quickly on the floor after that final bang, his gaze intent on the handle.

"Is it locked?" Zayvan asked, leaning forward to see.

"I think so..." He slowly worked the handle, running his hand over the surface of the door near it.

It was hard for Zayvan to see what he was doing. The door and handle were both in dark shades that melded together in the dim lighting.

"I think..."

A loud metal on metal sound reverberated through the corridor. Zayvan winced and jumped back, swinging his gun wildly up and down the hallway, expecting villains to come running at the noise they'd just made.

They had to hear that.

"Sorry," Veshuu muttered, but as he stood and lifted his gun once more, he reached for the door, and this time it opened. It was just a small gap, but it was enough to see that light was already blazing beyond.

It shouldn't be doing that, he thought, excitement rushing through him.

Zayvan crowded forward as Veshuu half turned to him, giving him direction by counting down on his fingers. He reached zero, and they stormed in, pushing through almost shoulder-to-shoulder.

He didn't believe his eyes at first. Justine sat, dirty but whole, on a small cot on the far wall, her arms raised and eyes wide. He rushed forward, wrapping her in his arms. He couldn't speak, the words locked behind a boulder of emotion in his throat, but it didn't matter.

She's safe.

"Let's go," Veshuu said.

Zayvan pulled back at the admonishment, but couldn't bring himself to completely let go, his hand touching lightly on her arm.

She didn't brush him off.

"We need to go," Veshuu insisted, his gaze darting to the doorway.

Zayvan turned to Justine. "Where is he?" he whispered gently.

"Not here," she whispered back.

Zayvan smiled, loving the sound of her gentle voice in this dreary place. He offered his hand and pulled her carefully to her feet. His gaze roamed over her, checking her for injuries, but there was nothing obvious. "Come."

She took his hand, the small weight setting his heart at ease even though they were not out of danger yet.

Veshuu slipped through the door, his body standing sentinel as he scanned the hallway in each direction for threats. Zayvan stepped through a few moments later, Justine a bare breath behind him.

"Wait," she said as they left the cell.

He urgently pulled her forward, determined to get her to safety, and she gave little resistance, though she continued to protest.

It broke his heart that she seemed so resistant to leaving

with him, even after everything she'd been through.

Did you think this would change anything?

Did you think she would suddenly love you, forgive you?

He pushed those thoughts from his head, focusing instead on their escape. They traveled more quickly on the way out, Veshuu urging them ahead of him, insisting on protecting their backs. Zayvan was no longer aware of the sounds they made. He was consumed by his wildly vacillating emotions, swinging from heartbreak to elation and relief and back again. When focused on the latter, his hand would flex on Justine's hand. He wanted to pull her into his arms and never let go. He wanted to drop to his knees and beg her forgiveness.

We need to get out of here first.

That thought drove him forward like a daemon at his back. He could feel how uneven Justine's gait was, but it didn't slow him down, not even for a moment. Ordinarily, he would be more considerate of her injury, but they needed to get out of here, and the faster the better.

They turned and turned again, and now he could see faint daylight up ahead. "We're almost there," he whispered to Justine.

Then a gun went off behind him, and he broke out into a run, pushing Justine forward as he looked over his shoulder, ready to fire backward and cover their escape. Veshuu stood at the last corner, firing around it into the darkness. His face was mostly in shadow and alarmingly intense, making him seem like the stuff of legends.

Zayvan faced forward again, nearly trampling Justine's heels as he urged her forward, wondering if he should pick her up and carry her the rest of the way.

It ended up not mattering as, moments later, they ran out into bright sunlight. He rushed her away from the entrance, making several turns in the maze of hedges before stopping, feeling slightly out of breath.

If he was out of breath, Justine was even more so, gasping for each inhale as she stared in the direction they'd come. She hugged herself, and he could see where the damp had soaked into her shirt.

"Justine?" he asked, suddenly hesitant to reach for her now that they were out of immediate danger. He contemplated offering her his shirt, figuring she was probably cold.

She turned to him, her eyes big and round with whatever she was feeling. She looked like she was a heartbeat away from bursting into tears.

"I'm sorry," he said, not sure what else he could say.

She rushed rushed forward and hugged him, her hold surprisingly tight. He curled his arms gently around her once more as joy rushed through him and a fledgling hope for the future started to bloom.

Maybe we have a chance, after all.

CHAPTER FOURTEEN

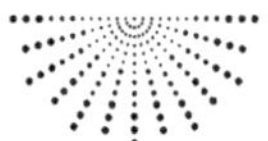

Justine was... fragile after the kidnapping. She didn't want to be, but she couldn't deny a part of her was traumatized by the experience. She didn't want to step out onto the grounds, even when the apartments and palace grew increasingly claustrophobic, and Zayvan's sudden overprotectiveness failed to alarm her, even though it should have.

If anything, she cherished it at first. She forgot for a time why they'd been fighting. She forgot her past, her issues, her fears. Instead, she focused on how good it felt, even if only for a little while, to be treated like something beautiful and breakable.

That didn't last long, though. Within a few days, his attentiveness became oppressive. She started snapping at him, and every time, she felt like the villain when Zayvan would jerk back, looking like a wounded puppy. She even apologized a couple times, trying to get him to scold her or something.

Within a week, what little sympathy she had for him evaporated. He hovered around her all the time, and while she knew it was different from her experiences with Brian, little whispers still tickled the corners of her mind. It would be easy to question her judgment, to let the whispers win, but she refused to let that happen. She *knew* Zayvan wasn't her ex, and she found it easier and easier to dismiss those thoughts as time went on.

Even so, she still couldn't decide if she could trust him. She wasn't sure if their relationship was healthy. She wasn't sure what a healthy relationship even *looked* like anymore. Could they work through this? Could they make something of their promising start? She didn't exactly relish the idea of starting over, but when she looked at him, she couldn't help wondering what else he was hiding. She honestly knew so little about him, and everything she didn't know felt like this great gaping void, this shadowy realm of darkness that threatened to consume them both.

I need answers.

But asking seemed almost impossible. A part of her was afraid of what he might say. Another part was afraid she wouldn't believe him. How could she? He'd already broken her trust. How could they ever move beyond that?

"Do you need anything?" Zayvan asked, looming in the doorway to her room.

She was tempted to close the door in his face and lock it, but that would just be mean. "No, I'm good."

He hesitated, like he didn't know what to do with himself if he wasn't coddling her.

"Maybe you should go to the office."

The wounded puppy look returned. "You want me gone?"

"No," she said, surprising herself with her tone. She barely recognized it as her own voice. It didn't *sound* like her voice. She was so used to the meek little mouse she'd become, her voice soft and high-pitched, that the much firmer tone she'd used for that one word seemed shocking. It was deeper, an alto, and suddenly she remembered that's how she used to sound. Before Brian. "That's not what I said," she continued, growing more confident.

That voice again.

It made her want to keep talking. Her voice sounded assertive, and she couldn't help smiling inside, remembering the phoenix image from earlier.

I'm flying now.

She straightened, standing just a bit taller than before.

You've got this.

"You're hovering," she said, feeling more and more empowered with every word that passed through her lips. "You don't need to watch me every minute of every day. Do you think I'm just gonna disappear again?"

"No," he said, shaking his head vehemently.

"No, I'm not. A lot's uncertain right now, but I don't need you here. I'm not a child. I'm an adult. There are guards at the door. I'm sure you can assign someone to guard me if I leave the apartments. I'm safe. I'm fine. I promise."

He hesitated. "I... just..."

"Yes?" she said, encouraging him to keep speaking.

"I don't want you to fall apart."

She laughed, the sound full-throated and strong. "I'm not gonna fall apart."

Not again.

Never again.

He looked incredulous.

"I'm not." She grew more serious and realized she even *felt* stronger now, like that phoenix was burning deep inside her, providing her with its strength. It was surprisingly exhilarating. She looked up at the excessively decorated ceiling as she tried to think of an argument that would convince him. She'd started out this journey in a bad way, she couldn't deny that. When he'd first met her, she'd practically been scared of her own shadow. It had taken time, patience, and distance to overcome that, but she *had*. She *had* overcome her fears, though she could still feel them like restless beasts roaming her psyche. They were there, looming on the fringes, ready to ambush her in a moment of weakness, but she didn't feel weak anymore.

She still didn't have a job, and she definitely still wanted one, but she didn't feel trapped. *Trapped* was being in a relationship with someone like Brian. *Trapped* was being locked in a room with a psycho. No, she wasn't trapped. The very nature of the matching service meant she had options if it came to that. Many, many options, in fact. How many people were in the database? Maybe there was an even better match waiting for her now.

But she didn't *want* a better match, at least not yet. If she left, she would always wonder. She would wonder if she'd given up too soon. She would wonder if he really was the man she'd started falling in love with. There was *promise* here, and while she knew hoping for *change* was a dangerous thing, hoping for the right *answers* wasn't.

But then, what answers was she hoping for? And what would it take for her to trust in those answers? She feared she would never truly believe something that slipped from his own lips. What if he lied? What if he continued to hide things? She couldn't take another surprise like that, not if it was avoidable.

If she was going to get the answers she needed, she needed to get them from someone else, someone who knew him better than they knew themself, ideally. But who could that be?

His brother.

She stiffened as the thought struck her and reflexively reached for her bruised hand. It was like lightning out of nowhere, and it was just as painful, because guilt immediately hit her. His brother, Crown Prince Rekhem, was still missing, out there under the control of the Silent Majority, whoever they may be. She'd spent the last week wallowing in her own inner turmoil while Rekhem was still under their control. And she hadn't said a word. She hadn't told anyone. What if something had happened to him? What if speaking sooner could have saved him? How could she ever forgive herself?

How could Zayvan?

She looked at him, compassion crossing her face as guilt continued to churn in her stomach. Here she was, giving him a hard time, but he wasn't just dealing with their fight, her disappearance, and her rescue. He was dealing with his brother's disappearance as well.

Justine tried to focus on what she remembered, her fingers digging into the abused skin on her hand, a part of her relishing the pain.

Think.

Remember the path from my cell to where Rekhem was held.

She tried to imagine every twist and turn, but it all felt foggy, some of the details lost after a week. She had a hard time visualizing the path in her head, but there was another way.

Justine looked up at Zayvan, nervous as all get-out. "I think I know where he is."

Zayvan didn't at first believe it.

I think I know where he is.

It seemed too good to be true. First, Justine was back and safe, and she didn't even seem to hate him anymore. And second, they might actually be able to save his brother now. He'd been beyond frustrated with the abysmal lack of progress on that front, and the only thing that had kept him from shouting his head off at everyone was all the drama with Justine.

"What do you mean?" he asked, barely able to breathe for fear that her words would prove to be a mirage.

"They showed me where he was. I think I know how to find him, your brother."

Zayvan's first instinct was to rush forward and drag her behind him, insisting she show him where Rekhem was. He had to take several deep breaths to control his urgency. *She's fragile. She's just been through a terrible ordeal.* Controlling his tone, he softly and calmly asked, "Would you be willing to talk to the Guard?"

"Of course."

He sighed a breath of relief and straightened, pulling his phone out of his back pocket and dialing Captain Veshuu.

The phone rang a couple times before being picked up. "How may I help you, Your Highness?"

"I need to meet. We have new intel on my brother's disappearance."

Suddenly, Veshuu's voice sounded a lot more urgent. "What do you have?" he barked.

"I don't know. Justine just said she might know how to find him."

"Meet me in the meeting room in Royal Guard Headquarters."

"Will do. And feel free to invite anyone who may be useful to the conversation. Considering how long Rekhem has been missing, I would rather we not waste time reiterating information."

"Agreed." Veshuu ended the call, and Zayvan pocketed his phone, turning to Justine. "Ready?" he asked, offering her his hand.

She nodded and took it, and he shifted his focus to reaching the other side of the palace as quickly as Justine's shorter legs could take them.

It took precious minutes to get to the meeting room, minutes he feared they couldn't afford to waste. He was painfully aware of how long his brother had been missing. How many more minutes did Rekhem have?

He entered with Justine into a room that was already mostly full. Captain Veshuu was there along with quite a few other people in Royal Guard uniforms and a couple royal advisors. Zayvan tugged Justine along by her hand and pulled out a seat for her, then sat next to her. She placed her hands on the table, and he hesitated before carefully resting a comforting hand on her own, wondering if she would object.

She looked over and smiled, though it seemed a little reserved.

We'll get beyond this, he told himself.

"Thank you all for coming," Captain Veshuu said, standing tall at one end of the table. "We all know why we're here. Let's get started. Justine?"

She sat there in silence for several beats. Zayvan looked over at her, saw the slight alarm on her face, and squeezed her hand lightly in encouragement. She looked over at him, her crooked smile tremulous this time, then turned back and focused on Veshuu.

"When I was in that cell, I had the opportunity to talk to my captor."

As she started talking, he couldn't help seeing that fragile little thing he'd first met weeks ago. She'd seemed so vulnerable and breakable, like she was only one rough experience away from falling apart entirely.

How has she not fallen apart yet?

He'd been watching her like an anxious mother, watching her moods and seeing to her every need. Even coming here felt like too much to him, but what else could he do? He scooched closer, his shoulder brushing hers, and she looked over at him, but he couldn't quite read her expression.

Then several voices started booming over hers. She faltered, and he reached out, pulling her into his side to comfort her, but she pushed back, shimmying out of his arms and shoving to her feet.

"Enough!"

CHAPTER FIFTEEN

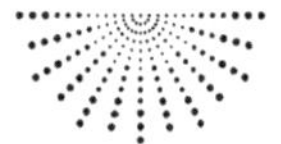

I didn't actually expect that to work.

The room quieted, the collection of people in uniforms and clearly expensive dress staring at Justine as if she'd grown a second head. She wrung her hands a little, wondering why she'd snapped like that, but she couldn't take it back.

After several moments passed, she noticed that the people in uniform actually had small grins on their faces while those in fancy clothes looked offended. She glanced over at Zayvan. He again had that wounded puppy dog look on his face, making her feel guilty for pushing away from him, but she was tired of being coddled. She needed to stand up for herself, to prove herself, even if at first it was only in small ways.

"What does the Lady Justine have to say?" a man in a purple silk shirt said.

She tried to ignore him, instead, focusing on the only person in uniform she actually recognized, the one who'd helped rescue her from that cell. "You know where I was kept?"

He nodded. "I'm familiar with it."

224

"Good. That'll be our starting point. From there, I can lead you all to where they were keeping him a week ago. Hopefully, he's still there."

Zayvan practically squawked at her side, but she ignored that, too.

"With all due respect..." her rescuer said, side-eying the man in purple, "...Lady Justine, it would be best if we can gather all the necessary intel here and not risk any civilians."

"With all due respect," she snapped back with a pointed glare, "I'm not sure that's possible." She leaned in, but had no hope of intimidating him. And while he was right for the most part, there was no guarantee she could stay behind *and* lead them to the Crown Prince. She might very well have been able to direct them using maps or cameras, but what if the maps weren't accurate or the cameras lacked the detail necessary? Those corridors had seemed old. She knew there were places on Earth where no accurate maps existed. Information was lost or never documented. Or maps were created for specific purposes that distorted reality in all other contexts. She wasn't even sure she wanted to do this, but she felt like she had to, for Rekhem and herself.

"I don't intend to fight or be in harm's way. I fully respect the role you have in this situation, but I would also expect you to respect my *own* role."

The smallest of grins tipped the edges of his lips. "Very well. You are certain you know where he was a week ago?"

She nodded her head. "Yes. If you can get me to the cell you found me in, I feel confident I can retrace my steps back to where they were keeping the Crown Prince." She looked over at Zayvan, unable to even *think* about the missing man without also thinking about his brother. She bit her lip and looked back up at the clear leader of the group. "Hopefully, we'll find him.

If not, maybe there will be additional clues there. Either way, it's a step in the right direction."

"Indeed." He turned to the rest of the table. "Since we are not needing to search the entire system, we are going in with one large team." He started calling out names and assignments. Each person saluted, stood, and left the room. By the time he stopped speaking, he was the only person in uniform left. He turned to the people in expensive garb. "Dismissed," he said, then turned to Zayvan and herself and waved at them, indicating they should follow.

"The same rules as last time, Your Highness. Stay with me, follow my orders, and no heroics." He turned to Justine. "I expect the same out of you, my lady."

"Of course."

"The name's Captain Pazran Veshuu, by the way."

"Nice to meet you, Captain."

He nodded. "Now, let's go rescue a prince."

Justine was nervous. They geared up while Zayvan gave Pazran dirty looks for giving her a weapon.

Pazran lifted his chin and completely ignored the looks, making Justine smile, even if the weapon itself was a bit daunting. She'd never had any experience with weapons back on Earth, and this wasn't exactly designed for humans. It was a little too big for her hands, even though Pazran had given her a smaller one than either he or Zayvan carried, and shaped more or less like a gun. She gingerly placed it in its holster, then proceeded to follow the group as they left Royal Guard Headquarters.

When they reached an exterior door, she paused. The last time she'd left the palace building, she'd been kidnapped, and the black hole of night that waited for her didn't exactly instill in her the confidence she needed to proceed.

The group filed through the door one by one, giving her time to get her gumption up.

It's not gonna happen again.

I'm not alone this time.

Plus, I feel like they put me in enough protective gear to survive a nuclear blast.

She took comfort in the heavily armed people she was traveling with. Each of them could easily take on an aggressor, she suspected, and that gave her an added layer of courage. She stepped forward with ease when it was her time, following the guard members out into the darkness. There were deep shadows, and some animals were calling out into the night. She had no idea what they were, but it was simultaneously familiar and alien.

Justine shivered a little as the cool night air hit her, but stiffened and pretended she was fine when Zayvan looked back to check on her. It was cold, but she wouldn't let that stop her.

Even so, goosebumps ran up her arms as they moved through the gardens. Within a few minutes, they stopped, and Pazran's voice filtered to her from up ahead. "I expect silence until further notice. I don't want the enemy alerted to our presence if we can help it."

That seems... unrealistic, she thought as she stood there, waiting for them to get going again. Her captors were bound to have noticed her disappearance, meaning they might be expecting the Guard to return.

She didn't say anything, though, because at that point, the group surged forward, and she rushed awkwardly to catch up. After only a few steps, she was engulfed by darkness, and she reached out, desperate for someone to anchor her. She found a hand. It gripped hers, and she looked up, seeing the heavily shadowed visage of Zayvan. He smiled down at her, and she let him guide her through the darkness, because she sure as shit couldn't see a damn thing herself.

Was this the same tunnel she'd escaped through only a week ago? She didn't remember it being this dark, though it *had* been daylight outside, and she'd been facing the other direction, so she supposed it was possible. Looking behind her, she was surprised by just how little light leaked into the tunnel from the entrance. Even in that direction, she could see nothing beyond that dim night glow that barely illuminated the first few feet.

Justine stumbled along blindly next to Zayvan for quite some time before they turned, entering a new tunnel, this one with track lighting. She still had to squint to see anything, but it was better than nothing, and before long, her eyes started to adjust.

She was so focused on seeing *anything* in the dim lighting, she didn't even notice when Pazran approached, tapping her on the shoulder. Justine jerked backward, but he waved his hand, and she realized he was signaling for her to stay quiet.

She nodded, and he smiled, then motioned her forward. She walked through the crowd, bumping shoulders with person after person. Every one of them was wearing something dark, thick, and heavy. Body armor?

They reached the front of the group, and she immediately spotted the vague outline of a door to her right. She'd only seen it from this side once, and then, when it was open, but it definitely looked familiar. She looked up ahead, then over at Pazran. He nodded encouragement, and she took a deep breath to clear her mind before she started walking, looking for landmarks.

Fortunately, the lighting was identical, making it easy to recognize each turn, building her confidence as she went.

Justine finally stopped when they were almost there. They

had to make one more turn and then go down a short hall that opened into a large space with no door. She looked over at Pazran and tried to use hand gestures to signal where to go.

He nodded and turned to his team. Every one of them got serious real fast. Guns were withdrawn and readied, shoulders were pulled back and tensed, and eyes grew flinty in the gloom.

With an open hand on her upper arm, Pazran ushered her back until she was next to Zayvan once more and lifted his own weapon to shoulder level. Everyone rushed forward, surging around the corner like a hive-minded mob.

Then a loud crack echoed off the walls. Justine covered her ears even as the single crack turned into a thunderous cacophony of sound that distorted in her ears, making her wonder if her hearing would forever be damaged by the experience.

The guards spread out, continuing to fight as Justine silently waited a couple steps behind Pazran. She could see nothing of the battle except the jerking motion people made when they were hit with something, though their gear must have protected them, because they kept going.

Justine was alarmed and exhilarated as the battle continued. She didn't even think to reach for her weapon, though. She wouldn't want to hurt one of the good guys by mistake.

Maybe I should head back around the corner, she thought, but quickly nixed the idea, remembering how Pazran had insisted on her sticking by his side. She might not be much use in a fight, but she could at least follow orders.

Then it was like the Red Sea parting. Suddenly, there was an opening between the guards, and she locked eyes with the guy who'd taken her.

It was strange. That moment became burned into her brain, and while it might have been nothing more than a fraction of a second, she could remember every detail. The color of his skin.

Every fold in his clothing. The way he styled his hair. The way his finger twitched on the trigger. She stared at him as recognition filled his eyes. She couldn't hear it, but she saw his weapon fire. It was so fast. Her mind whited with pain. There was a moment of bewilderment, then her brain clicked into gear.

I've been shot.

Justine felt lightheaded, her mind skipping over things like a badly scratched disc. The pain, though, *that* she could feel. It both grounded her and made her feel light and floaty, like she wasn't completely attached to her body.

Am I dying?

She couldn't tell if she was still standing or if she'd fallen after being shot.

Right. I got shot, didn't I?

The thought was fleeting as her mind continued resisting reality, wanting instead to retreat and curl into a ball like a child overwhelmed by the world.

And yet the things that flitted through her consciousness were no better.

"Of course, doctor. I'll make sure she follows your instructions," Brian says, gripping her shoulder so intensely it hurts as he smiles at her doctor, being the charismatic man she no longer believes is real.

Justine's stomach roiled at the memory triggered by the pain in her shoulder. She'd felt his hand on her shoulder for days after that.

"I'm sorry, Justine, but this is for the best," Brian says as he takes her phone from the table, shoving it in his back pocket. He'd already changed the Wi-Fi password and set Parental Controls on the TV.

I'm furious, but no words escape my throat. I see the look in his gaze, and it sends chills through me. Right now, I have no illusions about who the monster in front of me is. All I can do is cooperate and hope that saves me.

There is no escape.

She gasped as someone pulled at her, sending shooting pain out from the wound she'd forgotten she had. She could feel each finger digging into her skin, her vision again whiting out from the pain.

I'm yelling at him. I'm not even sure why I'm yelling, but I'm so mad, I can't see straight at this point. I'm fed up with his bullshit, fed up with his fragile ego, fed up with his every insecurity.

"Don't talk to me like that!" he yells back, his stance rigid, making the muscles in his arms and the tendons in his neck stand out.

"I'll talk to you however I damn well like, Brian," I yell back, inching closer and closer, seemingly with each word. We're nose to nose now, and I suspect we're practically spitting on each other with every word, but I'm too mad to care.

"I'm warning you," he says, his voice low and threatening.

I shove him. It actually surprises me that I did it. I'm not a violent person. In fact, I'm not usually the type to raise my voice unless I've been backed into a corner. Our relationship has been going downhill for a while. The shove wakes me up, snapping me out of our argument.

I take a step back, but it's too late. Brian's face darkens with anger, and I think he even growls. He lurches forward, and instinctually, I just know he isn't playing anymore. This is real. I'm in danger. I turn to run, but the bed is between me and the door. It feels like miles away, and I know he'll catch me.

Instead of trying to run around the bed, I just jump on top of it, each step awkward. Then the mattress bounces, throwing me off balance, and Brian grabs my leg. His fingers are like an iron manacle, and I go down face first, but I'm too close to the edge, and I roll. He pulls on my ankle as I fall. Something twists, something that's not supposed to, and I scream.

Justine was panting, the pain in her shoulder dimmer than before. She stared up at the ceiling, barely processing the rough stone above, but she could see it now. The room was still loud, far too loud, and the person whose lap her head was currently resting on had to yell to be heard above it.

"Are you okay?" he asked as his face shifted into her visual field.

Are you stupid?

And yet she nodded anyway as her brain started putting pieces together.

Rekhem.

"Hi," she said, her voice not even a whisper and immediately lost in the din.

He smiled, then looked down at her shoulder with a frown.

That bad, huh?

She tried to look, but her body didn't want to twist that way, so she gave up and continued to stare at the ceiling. The pain was continuing to dim more and more, and fortunately, it wasn't going numb. Numb would be bad. She flexed her fingers on that side. It hurt, but she could move them.

Another good sign.

She frowned as she noticed a stone digging into her back. She tried to move, but her shoulder screamed at her, so she stopped, but the stone was still there, trying to bore its way into her kidney.

To make matters worse, the ground was also damp, slowly soaking into her shirt and pants, and the air this low to the ground smelled dank and redolent with mold.

Great. It's probably gonna get infected, isn't it?

"What's wrong? What can I do?" Rekhem said.

"Stone," she whispered, not holding out a whole lot of hope that he would understand, but he did, and she sighed in relief as the pain there abated.

"Thanks."

Now that the pain has settled, her mind was a bit clearer, but the echoes of those past traumas continued to plague her. They were their own sort of pain, their own sort of torture, and her mind wanted to shy away from them.

Promise me you'll really *put this behind you.*

Amira's words resounded through her brain. Her mind was blank for several long seconds.

"Promise me you'll really put this behind you," she mouthed to herself.

It was strange. The words seemed different now after everything that had happened. They had more weight, more gravitas, and those past traumas seemed to wither away in their presence. She *wanted* to let it go. She *wanted* to put it behind her.

Was it that simple? Justine doubted it, but even so, the bad memories were fading and the good ones started taking their place. She remembered going to the movies with Amira and laughing while trying not to disturb the other patrons. She remembered going out with her friend then snapping at men when they tried to buy Amira drinks. She remembered asking Amira how to pronounce things in Arabic, and the way her friend would smile at her efforts, then laugh when she got the words brutally wrong.

A smile slowly crept onto her face.

Then she started thinking about Zayvan. She remembered playing games for hours, going for walks, picnicking, cooking meals together, talking until it seemed like they shouldn't have anything more to say. Oh, how desperately she wanted that to be the real Zayvan.

But even if it wasn't, even if their relationship died, they'd had good times together, hadn't they? Her time with him had helped her, maybe in more ways than she could ever put into words. That was a good thing, right? That was worthwhile, right? Even if it ended?

She tried again to sit up.

"Careful," Rekhem said, supporting her shoulders from behind.

She didn't listen, continuing until she was fully upright. The pain was intense, but she managed. She lifted a hand and pressed it against the wound. Blood seeped through her fingers, her shirt already saturated.

That's probably not good.

But she could move her arm. She gingerly lifted it, feeling the pain in her shoulder and determining it was manageable. "Help me up."

"I don't think that's such a good idea."

She turned and glared at Rekhem. "Well, I do. Help me up."

He nodded, and they awkwardly stood together. She swayed slightly when she was finally standing, but then staggered her feet and found she felt pretty stable that way. In pain, but not like she was about to keel over. She pressed one hand to her wound again and pulled the gun out of its holster with the other. Pain flared, but dimmed quickly to tolerable levels again.

I'm such a badass, she thought with a smile.

Justine had no plan except getting up, so when she was finally standing, gun in hand, in total badass mode, she just stood there for a moment like an idiot. Around her, guards and kidnappers were still fighting, probably because the good guys were blocking the only exit and the bad guys were holed up behind cover.

Meanwhile, she and Rekhem were just standing there in the open, and she wasn't at all comfortable with that.

"Move," she said, nudging Rekhem with an elbow.

He nodded, and she led the way, painfully raising her gun, her arm shaking in the process. Fortunately, there didn't seem to be anyone paying attention to them. She breathed deeply and a little too quickly as she walked slowly toward the tunnel up ahead.

Her focus being on the seething violence to her right, she had a hard time walking a straight line, eventually running straight into a wall, her good shoulder grinding against the rough stone, abrading it even through her shirt.

"Fuck!"

"Are you okay?" Rekhem said, whispering in her ear.

She nodded, straightened, and rolled the shoulder. It barely stung and was completely eclipsed by the steady pain on the other side. It was growing harder and harder to lift the gun, her arm shaking as she stared warily at the action that was uncomfortably close. She couldn't see Zayvan anymore, had no idea where he was in all that mess.

And it was a mess. There was a constant din of gunshots serenading the air, but not everyone was fighting with guns. Two men were grappling each other, occasionally swinging a fist. Another was whaling on their opponent with some sort of baton. It was big and nasty, and she winced as it caused the bad guy's head to snap to the side from the force.

"We have to get out of here."

"Agreed," he said, his face stern.

Justine pushed off the wall, focusing on the narrow opening

where this room met the hallway. The hand holding her gun had now dropped to her side, and she pressed harder into the wound with the other. It hurt, leaving her almost breathless, but she was determined. She was in over her head, but the least she could do was get herself and the Crown Prince to safety.

As they passed beyond their guards, putting the violence behind them, her vision started to tunnel, while her hearing was growing distorted. *We can't stop now. It's not safe.* They were still only one stray bullet away from disaster.

She sighed a breath of relief as they reached the hallway and leaned her shoulder against the wall. She took several deep breaths, grateful to have passed through that crucible with no more injuries, but as she looked behind her, she realized they weren't out of the woods yet. From her vantage point, she could see several kidnappers, which meant they could still be shot. She pushed off, now clumsily plodding forward.

"You should rest," Rekhem said as he loomed over her.

Justine shook her head, but regretted it as the room began to spin a little. She groaned as she lifted her gun-wielding hand to her forehead to steady herself, the metal pleasantly cool against her skin. She took a deep breath and let her arm drop. It was too exhausting to keep it raised, anyway.

Each step got harder and harder, but that didn't really slow her down. It just amplified her determination to get them to safety. She focused on each step, on adding every bit of distance she could.

Every step counts.

It was easy to narrow her existence down to that principle. One step at a time. Just keep going. Keep moving.

After a while, she realized she was no longer holding her wound or the gun. Had she dropped it? She was tempted to look for it, but even the slightest movement of her head threatened to end her journey.

She was panting.

When did that start?

"You can stop now," someone whispered in her ear.

She stopped, still panting, and nodded her head. The head nod was her undoing, and she swiftly lost consciousness.

CHAPTER SIXTEEN

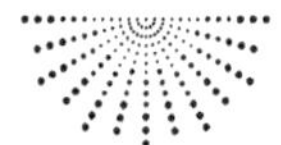

*R*ekhem was relieved to be back, but not like this. Somehow, in the heat of the moment, it hadn't occurred to him that the small woman who'd saved him was his brother's human bride. When his captors had used her to threaten him, all he'd really noticed were her hair and skin tone, neither of which had been easy to spot under the tactical gear she'd been wearing during the rescue. When she'd collapsed in that tunnel, he'd been worried as he would have for any person, even more so when he saw where she was injured. At first, with loud blasts of gunfire echoing off the walls and complete chaos reigning, he'd paid little attention to where she'd been injured, only that she *was* injured and had seemed out of it immediately afterward.

But when she'd collapsed in that hallway, the battle now nothing but distant background noise, he'd had more time to really see her *and* her injury. An alarmingly large blood stain colored her upper chest on one side, right over where the heart was in a Savalan. In the dim lighting, he couldn't tell how much blood she'd lost, but it didn't look like a small amount. He'd immediately pressed both hands to the wound, hoping to staunch the flow of blood, but his mind kept running over all the distance they'd covered and how long she'd been like this without treatment.

The blood had felt like it was seeping slowly between his fingers, and he couldn't tell if that was because her heart was slowing, or the wound wasn't as bad as he feared. He was terrified she might be dying, and he couldn't bear the idea of her dying because of him.

Rekhem never wanted *anyone* to die because of him.

Sitting at her bedside now, he pressed his ice-cold fingers to his mouth. She was asleep, her red hair haloed around her head. Zayvan was currently away getting a shower and some rest at Rekhem's insistence. Anything short of a royal command would have fallen on deaf ears. He felt bad for even insisting, but no one could go on like that forever, and it had been days.

Besides, Justine was stable now, so there was no need to keep watch. The doctors had assured them of that. But looking at her in that bed, she just looked so small and delicate and pale. And while the hospital was knowledgeable about all the known sentient species, it wasn't prepared to handle her blood loss. Humans just weren't that common in this sector of space, forcing them to scramble to get blood synthesized. For now, they were making do with saline fluid replacement, which prevented shock, but meant she was currently being supplied oxygen.

Rekhem sighed and looked out the window on the other side of the bed, surprised to see it was close to midday. Time had seemed to blur as they'd waited for Justine to recover.

Will she ever wake up?

That was what kept running through his head. Every time that thought struck him, he imagined his brother's reaction if she didn't. He imagined him stunned, then completely destroyed. He alternated between imagining a grand display of grief and his brother completely shutting down, maybe never speaking again. Certainly, he would never speak to *him* again. How could he? It was because of Rekhem that Justine was in this bed right now. If he hadn't been taken, if he weren't the Crown Prince, would any of this have happened at all?

No. No, it wouldn't have.

A part of him knew that this was all just emotion getting the better of him, that he didn't hold any blame in this situation. He was taken against his will. Bad people had acted, and this was the consequence. But he also couldn't help wondering if he could have done *something* to prevent it. Maybe more security?

But he'd always felt safe in the palace. They were at war with no one, and the people seemed to love the Royal Family, so why waste their money on more security? He would rather protect his *people* than himself. It had never really occurred to him that his people could be the threat. He did absolutely *everything* for them. Why would they turn against him?

"Who are you?" a scratchy voice whispered, barely audible.

Rekhem tensed, immediately jerking his gaze away from the window and dropping it onto the figure in the bed, who was now blinking the sleep from her eyes. She looked groggy, like she had half a mind to roll over and fall back asleep, but she was awake, and he smiled down at her, relieved to see this sign of progress.

"Rekhem, Zayvan's brother."

She seemed to think for a moment, her mind sluggish, before slowly nodding her head. "The tunnels."

"That's right. You rescued me."

"I did."

"Thank you for that. How are you feeling?"

"Tired."

He nodded. That was probably to be expected. "I sent Zayvan away for a shower and some rest."

Justine nodded slowly again, gradually waking up more and more, her eyes clearer, her movements a little less lethargic. She looked down at the bandages peeking out from beneath her hospital gown. "What do the doctors say?"

"Blood loss mainly. You're on fluids, and they're currently synthesizing some blood for you. There wasn't a stock on hand."

"How long does that take?"

Rekhem scratched his head. "I don't know. Never been something I needed to know. I'll ask the doctors, though." He stood up to leave.

"No, wait." Justine reached out with her unbandaged arm.

He stopped halfway to standing and sat back down. "Yes?"

She paused, chewing on her lip. "How well do you know your brother?"

Rekhem was taken aback by her question. "We've known each other our entire lives. We work together. We see each other every day. Why?"

Her expression grew even more intense. "What type of man is he?"

Rekhem wasn't expecting that question. Justine had been spending all her time with Zayvan for weeks. Didn't she know him at least a little by now? Why would she need to know that? "He's a good man." At first, he didn't know what else to say. He'd never had to think critically about who his brother was before. He was just... Zayvan. To him, that was all that really mattered. What did she want to know? What did she *need* to know?

He remembered that call with Zayvan, when his brother had intimated that something bad might have happened to her. She was skittish. The match was rushed. She tended to apologize all the time. Rekhem had told his brother he should focus on helping her and building their relationship, but maybe she needed more than that. Maybe she didn't trust herself. But if she couldn't trust herself, why would she trust him? Why would she trust *anyone*? What could he ever do or say to convince her? He was hesitant as he started talking. "I'm not sure I know how to answer your question. I'm not sure what you need. I've known Zayvan since the moment he was born. He's loyal and dedicated to a fault." He smiled. "I often have to command him to take a break. Nothing short of a royal decree will do."

"That fits."

"Oh?"

She looked up at Rekhem. "When the guards showed up, he just sort of... stopped being Zayvan. Like he was going through the motions or following a script. I needed him, but he wasn't there."

His heart twisted in his chest. Zayvan could definitely be like that at times. "It's probably one of his best and worst features, depending on who you ask."

"I'd say worst."

"I imagine so." He paused, taking a breath. "What do you want to know about him?"

She swallowed heavily. "Is he trustworthy?"

Rekhem knew immediately she'd dived straight for the issue at the heart of everything. It made so much sense, and she looked so vulnerable and hopeful. He could see she *wanted* to believe his brother was trustworthy, and if he could say something to reassure her, he would. "Yes, he is. There's no one I trust more. Like I said, he's loyal and dedicated. To a fault, in fact." He thought again of his call with Zayvan, of her potential past. "He's mild-mannered, laid back, and a bit of a nurturer. I've never heard him so much as raise his voice to someone.

"It's part of the reason I've always wondered if following me into government service was the right choice for him. Zayvan was never really ambitious growing up. He didn't have any real passions or subjects he was especially good at. He liked to," he chuckled thinking about it, "take forever making a decision. Still does. He'll mull over it for ages, spending hours doing research, weighing each option ad nauseam. I often wonder if he fell into government work more out of indecision than anything else."

Rekhem looked over at Justine. She had shifted some on the bed, her head bent toward him now. "I think choosing you was the most decisive he's ever been. The day he received the match, he showed up in my office and just started pacing. Wouldn't even explain why he was there at first. The whole thing just wound him up in knots.

"You see, ordinarily, people can take as much time as they like when reviewing a match. Zayvan was fully expecting to take weeks poring over your profile, but they were giving him less than a day. He agonized over that decision." Rekhem paused. "But it was also the fastest I've ever seen him make a decision.

"I listened to him as he worked out his thinking in my office. What he was feeling, his misgivings, and frankly, there weren't many, and they were all because he didn't like being pressed to decide so fast. He didn't have a single negative thing to say about your profile. I saw him agonizing over the decision, but deep down, I suspected you two were perfect for each other. I still think that.

"He needs you." He sighed. "My brother was lonely for years, and I suspect that was part of the reason he pushed himself so much in his work, why he seemed so invested in me and my career. I was his only close family. I knew he wanted to get married eventually, but growing up, there were just so many marriages around us going horribly awry. We had practically no good examples to model our hopes on.

"Zayvan always blamed it on arranged marriages. Sometimes, he asks me how I can tolerate being betrothed to someone I don't even know. From a pretty early age, he was *determined* to find a love match. But, it's not that simple for people like us. We're not just men, we're royalty. There's always going to be that extra baggage there, that question in the back of your mind."

"What question?"

He looked down at her, suddenly very serious. "Do they want you or your title?"

Her eyes widened, then her face settled into an expression he couldn't read. "He didn't want someone to want him for his title?"

Rekhem shook his head. "No. He dated a lot of women when he was younger. He thrived on the attention he got, but none of the relationships ever lasted long. It always became pretty obvious what the women were truly after, and it broke his heart every time. Every time it ended, he would bury himself in his work and not resurface for weeks. Eventually, he stopped trying. I thought he'd given up for good.

"I hated that. I wanted him to be happy. It was the only thing he wanted for himself, and the fact that he seemed to have given up just killed me." He shook his head, laughing a little. "I didn't know he'd signed up for the matching service. I don't know when he did. Just one day, he stormed into my office with an impossible decision looming over his head, whether or not to bring you here."

Justine nodded and looked away.

Rekhem leaned back in his seat, wondering if he'd given her what she needed or if he should keep talking. It felt like a jumble in his head, a complicated mess that had no hope of making sense, but if he needed to, he would do it again. He would speak with her again and again if it meant making his brother happy.

Justine didn't stay in the hospital much longer. The next time she woke up, it was to the sound of the medical staff bringing in the synthesized blood and setting up the transfusion. She'd watched them connect the blood to the saline drip, then continued to watch as the red liquid slowly migrated through the tubing. Just seeing that progress was reassuring, even if she was still exhausted.

The next day, the doctors let her go home. She'd tried to calmly ignore Zayvan's hovering as she left the hospital bed for the first time, but he quickly got on her nerves, and she snapped at him. The wounded puppy dog look returned, and she looked away.

How can this possibly work if I keep hurting him?

Justine stood without his help and slowly made her way out of the hospital, feeling like shit, and not because of her injuries. She thought back on her conversation with Rekhem while she walked, trying to reassure herself. *He is who I think he is. He is a good man. We were matched for a reason.* Remembering that they'd been matched helped some. It reminded her that they weren't a perfect match, but that no one was. And remembering what Rekhem had told her helped even more. It alleviated her concerns about not truly *knowing* Zayvan. No one could show you all of who they were in a matter of weeks. That was just unrealistic, and what he *had* shown her *was* a part of his character. Probably, it was a part of himself that few other people ever got to see or appreciate. But she did. She appreciated it so much.

So how are we going to bridge this distance between us?

As she'd lain in the hospital bed, she'd wanted him to hold her hand, to be the sweet man she'd known back at the cabin, the one she now believed he was at his core. Finding out about his title had shaken her, but after talking with Rekhem, she could forgive his omission. She could see his side of things. When so much emotion was attached to something, it could be hard to speak. She knew that from her own experiences. After all, she'd never told him what had happened to her. She'd held it close to her heart like some dark secret that would destroy her if it ever got out. Most of the time, it felt like that.

So how do we do this?

She knew it was something they both wanted. She could see the yearning in Zayvan's eyes. The same yearning Rekhem had mentioned. The same yearning she, herself, felt. It made her want to comfort him and tell him everything would be okay. It made her want to pull him in for a big hug, but her shoulder just wasn't ready for that yet.

So, instead, she kept quiet, looking for the right moment. There was an awkward silence between them as they left the hospital that continued into the car, through the palace, and even into their own apartments. When they arrived back home, they stood there in the foyer like idiots, the impossibly opulent decor seeming to put one more nail in the coffin of their relationship.

Without another word, Zayvan ushered her into her room, set her up with everything she would need within reach, and left.

She wanted to scream.

Justine had a plan.

It had been over a week since she'd returned to the palace. Zayvan had been little more than a ghost, slipping in and out of the apartments without being seen or heard. She needed to talk to him, but she only ever seemed to find him when he was asleep in bed, which wasn't exactly helpful. She was often tempted to wake him up, but he just looked so damned peaceful and adorable, and she couldn't do it.

The *plan* actually came to her with almost no forethought, just a lightning strike out of the blue, charged by all her frustrations.

"This is ridiculous," she muttered to herself before dialing up Rekhem on her phone.

"Hello?"

"I need your help," she said, not even bothering with a greeting.

"How may I be of assistance, my future sister-in-law?"

"Well, that's part of the problem. Zayvan and I need to talk, but he's never here."

"It's not my fault," Rekhem said defensively. She could imagine him raising up his hands.

"I'm not blaming you. I remember what you said about him. It's just... there's this rift between us, and he's probably giving me space, but that's not what we need right now."

"Yeah, that sounds like him."

"Can you, I don't know, force him not to work?"

He laughed. "Not on my life. I can force him to leave your bedside to get some rest. I can force him to leave the office. I can force him to stay at the cabin longer. I don't think anyone can force him not to work. But I can definitely get him to the apartments, if that's what you need."

"That'll do." Justine hung up, trying to decide exactly what she would say. She looked around her, as if her surroundings might give her inspiration, but her room was covered in the chaotic leavings of her illness. Dirty cups with dregs of beverages in them, rumpled bedding, and some trays on the far dresser that still had some food left on them.

"This is disgusting," she muttered to herself.

Justine started loading everything up on the food trays, hoping that a little manual labor would help her think. Her shoulder, no longer bandaged, barely even twinged at the strain, and she smiled, happy to be mostly back to her normal self again. She walked briskly across the apartments, dropping the items in the mysterious compartment that returned things to the palace kitchens. She had no idea how it worked, but if you closed the door, it hummed, then nothing was in it when you opened it again.

With that taken care of, her nerves started getting the better of her. Justine walked through the rooms, organizing her thoughts as she went. She supposed the first thing they should address was their fight, but how? She didn't want to start up another argument. So then, what could she say that would express how she felt but wouldn't cause another fight? She wasn't really sorry. Maybe sorry for yelling, but not sorry for what she'd said. It was true, after all. He *should* have told her. She might forgive him and understand why he did it, but that didn't change the fact that he'd been in the wrong.

And yet, she'd kept her own secrets, too, hadn't she? She was pretty sure she hadn't told him about her past yet. Could she really blame him for withholding information when she'd been doing the same thing?

Maybe she should start with that? Maybe she should open up about Brian and put all the cards on the table, so to speak?

Justine started pacing the foyer. The wait was really getting to her now, and she could feel her anxiety growing with every second. She just wanted Zayvan to *be* here already. Why wasn't he? How long had it been?

Damn, I wish I knew how to tell time here.

"Stop that," she said to herself, ending her inner recriminations and pacing at the same time. "This isn't helping." She looked around at her surroundings once again. "I hate this room."

She jumped when the door opened. Embarrassment rushed through her.

Did he hear me talking to myself?

Zayvan walked through a moment later, already speaking, clearly not having heard her. She sighed in relief.

"Rekhem, what was so important? Why did you need to meet me here?"

Justine froze. The time had arrived, but suddenly, all possible discussion points fled her mind.

Shit, what do I do?

Zayvan froze, too, his hand still on the door. "Justine."

She couldn't move, couldn't even think.

Why can't I think?

Just say something. Anything.

"Justine? Where's Rekhem?"

Her words failed her.

Zayvan started crossing the room. "Shouldn't you still be in bed? You were in the hospital a week ago." A concerned expression settled on his face.

That was what broke her out of her paralysis, the concern. It both reminded her of who he was and annoyed the everloving crap out of her, all at the same time. She didn't *need* concern right now. She *needed* them to get past this *thing* that was keeping them apart.

When he was only a few feet away, she acted without thinking. She still couldn't remember what she'd wanted to say, but she could act, and she did. She stepped forward, reached up to grab him by the hair, and pulled him down for a kiss.

The kiss was awkward, neither of them yet in the mood, but it was the right thing to do.

Zayvan pulled back gently. "Justine?" He sounded a bit confused, but there was a gentleness to his expression, and the overprotective concern was gone.

Justine leaned up on her toes and kissed the edge of his jawline, then pulled back without a word, waiting for him to respond.

His eyes seemed to shine, almost as if he had tears welling in them. "I'm sorry. I should have told you. I shouldn't have broken your trust like that." He shook his head. "I knew you'd been through some bad things. I should have realized you might have seen that as a betrayal."

Relief flooded her at his words, and she leaned into him, pulling him close. His warmth seeped into her and, soon enough, his arms wrapped around her.

This *is why we're such a good match.*

Zayvan had figured it out on his own. She'd never managed to tell him, but he'd figured it out. Given enough time, he'd realized how his actions could feel like a betrayal to her, and she couldn't imagine being with anyone else. *He* was the only man for her, her forever after. It made telling him her own secrets surprisingly easy. "I was abused."

He tensed, but didn't speak, thank God.

"His name was Brian. I never saw it coming. He seemed perfect at first, but eventually his true self came out. He's the reason... he broke my leg."

Zayvan's arms grew tighter around her, and he started to rock her back and forth. As if knowing exactly what she needed, he didn't speak. He just held her, giving her however much time she needed. And what she needed more than anything else was just *him,* being there.

For her.

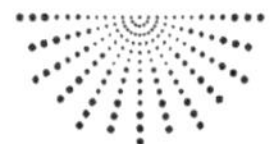

CHAPTER SEVENTEEN

"Justine, I have to go. I have a meeting, and at this rate, I'm going to be late."

Justine smiled against his lips, little butterflies taking off in her stomach. They were naked in bed, and she was enjoying the feel of skin on skin, even if they had no time for anything else. A part of her was tempted to make him late, but she couldn't do that to him, so she sighed and rolled over, staring up at the ceiling.

They were in their bedroom, once Zayvan's room, and she smiled up at the new ceiling. The entire apartment had seen a renovation after she'd mentioned how uncomfortable she was with the extravagance. Zayvan had admitted he'd never been overly fond of it either, but had also never had sufficient motivation to change it.

Now, the ceiling was hardly plain, but it *was* much more subdued. There were intricate designs of white, silver, and black, but in the dark, you couldn't even tell. In daylight, you could see it, but you barely noticed it unless you looked straight at it. The walls had taken on a similar redesign and the horrible couches in the foyer had been replaced with ones she actually enjoyed sitting on.

She watched with a smile as Zayvan got out of bed, his bare body giving her a show as he entered the bathroom to take a shower.

With another sigh, she pushed back the blankets and slipped out of bed. She grabbed a green robe off a chair in the corner and slipped it on, cinching it tight as she wandered through the apartments and into the kitchen. She blindly went through the motions of making a couple cups of hal while she listened to the shower running, imagining water pouring over Zayvan's naked body as he rubbed soap all over himself.

Justine smiled as she lifted a cup to her lips. The fumes hit her nose, immediately summoning the memory of that first bitter sip back at the cabin. She'd learned since then, and now she doctored hers with a little fruit extract to make it more palatable. She was taking that first sip as Zayvan stepped into the kitchen, now fully dressed.

Pity.

"You really *are* in a rush. How much time did you spend in the shower?"

"Probably not enough," he said, chuckling. As he walked past her to the cup on the counter, he kissed her temple.

A flood of warmth filled her chest at the tender action, and she practically hugged her cup to her chest, her smile growing. "When will you be back?"

"I just have the one meeting, then I'm going to spend a few hours in the office." The "office" now referred to a space here in their apartments. They'd converted two of the bedrooms into home offices.

She had one herself, and she'd been using it to look for work.

Zayvan downed his hal in record time, kissed her temple

once more in passing, then muttered a farewell before rushing out.

Justine shook her head, took another sip, then walked into her office. It was pretty basic still, with just some office furniture, supplies, and personal touches. She didn't have a specific career path in mind yet, so this space felt a little like a blank slate, waiting to be filled in. She was currently looking for work, but Zayvan had insisted she take her time. A small part of her brain had still bristled at the suggestion, that residual fear of being controlled still present, but it no longer had any real power over her, and she let it go without saying anything. He wasn't trying to control her, and there was no rush. She didn't need the money, and she had no interest in leaving Zayvan.

She sat down in her chair with a smile and set the cup down. The desk was made of metal and glass, with gentle swirls etched onto the surface. She powered the computer on and realized as she pulled up the job site that she'd never felt this way before. She was actually excited.

On Earth, when she'd looked for work, it had always been stressful, almost manic. She was always either reeling from recently being let go or worried about how she was going to make ends meet. She would be worried about if she would get a response or if they would like her. The question was never whether the job would be the right fit for her or even if she would be the right fit for the job. No, she only ever seemed to care about getting a job as fast as humanly possible.

But now? It was different. Every job was an opportunity, something potentially special. There was no rush because she realized she felt completely secure in who she was and what resources she had at her disposal. It was somehow beautiful.

She wasn't afraid that not having a job would be used against her. She knew Zayvan would never do that.

And even if he did, she was fairly certain his brother would rip him a new one for it.

For the first time in a long time, she felt completely safe.

Suddenly no longer in the mood to look for work, she left the job website and opened her messaging app, starting a new letter to Amira, eager to tell her about this latest development.

She'll be so happy for me.

EPILOGUE

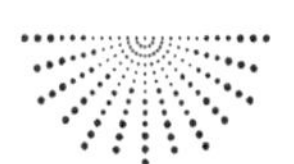

Michelle waited as the scheduled communication tried to connect. This was a normal part of her process, but she couldn't deny it was also frustrating. Nothing short of a TAT system, which required terminals on each end and was a *bit* out of her price range, could handle instantaneous communication over such long distances.

Ah, that would be the day, wouldn't it?

The comm finally connected, and a face she only vaguely recognized from her Savalan partner's offices filled the screen. He gestured for her to wait. The image glitched as he moved off to the right.

She frowned, her nails tapping on her desktop.

Then Justine and a blue Savalan appeared. Justine was relaxed and all smiles, and Michelle couldn't help smiling back. The man had an arm around Justine's middle as they sat down. Even she could see the way they were leaning into each other, like they couldn't stand being apart, even by a few inches.

"I hope things are going well," she said, waiting for the translation and response.

"Fantastic," Justine finally said. "Better than I could have ever hoped."

The man looked over at Justine, a slow smile forming on his lips. "She's perfect."

"I'm glad."

They talked for about half an hour, Michelle asking carefully worded questions meant to clue her in to any potential issues, but no red flags appeared. If anything, they seemed completely smitten with each other.

This is why I do this.

This was also one of several reasons she insisted on a visual final interview. Some things you just couldn't pick up on in text, even if it was easier. With this, she could make out inflections in Justine's voice, read facial expressions and body language. If something was wrong, she just might see it. And with Justine, she was more concerned than most about something going wrong, but it seemed she needn't have worried. This had been yet another good match. Perfect, he'd said.

"Thank you for speaking with me. And before you go, I was wondering if you wouldn't be willing to participate in a case study, a sort of testimonial for the agency?"

She waited anxiously for a reply, reminding herself again and again to be patient, that the audio had to be translated *twice* and cross distances that took *months* by spaceship.

Justine looked over at her partner, a little surprised, but a small smile crossed her face. "Should we?" she asked him.

"If you'd like."

She nodded and turned back to the camera. "I'd be happy to help."

"Great. I'll reach out to you via IS Messenger."

Justine nodded. "I look forward to it."

"Well, if that's everything, I'm going to sign out."

They each said goodbye, and then she closed out the connection.

Michelle pulled up the messager app, started typing up some quick prompts to get Justine started, and hit send, then moved on to her matching software where a profile was waiting.

Sarah Watkins. The eager woman had shown up a few weeks ago. She was a chatterbox, going on and on about how much she liked alien romance books and how she dreamed of being the heroine in one of those novels.

It had made Michelle a little hesitant to work on her profile, but beggars couldn't be choosers, she supposed. Sarah might be a bit over the top, and Michelle had more than a little concern that a woman who dreamed of being the heroine in a romance novel was bound to be disappointed by the real thing, but she was just as deserving of love as anyone else, and while she found the woman's obsession with aliens a little unnerving, if it got people signing up, she couldn't say it was completely unwanted.

She refreshed the search, looking to see if any new matches had shown up since the last time she'd checked.

One new match was highlighted, and Michelle leaned forward in her seat when she saw the 99% SS. She clicked it and started reviewing the profile one item at a time. Little by little, she started to smile, and finally, she picked up the phone and dialed.

After two rings, Sarah's bright voice said, "Hello?"

"Hi, Sarah, this is Michelle Mackey with the Best Life Interstellar Matchmaking Agency. I'm calling to let you know that I've found a match." She clicked the button to send the profile and match information via encrypted email. "I'm sending it to you now."

"Right, one sec. Um, I see it. How do I unencrypt it again?"

Michelle rolled her eyes, wondering if anyone would ever remember. "Click the link."

"Okay, now?"

"It should have a button that says 'Begin Facial Recognition.'"

"Oh, right."

Michelle waited as Sarah presumably tapped the button and tilted her head back and forth, letting the software do its work.

"Got it. Um... Opening now. Okay. Pazran Veshuu. Is that a name?"

Michelle pulled the receiver away from her mouth and sighed, then pressed the handset back to her face. "Yes, that's a name." She looked at her screen. "Pazran Veshuu." She frowned as she looked at the translated part of the profile that gave biographic information. "Says Guard Captain."

"Oohh, nice," Sarah cooed.

Michelle closed her eyes, praying for patience.

Lord, give me strength.

She took a deep breath. "Yes, just go over the profile. If you're happy with the match, let me know, and I'll send the information to my Savalan partners to see if he's interested as well."

Michelle could hear Sarah's smile over the phone. "I can't wait."

DID YOU ENJOY THE BOOK?

IF SO, YOU CAN MAKE A BIG DIFFERENCE...

Reviews are among the most important tools in my arsenal for getting my books in front of readers like yourself. I'm just one person. No matter how much I shout, my voice can only carry so far.

But do you want to know what does carry?

A crowd.

When one voice joins another who joins another, that matters. *That* gets heard.

Let your own voice be heard by leaving an honest review. It only takes a few minutes, but makes a major difference not just to me as an author, but to readers like yourself who are trying to decide on their next read.

I love building relationships with my readers. As part of that, I regularly send emails with deleted scenes, never before seen excerpts, pre-order and new release announcements, and more.

If you sign up to receive these emails, I'll send you Mila's Flight, the prequel to the Darkest Day series, and Shifting Sides, the prequel to the A Shift in Space series, FREE.

Join Now to Get Your Free Ebook

www.theeternalscribe.com

ABOUT THE AUTHOR

Danielle Forrest is a Paranormal SciFi author and Medical Laboratory Scientist based out of Indianapolis, IN.

She has dedicated her life so far to two things:

Science & Books

So it really shouldn't be a surprise if science finds its way into even the most fantastical examples of her writing.

Sign up for her mailing list at www.theeternalscribe.com to get access to exclusive content and updates.

facebook.com/theeternalscribe

twitter.com/theternalscribe

instagram.com/theeternalscribe

goodreads.com/theeternalscribe

amazon.com/author/danielleforrest

bookbub.com/profile/danielle-forrest